A
STUDY
IN
MURDER

ALSO AVAILABLE BY CALLIE HUTTON

SCOTTISH HEART SERIES
His Rebellious Lass
A Scot to Wed

NOBLE HEART SERIES
For the Love of the Viscount
For the Love of the Marquess
For the Love of the Baron
For the Love of the Lady
For the Love of the Duke
For the Love of the Gentleman

PRISONERS OF LOVE SERIES
Adelaide
Cinnamon
Becky
Miranda
Nellie

LORDS AND LADIES IN LOVE SERIES
Seducing the Marquess
Marrying the Wrong Earl
Denying the Duke
Wagering for Miss Blake
Captivating the Earl

MCCOY BROTHERS SERIES
Daniel's Desire
Stephen's Bride

OKLAHOMA LOVERS SERIES
A Run for Love
A Prescription for Love
A Chance to Love Again
A Wife for Christmas
Anyplace but Here
A Dogtown Christmas

MARRIAGE MART MAYHEM SERIES
The Elusive Wife
The Duke's Quandary
The Lady's Disgrace
The Baron's Betrayal
The Highlander's Choice
The Highlander's Accidental Marriage
The Earl's Return

THE MERRY MISFITS OF BATH
The Bookseller and the Earl
The Courtesan's Daughter and the Gentleman
Lady Pamela and the Gambler

OTHER NOVELS
Caleb
Heirlooms of the Heart
Julie: Bride of New York
Miss Merry's Christmas
An Angel in the Mail
Emma's Journey
A Tumble Through Time
The Pursuit of Mrs. Pennyworth
Choose Your Heart

A
STUDY
IN
MURDER

A VICTORIAN BOOK
CLUB MYSTERY

———◆———

Callie Hutton

CROOKED
LANE

NEW YORK

Copyright © 2020 by Colleen Greene

Published in the United States by Crooked Lane Books, an imprint of The Quick Brown Fox & Company LLC.

Crooked Lane Books and its logo are trademarks of The Quick Brown Fox & Company LLC.

Library of Congress Catalog-in-Publication data available upon request.

ISBN (hardcover): 978-1-64385-302-4
ISBN (ebook): 978-1-64385-323-9

Cover design by Lori Palmer

Printed in the United States.

www.crookedlanebooks.com

Crooked Lane Books
34 West 27th St., 10th Floor
New York, NY 10001

First Edition: May 2020

10 9 8 7 6 5 4 3 2 1

To Doug. You know why

CHAPTER 1

Lady Amy Lovell, only daughter of the Marquess of Winchester, hurried up the steps of St. Swithin's, the old and stately church on the Paragon in the Walcot area of Bath, barely on time for the Sunday service. As usual, she arrived ten minutes past her aunt Margaret, who had never in all her life been late for a church service. Or anything else.

Her aunt shifted over in the family pew as Amy slid in alongside her. She offered her a hymnal, a Bible, and a slight roll of her warm brown eyes.

Amy looked around the church, comfortable with familiar faces. There were the Misses O'Neill, Miss Penelope and Miss Gertrude, who made it their responsibility to make sure everyone knew of their particular devotion to the church. Their usual flowered dresses matched each other's, as did their blue-and-pink straw hats. They were not twins, but for some odd reason pretended to be, although they looked nothing alike and their heights were separated by almost a foot.

Mrs. Edith Newton played the organ with gusto, fingering the wrong chords only a few times. Amy smiled. The woman was half-blind, but no one had the heart to tell her it was time to retire. So, they all sang off-key half the time.

Amy's heart slowed down from the race to church, and she settled her hands in her lap as the pastor, Mr. Palmer, began his Sunday sermon.

Despite her best intentions, Amy's mind drifted to her latest novel. Like her other self, the famous mystery author E. D. Burton, her mind was always filled with murder and mayhem. In her most recent work, she was stymied by the last red herring she'd thrown into the mix. She needed some guidance and knew exactly what research book would help, but she'd been unable to find a copy anywhere in Bath. Or even in London when she'd made the trek there to search for the tome.

Mr. Palmer was finishing up his sermon when Amy realized she'd spent the entire time dwelling on her story and hadn't heard a word the man had said. She made a quick apology to God as the congregation stood and sang the last hymn.

"Good heavens, Amy, are you aware that you are wearing two different shoes?" Aunt Margaret pointed to Amy's feet as the last note was sung.

"Yes, I know, Aunt, but they are actually the same shoes, just different colors. I purposely bought them that way in case something like this happened."

"Something like what happened?" Aunt Margaret smiled and nodded at the pastor as they made their way out of the church and down the steps.

"That I can find only one shoe when it is time to leave the house." She did try to be more organized and had often thought of hiring someone to just help her keep track of . . . well . . . herself. But her last lady's maid had left the year before to marry, and Amy never seemed to find the time to interview new candidates for the job.

Aunt Margaret, younger sister of Amy's father, had practically raised her once Lady Winchester passed away of an ague when Amy was ten years old. Aunt Margaret had only been Amy's present age, five and twenty, when her role as surrogate mother began. As much as they loved each other, Amy and Aunt Margaret could not have been more different.

While her aunt was willowy and above average in height for a woman, with ordinary yet lovely features, straight brown hair, and a gait that caused her to almost glide rather than walk, Amy was of less than medium height, and while not plump, she certainly possessed enough curves to fill out her clothes. Her always-in-disarray curly auburn hair and hazel eyes had come to her from her Scottish mother, as had the light freckles peppering her cheeks.

Amy was the devoted owner of a yapping, white fluffy Pomeranian dog with a missing tail and a propensity for hiding slippers all over the house. Aunt Margaret, meanwhile, possessed a thirty-year-old cockatoo who quoted Shakespeare. Nevertheless, the two women lived in harmony in Winchester Townhouse on fashionable Westgate Street in Bath.

Amy took in a deep breath of fresh air in the bright sunshine as they strolled arm in arm to the Friendship Hall for lunch, greeting other church members on the way. The first Sunday of every month was Social Sunday, when the congregants shared a meal that each woman had contributed to.

"If you would set some sort of a schedule for yourself when you are involved in a new book, it would certainly help to tame your life. So many hours of writing, so many hours of other activities." Aunt looked pointedly at Amy's shoes. "Like taking care of yourself."

"Good morning, ladies." Viscount Wethington, a longtime friend and fellow Mystery Book Club member, stepped into their path and removed his hat as he greeted Amy and Aunt

Margaret. Offering a slight bow, he said, "You are both look-ing quite fetching. Almost as lovely as the day."

"Good morning to you, my lord." Aunt Margaret returned the greeting, flashing a bright smile. His lordship had always been a favorite of her aunt's. More than once Amy had felt the slight—or not-so-slight—nudge from Aunt toward Lord Wethington, better known by his friends as William.

Although a viscount, William had never been one to stand on titles. He was a pleasant-looking man in his early thirties, with light-brown hair and blue eyes. His perpetual smile made him a favorite among their circle of friends. Particularly the ladies. To whom he never seemed to grant much attention.

Amy had once asked him why he had never married, and after a lengthy, silent stare he had asked the same question of her. Which had brought an abrupt end to that conversation.

"May I escort you to the hall for lunch?" Ever the gentle-man, William extended both elbows so the ladies could walk with him. Amy could not help but compare him to her betrothed, Mr. St. Vincent. Not that St. Vincent would not have acted the gentleman, but his actions always seemed to speak more of impressing those observing him. She pushed thoughts of him and that yet-to-be resolved problem from her mind to deal with later.

The hall quickly filled up, the noise of laughter and con-versation filling the space. William held out a chair for Aunt Margaret and then another for Amy. "Have you finished read-ing *A Study in Scarlet*?" He settled next to Amy and turned to face her. "I have found something quite interesting about the story."

Both she and William were longtime members of the Mys-tery Book Club of Bath. The group met every Thursday to discuss various mystery books. They were currently reading Arthur Conan Doyle's story of detective Sherlock Holmes.

"I am in the process of reading the story. What is the interesting thing you discovered about the piece?"

William nodded his thanks to the young girl who placed two glasses of lemonade in front of them. "Ah, I am not going to reveal my discovery until the meeting. I want to know if you notice the same thing I did."

"Goodness. How am I to know that I've discovered the same thing you've discovered if you don't tell me what it is you've discovered?" They served themselves from large platters placed on each table. Today's array of food consisted of various salads as well as ham, chicken, and roast beef. Since neither Amy nor Aunt Margaret knew her way around the kitchen very well, they had contributed warm rolls and sweet buns Cook had made.

Amy eyed her plate, her stomach rumbling, as she thought on William's question. "You know I hate it when you toss out these innuendoes. And you do it all the time." She placed her hand over her middle, hoping to quell the embarrassing noise.

"No, fair lady. I do not do it *all the time*. Sometimes I sleep, sometimes I go for a walk, sometimes—"

"Enough!" Aunt Margaret smiled at the two of them as if they were children needing a reprimand. "We are about to have the blessing."

Feeling like a child bickering with her sibling, Amy bowed her head while she wondered what interesting fact William had uncovered that she had obviously missed.

★   ★   ★

Amy glanced up from her conversation with Mrs. Morton and smiled at William as he strolled into Atkinson & Tucker Booksellers, the location of the weekly meeting of the Mystery Book Club of Bath.

William wandered in her direction, eyeing but not selecting a glass of watered-down lemonade from the table against the wall. "Good evening, ladies." He offered a slight bow and a warm smile at the group. "Are we prepared to discuss another facet of *A Study in Scarlet*?"

"Indeed we are," Amy said. "I am very impressed with Mr. Holmes's deductive reasoning. The man makes it all seem so easy."

"Ah, you know the saying: the easier it looks, the harder it is to do," William said.

Amy shrugged. "One can apply deductive logic to anything."

"Excuse my ignorance, Lady Amy, but what precisely is deductive logic? Although Holmes mentions it, I'm not quite clear on it." Mrs. Miles had joined the group, while her son had sauntered over to Mr. Colbert, a solicitor and fellow book club member, who conversed with Lady Carlisle, another member.

"Deductive logic is a well-ordered method that provides strong support for a conclusion." Amy would have loved to add that she used it all the time in her books, but that subject was not one she could address.

Five years ago, when she'd waved the contract for her first book at her father, full of excitement and joy, he had made her promise that she would use a pseudonym and keep her connection to the book a secret.

"I am afraid that is beyond my woman's brain." Mrs. Miles shook her head and glanced around the group.

Amy raised her chin. "I disagree. I think a woman could do just as well as any man in solving crimes." She did it all the time in her work.

"Indeed?" William's smirk started her heart thumping with anticipated anger. "Surely a woman would not have the—"

Amy held up her hand to interrupt the fool man before he said something for which she would make sure he was sorry. "Please don't say *brains*, my lord."

"Ah, why would I ever be so foolish as to put myself in the line of fire by saying that to a woman who is so set on women's rights?" William nodded a greeting at Mr. Colbert, Lady Carlisle, and Mr. Miles, who had just joined their circle.

"Well done, William. I don't know for what you were defending yourself, but I almost think you have developed some sense in your old age," Mr. Colbert said.

William turned toward Lady Carlisle. "And you, Lady Carlisle. Do you believe women could solve crimes by applying logic?"

Lady Carlisle was a beautiful woman in her early thirties. Her husband, the Earl of Carlisle, held one of the oldest titles in the kingdom. He cut quite a figure in Parliament and was rumored to be in a fine position to be named the ambassador to France. Lady Carlisle enjoyed her husband's consequence and took every opportunity to flaunt her position in society. "I don't believe so. Personally, it is my conviction that women should remain in the background and support their husbands." She smiled sweetly in Amy's direction. "Is that not true, Lady Amy?"

Amy gritted her teeth at Lady Carlisle's condescending tone. "I'm afraid I must disagree once again. I don't believe that women should remain in the background. That is why my women's rights group is working to gain the vote. We need to make sure other rights are granted as well. We are not children, and why should a woman need a husband to make decisions for her? 'Tis humiliating." She took a deep breath, aware that her voice had begun to rise. It was a sore spot for her.

"But, are not all women eager to enter the wedded state?" William grinned at them, immediately raising Amy's ire further.

"I imagine as excited as a gentleman is to succumb to the parson's noose." Amy sniffed. "I intend to live my life as I choose, not how a man decides to *permit* me."

William glanced quickly at her hand. "I thought you were betrothed."

Betrothed. There was that word again.

Whyever had she been foolish enough to agree to her engagement to Mr. St. Vincent? Truth be known, she knew precisely why. Papa had come from London, marriage offer in hand, to badger her into it, calling her a spinster and waxing poetic about her lonely state in her old age.

He had blithely glossed over her observation that Aunt Margaret was quite happy with her spinster state and not at all lonely with all her friends, volunteer work, and social life. Papa's inability to get his younger half sister married off had been an annoyance for years. 'Twas only recently that he'd seemed to have given up on the idea.

Spinster, indeed! The word still echoed in her head with distaste. Perhaps at five and twenty she was considered a spinster by society's rules, and a bluestocking as well. However, she liked her life precisely as it was. She had no sooner accepted Mr. St. Vincent's offer of marriage than she'd begun to regret her decision.

Before she could respond to William's question, Mr. Colbert, acting as the club moderator, called the meeting to order.

The members drifted from their small groups and arranged themselves on the comfortable chairs, sofas, and settees in the back room of the bookstore set aside for various book club meetings.

The door between the bookstore and their meeting flew open and Eloise Spencer hurried in, nodding briefly to Mr. Colbert. She made a beeline for Amy, plopping down alongside her on the settee, bumping Amy's hip with hers, and almost sending her to the floor. "Move over."

"For heaven's sake, Eloise, I shall be bruised in the morning." Amy rubbed her side.

Amy and Eloise had been best friends since their school days. Papa had never approved of their friendship, since Eloise was what he referred to as a "hoyden." Perhaps Eloise's family was not of their class, but no truer friend had ever existed. Eloise's father owned several stores in both Bath and London, which put him in the merchant class.

Since Aunt Margaret was quite fond of her—which Amy sometimes attributed directly to Papa's disapproval—Eloise was always welcomed at their home.

Eloise was also the only person outside Amy's family who knew about her "other" life. When Amy had first told her about her hopes to one day be published, Eloise had encouraged her, read her manuscripts, and offered very well thought out suggestions.

Once he had the members' full attention, Mr. Colbert nodded to Mr. Davidson, who had his hand raised.

"I first want to say that I think Mr. Doyle did a wonderful job portraying the brilliance of Mr. Holmes," said Mr. Davidson. "A typical male way of thinking that cuts out all the nonsense and gets right to the bottom of the matter."

Amy bristled and scowled at the man. She never had cared for Davidson, a tall, gangly fellow with a moustache that covered almost the entire bottom half of his face. He looked toward the few women in the group and smirked as only a man who felt secure in his position in life would do.

Eloise leaned in to whisper into Amy's ear. "Are you going to let him get away with that?"

Before she could speak, William said, "Strange you say that, Mr. Davidson. We just had an opinion from Lady Amy that was quite the opposite." He turned to her, the twinkle in his eye revealing his attempt to begin a lively debate.

Part of the reason for the club was to discuss various elements of stories and their characters, but William was known for his propensity to throw out a provocative statement and then sit back and enjoy watching the furor he'd caused.

"I think both women and men are able to sort through a problem in a logical way." Lady Forester, another club member, spoke with a soft voice that forced most of the members to lean forward to hear what she said. Although she came to every meeting, she rarely offered an opinion. "Why can't someone write a book where a woman solves a crime? After all, Mr. Holmes doesn't go running around London chasing criminals. He sits in his chair and thinks, something a woman could certainly do."

"Yes, definitely." Amy nodded furiously. "Or perhaps even have a woman as a partner with a man in solving a crime."

"A partner?" Davidson crossed his arms over his chest and sat back, a sneer on his face. "What does a woman know besides how to order servants about, wipe children's noses, and drink tea with gossiping women? I would certainly not want a woman as a partner."

After a few moments of stunned silence, Wethington turned to Davidson. "I say, old chap. I'm not sure if it was your intention, but I believe you have just insulted every woman in the room." William's easy demeanor had changed from enjoying a lively debate to taking umbrage at Davidson's words. Thank goodness for at least one man who valued women for more than mere fluff.

"I concur with Lord Wethington." Amy smiled in Davidson's direction. She leaned in and said in a soft voice to William, who was sitting in the chair next to the settee, "I believe you grow smarter by the day. Certainly smarter than that numskull Davidson."

William attempted to cover up his laugh with a cough.

Eloise raised her hand. "I also agree with Lady Amy and Lord Wethington." She glared at Mr. Davidson. "There is no scientific proof that a man's brain and a woman's brain operate any differently."

Eloise was an insatiable reader. Before she reached her twentieth birthday, she'd gone through every book in the Bath Library. It didn't matter the content or subject; if it was printed between two covers, Eloise would read it.

"I think we have gotten off track here, ladies and gentlemen. Perhaps we can keep our discussion to the story." Mr. Colbert smoothly tossed out a question about Holmes's reaction to Dr. Watson's dismissal of the detective's article on the art of deduction based on observation.

After a discussion on that point, Amy leaned over to William. "You mentioned a matter you wanted to raise about the story."

He grinned. "Your curiosity got the best of you, Lady Amy?"

William raised his hand and was recognized by the moderator. "Yes, Lord Wethington, did you have a comment?"

"Yes, I do. One thing I would like to point out with regard to *A Study in Scarlet* is, if anyone has read 'The Murders in the Rue Morgue' by Edgar Allan Poe, the similarity between the two stories almost borders on plagiarism."

A few gasps followed, and Amy hurriedly added, "Mr. Doyle has indeed mentioned his inspiration came from Mr. Poe's work." She didn't know why she felt she had to defend William's statement. Perhaps because he had come to her defense about women.

"Lord Wethington, surely you are not accusing Mr. Doyle of plagiarism?" Mr. Davidson raised his arrogant voice, and the heated discussion began.

Despite the disagreements that came from William's observation, the rest of the meeting went quite smoothly, with Mr. Colbert's expertise in moving things along. Once the meeting was declared over, Amy remained behind with Eloise, Mr. Colbert, William, Lady Carlisle, Mrs. Morton, and Mr. Miles and his mother, Mrs. Miles, who all generally partook of a light supper at a nearby pub after each meeting. Lord Temple and his daughter, Lady Abigail, had elected to join the group this week as well.

They enjoyed a lovely repast of cold cucumber soup, various meats, cheeses, warm bread, coffee, tea, and small tarts. The conversation was lively and relaxed without the difficult Mr. Davidson present.

Amy wiped her mouth after taking her final sip of tea, wondering if she'd have to let out the skirt she wore. She really needed to cut down on these lovely desserts. In an ironic twist of fate, she often admired Aunt Margaret's lean, slim figure, while her aunt despaired of ever having proper curves to fill out her clothing as Amy did.

Laying her napkin alongside her plate, Amy addressed the group around the table. "I have been looking all over London for a book and cannot find it. I wonder if any of you have ever heard of *Unsolved Gruesome and Ghastly Murders of London* by Melvin Fulsom?"

William, sitting to her right, almost spit out his tea. "What?"

Expecting another discourse on the proper behavior of women, she sniffed and raised her chin. "I am interested in unsolved murders."

Eloise, the only person at the table who knew of Amy's alternate persona, said, "Yes. Even I couldn't find the book." That, itself, was a remarkable thing. Amy was quite sure there were no books Eloise hadn't read, or at least didn't know where to obtain.

Lord Temple frowned. "Is that not a rather unpleasant hobby for a gently reared young lady?" He glanced at his daughter, perhaps believing she should never have been subjected to such a conversation.

Gently reared young lady. How she hated that term. Those were the words that generally preceded comments on her personal lack of the married state. She shrugged. "I believe some would think so—"

"As do I," William said.

She glared at him. As much as she would like to reveal that the reason for her interest was research on the book she was currently writing, she was bound by the promise she'd made to Papa.

Yet another way that women were inhibited. If she had been writing romances like Miss Austen or the Brontë sisters, it would have been accepted. But the subject of murder and mayhem was not a ladylike pursuit. But then there was *The Modern Prometheus* by Mary Shelley, one of Amy's favorite books.

"But I find the subject fascinating." She glanced from face to face around the table. "Well, it appears most of you disapprove of my pastime."

Eloise snorted. "I don't disapprove. I think women should be permitted to read anything. After all, we are not children."

"I don't believe it is that we do not approve, my dear. I think, if anything, we are taken aback by your request." Mrs. Morton patted Amy's hand. "I am sure you can't find a copy because respectable people have no need for such horrible things."

William cleared his throat. "As a matter of fact, I have a copy of the book in my library."

Gasps came from those at the table. Except for Amy, who traded grins with Eloise. "Indeed?" She looked at the others. "I guess I am not the only oddity in the group. May I borrow it, Lord Wethington?"

"If you are certain you won't stay awake nights fearing an attack from a crazed knife-wielding maniac." She had to grant him credit for casting her a grin rather than a smirk.

Thinking back on some of the frightening scenarios in her books, she waved her hand in dismissal. "Nonsense. I am not subject to the weak sensibilities of other young ladies."

"Apparently not," he said, as he lifted his cup in a salute before taking a sip of tea.

Amy studied William as he continued to converse with the rest of the group. Although over the years they had enjoyed a warm and companionable friendship, at one time she'd thought perhaps he would request to court her. But he never had. He remained a bit of an enigma, never revealing much about himself.

He was a private man, and at a time when many large titled estates were floundering, their owners seeking rich American brides in search of a title, William had managed to keep his holdings profitable.

She'd heard from her brother, Michael, that William had gotten involved in railroads at a time when most gentlemen were skeptical of the new mode of transport. Being clever himself, Michael had convinced Papa to join in the venture, and consequently the Winchester house was doing quite well.

The conversation had veered away from her unusual request, for which she was grateful. William leaned in, close to her ear. "I must travel to London for a few days, but if you are at home next Tuesday evening, I can bring the book to you. That is, if you are absolutely certain you want it." His raised eyebrows made her laugh more than scowl. Even though he'd refuted what Mr. Davidson had said, like most men, he likely still held an ingrained idea of what women could handle. They were all so wrong. After all, women gave birth, didn't they? She shuddered. A messy business, that.

"Oh, yes, indeed I do." She quickly ran through her calendar and remembered the Bartons' musicale on Tuesday, which she didn't mind missing. The Barton daughters' idea of singing brought a whole new meaning to *self-inflicted torture*. "Yes, I will be at home Tuesday night."

He nodded. "Excellent. I shall call around eight, if that is acceptable to you."

Amy told herself she was looking forward to William's visit because she was relieved to finally receive the book she had been searching for, certainly not because she was anxious for a visit from his lordship.

CHAPTER 2

The next evening, Amy paced the deep-blue Aubusson carpet in the library of her family's townhouse, awaiting the arrival of her betrothed.

Soon to be ex-betrothed.

As she strode back and forth, her gown whipping behind her as she turned, she mumbled to herself the words she wanted to say to St. Vincent. In her fist she clutched the anonymous note she'd received two days before, repeating to herself the words etched in her mind:

My Dear Lady Amy,

I find it imperative to inform you of your fiancé's nefarious activities. Mr. Ronald St. Vincent has been involved in shipping, and in turn selling, opium to individuals who are unfortunately addicted to the drug.

His illegal activities have caused a great deal of harm to upstanding members of the community.

Sincerely,

A Friend

She'd done her own investigation. It had taken her only a short visit with one of her contacts in the criminal world to discover the truth of the missive, giving her the perfect reason to put an end to her betrothal.

Most young ladies of her rank would have had their father deal with the messy matter. However, she was not one to hide from her decisions or show anything but confidence. Instead of summoning Papa from London, she would do the dirty deed herself. Truth be known, she wasn't fully convinced Papa wouldn't try to dismiss the evidence she'd gathered and insist on proceeding with the wedding anyway.

Her insides roiled when Mr. Stevens, the night butler at the front door, entered the room. "My lady, Mr. St. Vincent has called."

"Thank you, Stevens. Please show him in."

She wiped her sweaty palms on her skirts, patted her hair, and raised her chin. She could do this.

St. Vincent entered, his hands extended. "My love. So very nice to see you. I always look forward to our visits."

Why had she not noticed his false levity before? Or the fake smile? So many things about the man annoyed her now. Thank goodness she'd discovered his unsavory deeds before they married. Her stomach muscles tightened at the thought of being stuck with this man for the rest of her life.

She regarded him coolly. "Please have a seat, Mr. St. Vincent."

He waved to the deep-red brocade settee. "After you, my love." Again, the artificial smile. Admittedly, he was certainly not difficult to look at, with his sandy hair, warm chocolate-brown eyes, and the little dip in his chin. But his good looks were too perfect. Along with the smile. She shuddered thinking about how close she'd come to disaster.

She settled on the settee, and he sat alongside her. When he reached for her hand, she drew it away from him. "I wish to discuss something of great importance."

"Anything, my dear."

She stood, unable to sit close to him and say what needed to be said. He stood as well. She drew in a deep breath, faced him, and removed the ring he'd given her on their betrothal, an ostentatious sapphire-studded band that had belonged to his grandmother. His brows rose as she held it out to him.

"What? Do you not like the ring? I can get you another one." His eyes shifted, and small beads of perspiration popped up on his forehead.

"No, I do not want another ring." She stiffened her spine and sucked in a lungful of air. "I wish to break our engagement."

His eyes grew wide. "I don't understand." Was that a lack of surprise in his voice, a bit of playacting? Had he guessed she'd discovered the truth? Did he know about the note?

"Let me see if I can say it differently so you do understand." She tapped her chin. "I do not wish to marry you."

He placed his hands on her shoulders. "You are over-wrought and not making sense, Lady Amy. Perhaps I should have your cook prepare a tisane for you."

She shifted her shoulders to release his grip. His hands dropped to his sides.

"I am never overwrought, and therefore, please accept that I want our betrothal to come to an end. You are free to pursue anyone else you wish. We"—she waved her hand between them—"are no longer contemplating marriage to each other. The wedding is off. I will not be your wife. You will not be my husband. There will be no honeymoon." She smiled her own fake smile. "Am I making sense now?"

He tried once more. "I have no idea why you are suddenly casting me aside. You have accepted my offer in good faith." His face twisted into an ugly mask she had never seen before. To the extent that she was almost afraid of him.

She stepped back. "You may leave now, Mr. St. Vincent."

He stepped forward, causing her to retreat a few more steps. "No. I deserve to know why."

"Very well." She placed the ring he'd refused on the table in front of the settee and crossed the room to her father's desk to fiddle with the pen in its holder. For some reason, she felt the need to create space between them. "It has come to my attention that you have been importing opium to be sold to individuals who are unfortunate enough to be dependent on it."

He looked as if he had been prepared for her statement and answered quickly. "Opium is not illegal. There are opium dens all over London."

How she loathed every minute he was in her presence. When he left, she would need to take a bath. "We are not in London, but in Bath. Additionally, your statement is not exactly true. The sale of opium and other drugs is restricted to chemists and pharmacists. You are neither. Therefore, you are breaking the law."

When he remained silent, she added information she'd picked up from her contact. "You are selling dangerous drugs to ladies and gentlemen who would never enter an opium den even if there were any such horrible place in our fair city. By doing so, you are helping them destroy their lives."

"If they wish to destroy their lives, that is their business."

She pointed a finger at him. "No. You have made it *your* business. It is immoral and ugly. I do not wish to subject myself to being awakened in the middle of the night by an angry father or husband, or possibly even the Bath police, as my husband is dragged from our home in the middle of the night. It would be most annoying and would leave one quite unsettled."

"That is not true!"

"I disagree. I am always unsettled when my sleep is interrupted."

He moved toward her, his lips curling. "You might make light of this, but you do understand I can sue you for breach of contract."

Well, then.

She'd had enough of Mr. St. Vincent. "Do not threaten me, sir. My father is fully aware of my decision and has already consulted with his solicitor." She offered a quick prayer to the heavens for her lie. "If you wish to pursue that avenue, we are well prepared."

He snatched the ring from the table and dropped it into his pocket. He straightened his necktie and tugged on the cuffs of his jacket. "Very well. I will leave now. But I must warn you that you will be sorry for this."

She nodded, only wishing for him to go, so her shaky knees would no longer have to hold up her body.

Mr. St. Vincent turned on his heel and strode from the room, closing the door a bit more enthusiastically than she thought necessary. Amy collapsed onto the settee and let out a huge breath.

Startled at the sound of the door slamming, her dog, Persephone, raced from where she had been enjoying a nap in the corner of the room and jumped onto Amy's lap. Amy tried to get herself under control as she petted her beloved animal.

Thank goodness that situation had ended.

After a few minutes, she placed Persephone on the floor, moved to the sideboard in the room, and poured herself two fingers of brandy. A most inappropriate drink for a lady, but when things were very difficult, she found it soothed her much more than the contents of a vinaigrette, which most ladies carried.

The door opened and Amy braced herself for Mr. St. Vincent's return. Her visitor, however, was Aunt Margaret, who frowned at the glass in Amy's hand. "Was that Mr. St. Vincent I just saw leaving?"

"Yes." She took another sip of the liquor.

"He looked a bit disturbed." Aunt glided across the room and poured herself a very ladylike glass of sherry. "To what occasion are we drinking?"

"The end of my betrothal." Amy wandered across the room and slumped in the blue-and-white-striped chair she always used when she needed comforting. It was in that chair that her mother had sung her to sleep at naptime when she was very young. She raised her glass. "To freedom."

"Heavens, Amy. Whatever made you end your betrothal? Does your father know?" Her aunt took the chair across from her, sitting on the very edge, her back as straight as an arrow.

"No, Papa does not know." She shifted in the seat. "He practically forced me into this marriage offer, you know."

Aunt smiled. "I hardly think anyone could force you into anything."

"All right, I concede that point—maybe not force, but he was very persuasive." At least if one could call insults and dire predictions of her dotage persuasive.

"What happened to make you suddenly decide to break your engagement?"

Amy swallowed the rest of her brandy and considered the empty glass for a minute, then placed it on the table next to her. She didn't wish to become sotted only to ease her nerves. "I received a note from someone—he or she did not identify themselves—that Mr. St. Vincent was involved in immoral and unacceptable behavior."

"Oh, my dear." Aunt took a large, and very ladylike, swallow of her sherry. "That sounds ominous. Did they identify this inappropriate behavior?"

"He is importing opium and selling it to people who are dependent on the drug and have no way to get it from a chemist or a pharmacist, who must abide by the rules." She shuddered just thinking about all those poor people whose life was a nightmare of addiction. She perked up. That would be a good plot in her next book.

"Not well done," Aunt Margaret said.

"Precisely."

"When will you tell your father?" Aunt placed her empty glass on the table in front of her and stood, brushing her skirts.

"Soon." 'Twas not something she looked forward to, since Papa would not be pleased. Amy rose as well, thinking of a long, hot bath, followed by tea, then bed. Persephone trotted behind her as they all left the room together.

Aunt Margaret offered a slight smile. "Good luck with that, my dear."

★ ★ ★

Tuesday evening, Amy was comfortably ensconced in her room with a book she'd been reading all week as she awaited the summons that William had arrived with the tome she wished to borrow.

In the few days since she'd had her scene with Mr. St. Vincent, she had begun to feel much better about her decision. She'd even written to Papa and expected to hear from him shortly.

Her attention was drawn away at a very inopportune part of the book by a light tap on her bedroom door.

"Come in."

Lacey, their parlormaid, entered. "Milady, you have a visitor."

Amy checked her timepiece. William was fifteen minutes early. "Very well, tell his lordship I will be down momentarily."

The maid shook her head. "No, milady, it is Mr. St. Vincent who has called."

"What?" Dratted man. She did not want to speak with him. Had she been in London, she would have had Papa deal with the man's visit this time, since he'd been the one to get her into the entanglement with Mr. St. Vincent to begin with. Her brother, Michael, who rarely spent time at their Bath home, was also in London, wreaking God knew what sort of havoc young men wreaked, so she was on her own. Although reluctant to admit it, even to herself, this was one time she would not have minded having a man to stand in front of her.

She had already had her say, and there wasn't anything else she wanted to discuss with him. Of course, she could instruct Lacey to refuse him admittance and send him on his way, but she might as well get it over with. She would emphasize that this was their very last visit and that she would no longer receive him, speak with him, or have anything at all to do with him.

"Very well, I will be down shortly. I am expecting Lord Wethington to call also, so please put him in the drawing room when he arrives and direct Mr. St. Vincent to the library. Once Lord Wethington arrives, please fetch me from the library."

She would just let St. Vincent cool his heels, since he had not been expected, and then be rid of him quickly once William was announced. She checked herself in the mirror and smoothed back the sides of her unruly hair—which was futile, since her locks never behaved as she wished, curls always popping out of her chignon. After checking her timepiece once more, assured that enough time had passed that she needn't spare her unexpected visitor more than a few minutes, she made her way downstairs to the library.

"I don't understand why you have called, sir." Her terse words bounced off the walls of the library as she flung the door open wide. The very empty library. Where had St. Vincent gone?

She quickly walked down the corridor to the drawing room, thinking Lacey had misunderstood. He was not there, either. She returned to the library, a slight draft coming from the open

French doors that led to the garden, drawing her attention. Odd, that. Perhaps he had taken a stroll outside. She rounded the desk in the middle of the room and stepped onto the patio.

"Mr. St. Vincent?"

Silence.

"Mr. St. Vincent?"

She walked the few steps down the patio stairs into the garden. Without a full moon, and with the typical English mist, she could see very little. She called again.

Silence.

The damp, chilled night air caused her to shiver. She rubbed her arms with her palms and returned to the library. Frowning, she placed her hands on her hips and surveyed the room. Perhaps he had thought better of his visit and had already departed. She shrugged and headed back to close the French doors. In her usual rapid gait, she had gone only about five steps past Papa's desk when she stumbled over something.

She fell forward, landing on her knees, her hands resting on a totally unfamiliar item that lay in the shadow of the desk. Had someone dropped a large object and not picked it up? She raised her hands to examine them, as they felt sticky. She climbed to her feet and stared down, her eyes slowly adjusting to the dimness of the shadowed corner.

Her hands came up to her lips as she screamed loud enough to tumble the walls.

CHAPTER 3

Amy backed away from the body on the floor just as a flushed and agitated William raced through the library door. "What happened? I heard you scream."

She shook her head back and forth as she continued to stare at the body of Mr. St. Vincent, a very large knife sticking out of his chest, his open eyes staring at nothing. All the blood left her head, and from what seemed like a vast distance, she heard William call her name just as her knees gave way and she slid to the floor.

Dear God, please don't let me fall on a dead body!

When she awoke, she was lying on the sofa with a very worried-looking William sitting alongside her, tapping her cheek. He waved something nasty under her nose, and she coughed. Her sweet Persephone, all white and fluffy, sat on her chest, staring at her with her yellow and hazel eyes. Before she was able to cuddle the little dog, William waved the obnoxious vial under her nose again.

Persephone turned to William and growled as Amy pushed his hand away. Whatever was she doing lying on the couch with William staring at her while her housekeeper, Mrs. Brady, and Stevens all carefully watched her as if they expected her to rise up and scream like a banshee?

As she was gathering her thoughts, Lacey entered the room and approached the group, her face pale, her eyes wide.

"Milord, I heard a scream. Is milady well?" Lacey glanced over the back of the sofa, sucked in a breath, and screamed herself.

Amy remembered as it all came rushing back. She struggled to sit up, dumping Persephone on the floor, banging her own head against William's chin. He rubbed the spot as she sputtered, "St. Vincent!" She looked at William and gripped his arm, her eyes wide. "Is he dead?"

"The man on the floor? The one I believe is your fiancé? Yes, I'm afraid so."

She waved her hand and coughed again. "Ex-fiancé."

He glanced over at the body. "I haven't checked the man closely, but blood no longer flows from the wound, so I am somewhat certain he has left this world."

How dare St. Vincent come here uninvited and then land on the floor in her library with a knife in his chest? The whole thing was so unbelievable, she wouldn't even use it as a plot in one of her books.

William looked at the group of servants who now stood huddled together, staring at her. Drawing on his consequence, he said, "Is Lord Winchester at home?"

The rattled staff ignored his question, but Amy closed her eyes as she pinched the bridge of her nose and shook her head. "No. He is in London."

"Perhaps your brother?"

"Not him either. He is making his presence known at the various clubs and gambling hells in London." She fisted her hands in her lap and sighed. Persephone jumped back onto her lap and flipped over, apparently wanting her tummy rubbed, which Amy ignored.

"*Bloody hell*." He might have mumbled the words, but she heard them. If only ladies were permitted to swear. She had a list of words she'd gathered over the years that she could use in this moment. One day, she vowed, when she was old, she'd let loose a torrent, and everyone would roll their eyes and say she was eccentric.

And she would drink as much brandy as she liked at any time of the day she chose.

"Very well, someone needs to take charge." He turned to Stevens, who Amy noted didn't look very well, his face as pale as new milk. The poor man was taking this hard. But then, she doubted his butler training had included guests being murdered in the library of one's employer. On the other hand, it was most likely the first murder for all present.

"Please send for the Bath police," William said.

Next he addressed Mrs. Brady, her ashen complexion making her a good candidate for the next woman to swoon. "Please fetch a blanket or sheet to cover the deceased." He turned to the remaining staff. "The rest of you may return to your duties."

They all shuffled out, leaving just William and Amy.

And a very dead Mr. St. Vincent.

She covered her face with her hands again. Perhaps she could pretend this was merely one of the scenes in her book. No, she reminded herself. Too unbelievable.

Gently, William pulled her hands down. "I think you might want to send for a wet cloth and clean yourself up."

Her brows furrowed; then she followed his glance to her hands and screeched once more. How had she forgotten they were covered with blood? She hopped up from the settee, dumping Persephone to the floor once again. The poor animal raced from the room at the rough treatment she had been subjected to. Amy danced around and jiggled her hands, as if to shake the blood off.

"Lady Amy!"

She waved frantically. "Get. It. Off."

"*Out, damned spot! Out, I say!*" he muttered.

She stopped her hopping about and glared at him. "This is no time for comedy, Lord Wethington." She took a deep breath to calm herself.

"Shall I send for someone to bring you a cloth?"

"No. If you will close the French doors, since the night air is quite chilly, I shall go wash."

As she left the room, William added, "Your face, too."

Still not too steady on her feet, Amy made her way to the kitchen, surprising Cook, who jumped as she entered. The room had been cleaned for the night, a lone lamp burning next to the bread for the morning, rising on the table with a cloth draped over the mounds.

"Oh, milady. My apologies." Cook's hand shook as she poured boiling water into a china teapot. Her portly body was covered in a pink flowered dressing gown, her hair hidden beneath a ruffled white cotton mop cap.

"No need to apologize. I merely need the sink."

The older woman placed her hand over her heart. "Is it true there is a dead man in the library, milady?"

Amy dipped her fingers into the soap tin and smeared it over her bloody hands. "Yes, I'm afraid that's quite true. But do not concern yourself. I am sure he will be removed before breakfast."

"He is your fiancé?" She whispered the words.

Amy sighed and nodded once. "My ex-fiancé."

She scrubbed her hands until they felt raw. *Out, damned spot*, indeed. Now that she was away from the library and more herself, she did find a bit of humor in Lady Macbeth's famous line. Very little humor, though, since a man was dead after all.

Her smile dimmed when her thoughts returned to the matter at hand. St. Vincent lying dead on her library floor. With a knife stuck in his chest. Had she ever considered that her decision to end her betrothal might not have been the correct one, the lack of sorrow she felt at seeing his lifeless form would have convinced her.

Not that she wished the man ill! And certainly not dead right under her feet. She shook her hands and then grabbed a cloth to dry them. Remembering the words William had tossed at her as she left the library, she dipped the cloth into the water once again and wiped her face.

"I will send in tea, milady. I find that always settles the nerves." Cook hustled around the kitchen, setting up a tray.

"Wait until the police leave." She was not going to entertain the Bath police department as if this were an afternoon social call. The sound of the door knocker reverberated through the house as Amy made her way from the kitchen back to the library. Two men entered.

So, this was it. The police had arrived and the questions would begin. Hopefully their first order of business would be to remove Mr. St. Vincent from the library.

"Bath police." The bigger of the two nodded to Stevens.

"This way, sirs." The butler turned and stopped when he saw her. "The police have arrived, my lady."

"Thank you, Stevens." She waved to the library door. "This room."

Taking a deep breath, she passed through the doorway, and they followed her. William stood near the French doors, a glass of brandy in his hand. She headed in his direction. "I would like a glass of something myself."

"Brandy or sherry?"

She leaned in close so the men who were examining the dead body couldn't hear. "I will have a small sherry now, but once they leave, I will require a very large brandy."

He poured a sherry and handed it to her, a slight smile of encouragement on his face.

The larger of the two detectives flipped the sheet back over St. Vincent's face. "May we sit, please." He took out a notebook and pencil.

They all sat in a circle around a small table, the two men dwarfing the chairs they'd chosen. "First of all, allow me to introduce ourselves. I am Detective Edwin Marsh, and this is Detective Ralph Carson."

She and William nodded in their direction.

The two men stared at her, forcing her to use all her control to not fidget in her seat. She might have a dead body in the library with a knife sticking out of it, but she'd done nothing wrong. She knew from her writing that detectives often used the tactic of silent intimidation to bully a suspect into a confession.

Except she was no suspect.

Detective Marsh had to be more than six feet tall, slender, with a well-lined face, even though he gave the appearance of being much younger. He had what Amy would call "sad" eyes. Until you looked deep into them and saw the strength and determination there. He was no one to fool with, reminding her of Shakespeare's Iago. In the play, Othello's man had appeared to be trustful but caused his master's downfall. She would need to watch herself around Detective Marsh.

His partner, Detective Carson, barely came up to Marsh's shoulders. He was round, bald, and had a perpetual smirk on his face, as if he intended to not believe anything he was told. She shuddered to think of how difficult the man could make her life if he so chose.

Marsh licked his pencil point and peered at her. "You are Lady Amy Winchester?"

"No. I am Lady Amy Lovell. Winchester is my father's title."

"Never could get all that stuff straight," he mumbled as he wrote. "Where is your father? Is he at home?"

"No. He and my brother, the Earl of Davenport—"

"Another title," Marsh groused as he scribbled.

"—only reside here on occasion. They are currently both at our home in London."

"Must be nice to be Top-of-the-Trees and have houses all over the place." Carson shook his head.

Truth be known, after only a few minutes she was growing weary of the man's surliness. Before she could speak with him about it, the man glared at her and leaned forward. "Did you know this man?" He waved in the direction of St. Vincent.

"Yes. I did."

"And who is he?" he growled. The detective had absolutely no finesse. And poor manners. There was certainly no need for him to speak to her as though she were a criminal.

"He is Mr. Ronald St. Vincent, third son of the Viscount Trembly." She paused for a moment and added, "Also, my former betrothed." She glanced sideways at William, who gave her an encouraging smile. There was no reason to not mention the connection, since it would become known anyway, and if she failed to mention it now, it would only cast her in a bad light later if they thought she was trying to hide something.

"Former?" Detective Marsh's head snapped up from his scribbling, studying her as if she'd just admitted to chasing St. Vincent around the room and plowing the knife into his chest.

She shuddered. She needed to pull herself together. She had nothing to feel guilty about. Perhaps she was entitled to feel annoyed at St. Vincent for getting himself stabbed in her library. Although he most likely hadn't planned it. She raised her chin, eyeing him with the look all ladies of the *ton* learned to perfection in the nursery. "That is correct. We were engaged, and I recently broke the engagement."

Carson leaned forward, his beady eyes examining her. "Care to tell me why?"

Amy glared at him. "I beg your pardon, sir? Did you just ask me why I broke my betrothal? Since that is none of your business, surely I misunderstood."

She didn't need to have known Detective Carson for long to realize he did not appreciate her answer. "No, you did not misunderstand, and it *is* my business. Someone murdered this man, and everyone who had a reason to do so is a suspect. I would say a broken engagement could be one of the reasons why Mr. St. Vincent is dead—and in your house, with no other family members present." There was nothing smooth or pleasant about the man. Honestly, was it necessary for him to be so very coarse?

She picked invisible lint from her skirts. "My reasons were personal." She wrestled with telling the detectives why she'd broken the engagement. If they uncovered that information during the investigation on their own, they would have no reason to assume she knew about it. In fact, admitting to knowledge of his activities might land her further up the suspect list if they believed she was involved in the sordid mess herself. The more distance she put between herself and that matter, the better.

Detective Marsh jumped in. "Did you have a fight with him and then stab him?"

Amy drew back and sucked in a breath. "Of course not. I broke the engagement a few nights ago. We did not fight then, and tonight I never even spoke with him."

"If you broke the engagement a few nights ago, what was he doing here?" Marsh continued to scribble, not bothering to look up at her.

"I have no idea. I wasn't expecting him at all." She hated that she'd begun to perspire. She kept reminding herself that she was innocent and the sooner they found the murderer, the faster she could put all this behind her.

And write her next book about a murder where she was not a suspect.

Carson jerked his thumb toward William but directed his comment to her. "Who is this bloke?"

"I am the Viscount Wethington." Apparently William was not going to be ignored.

Carson scowled, but Marsh wrote down the name. "You the new betrothed? Did she break up with this cur for you?" He gestured toward the shrouded body.

Amy was impressed when William merely smiled at the detective, not showing any surprise or annoyance. "No."

"Then why are you here?"

Maintaining his composed demeanor, he said, "I am here to deliver a book to Lady Amy that she requested to borrow."

"What book?"

Amy groaned when Wethington held the book out. Marsh took the tome, glanced at the cover, and looked at Amy, then passed it to Carson. "Interesting reading for a young lady. Have a need to discover why some murders go unsolved, do you?"

"Of course not. It is merely a hobby." Good heavens, if the man demanded to search her room, he would find a stack of books, newspapers, and other notes on murder that she used for reference for her novels.

"Unsolved murder is your hobby?" Marsh's eyebrows rose almost to his hairline.

William nudged her. "Might I suggest you don't answer any more questions until your father can be present?"

Detective Carson stood and approached St. Vincent's body. He looked around, and studying the floor, waddled, more than walked, from the body to the French doors. Once he had them opened, he returned to the table and picked up an oil lamp, then made his way back to the doors and walked through to the patio, studying the ground. Detective Marsh stood and wandered the room, examining books, the contents of the desk, and even sniffing the ink in the inkwell.

William took Amy's empty glass and returned to the sideboard, refilling both her glass and his.

"Your Mr. St. Vincent was stabbed in the garden." Carson returned to the room and placed the oil lamp back on the table.

"The garden?" She remembered now that the doors to the garden had been open when she'd entered the room. "Whatever was he doing in the garden?"

She hadn't realized she'd said the words out loud until Carson glared at her.

"You tell me. It looks like he was stabbed in the garden, then made his way back through the doors and collapsed here." He pointed to the body. "There is a trail of blood." Carson walked to her and went down on one knee. She batted his hand away as he touched her foot. "Sir, you forget yourself."

He looked up at her, a grin on his face. "The bottom of your shoe is wet."

"Of course it is. When I entered the library, Mr. St. Vincent was not here, but the doors were open. I went down the steps and called him, but he did not answer."

"He wouldn't. He was dead," the detective said unnecessarily as he stood and brushed his hands.

"I know that now," she huffed. "Are you always this obtuse?"

He scratched his head. "Not sure what that means, but probably."

So far the man had proven to be anything but obtuse. For the second time in less than an hour she reminded herself that Detective Carson could make her life difficult if he so chose.

"My good man, might I request that you have Mr. St. Vincent's body removed and allow Lady Amy to retire for the night? I am sure she will be more than happy to answer your questions in the morning." William had seemed to grow agitated as the questioning continued.

"I am sorry, my lord, but this isn't a high-class ball where you can come and go as you please. This is murder. And we have to investigate. Since she"—Marsh pointed to Amy—"admitted chucking the man, and he's dead in her house, and you are sitting nice and cozy alongside her, she is our main suspect."

Their main suspect? Amy had to fight the desire to either scream or slide to the floor once again in a faint. She fought the black dots that appeared in front of her eyes.

William stood and placed his hand on her shoulder. "If your only motive for this murder is Lady Amy breaking her betrothal, with no consideration of the sort of person she is, and disregarding all the other reasons why the man could have ended up dead in her library—"

"Yes. That is our case." Marsh snapped the notebook shut. "We are expecting the coroner any moment to remove the body, and then we will notify the man's family. Right now I want this room locked until he arrives. Once he leaves, the door to this room will be kept locked as well as the garden doors, with no one—and I mean no one—allowed to enter until we do a complete examination of the murder scene.

"I will leave instructions with your man at the door to do that." He pointed his notebook at her. "Right now, due to your station, we are not taking you to jail tonight. But you are to remain in Bath, no running off to London to any of your la-di-da events until we give you permission to leave. We will return in the morning, along with other members of the department, to examine this room carefully while Carson and I have a conversation with your father, who I suggest you summon from London. We will also need to speak with every member of your staff."

Still shaken at their blasé comment that she was a suspect, she licked her dry lips and attempted to slow down her heartbeat.

The two men nodded briefly and stood at the entrance to the room until she and William left with them.

Once the front door closed, she led unfortunate William, who had been caught up in this mess, to the drawing room. She took a deep breath and sat on the settee. "I will have that brandy now." She nodded to the sideboard in the drawing room, where several bottles of liquor sat. If the mess didn't end quickly, she might soon be storing spirits in her bedchamber.

He crossed the room and poured a splash into a tumbler.

"A little bit more, please."

After adding another finger, he returned to the settee and handed it to her. She took a healthy swallow.

They had no sooner settled into their chairs than their peace was shattered by a loud voice at the front door. Amy cringed and cast an apologetic glance at William. She drew herself up as Papa appeared at the doorway, a scowl on his flushed face.

Aunt Margaret stood alongside him, her elegant brows raised. "Oh my dear, dear girl, what have you done this time?"

CHAPTER 4

William stood as Papa and Aunt entered the room. Beginning to feel the effects of the sherry and brandy, Amy thought it best if she remained seated. The look on Papa's face as he cast his regard in William's direction had her wondering if William planned to take his leave. Desperate at what she assumed would be his imminent departure, she said, "Stay for tea, my lord?"

"Wethington, is it not?" Papa strode across the room in the direction of the sideboard. She'd forgotten how Papa knew just about everyone in the *ton*. "Care for a drink, my boy?" He tossed the words over his shoulder.

Boy? She didn't think William would care too much for that moniker.

"No, sir." Maybe William was also feeling the effects of the liquor, which was unlikely, since men seemed to handle it much better than women. Or maybe her father's supercilious presence overwhelmed him.

"Cook is sending in tea, Papa."

Papa ignored her and poured a brandy, then looked at Aunt Margaret with raised brows.

"No, thank you, Arthur. I believe I need a clear head to keep the two of you from adding to the body count." Aunt Margaret settled on a comfortable chair and regarded her and William with curiosity.

Papa poured a brandy for himself and waved William to the settee across from where Aunt Margaret sat, her back rigid. "Take a seat and see if you can explain to me why my daughter is in trouble once again."

"Papa, I am not in trouble *once again*."

"Is there a dead man in my library?"

She raised her chin. "Yes."

He waved his glass, the liquid swirling around. "Is he not the man to whom you are betrothed?"

"Not anymore."

"Obviously. 'Tis hard to marry a dead man. Was he dead when he arrived?"

Lady Amy shook her head. Heavens, the man could shoot questions at a person so rapidly she wasn't sure what was up and what was down. He'd done that to her for years, which was how she'd found herself betrothed to St. Vincent in the first place.

He gulped the rest of his brandy. "Then, to my way of thinking, you are in trouble once again."

Amy drew herself up. "Certainly you don't think I had something to do with his murder?"

"Of course not." Papa rose and headed back to the sideboard. He refilled the glass a bit more generously than the last time. "However, the fact remains, according to Stevens at the door, St. Vincent was hale and hearty when he arrived, and now he is cold and lifeless." He shook his head. "Nasty business."

Stevens entered the room, pushing a cart with a teapot and several cups and saucers, along with a tray of tarts and biscuits. Aunt Margaret motioned for him to bring the cart next to her, where she would pour tea for those who wanted it.

Amy needed a very strong cup of tea at that moment to clear her befuddled head so she could deal with her father.

Papa studied the liquid in his glass. "Perhaps you can enlighten me as to why I found a letter on my breakfast table this morning with a note from my lovely daughter that she had broken the engagement I had arranged for her. Then I take the day's last train to Bath to discuss this turn of events and find two members of the Bath police leaving my house and a corpse in my library."

Amy accepted a teacup from Aunt Margaret, her stomach rebelling at the idea of any of the tarts or biscuits her aunt offered her. William took a cup with a nod and a smile at Aunt.

"I informed Mr. St. Vincent a few nights ago that I wished to break our engagement."

"'Twas considerate of you to inform me of this before it happened."

"I intended to tell you. But I thought it best to get it over with when I found out some disturbing information about Mr. St. Vincent."

Winchester waved his hand for her to continue.

"Tonight he called on me. Unfortunately, I never learned what his intention was, because by the time I arrived in the library, he was already dead." She shuddered. "A knife in his chest."

Papa swung his attention to William. "How are you involved in this, Wethington?"

William straightened in his seat and placed his teacup and saucer on the table alongside him. Papa could do that to people. "I called to bring a book to Lady Amy that she wished to borrow."

"Continue."

"When I arrived, there was excitement among the staff and screams coming from Lady Amy, who seemed to be in distress. I found Mr. St. Vincent lying on the floor in your library with a knife in his chest. I asked one of the servants to summon the police."

Her father nodded and took another sip of brandy. Then he turned toward her. "I assume, given the facts as they are, that you are the suspect?"

No point in showing outrage at her father's words, since that was the case. "Most likely. The detectives who were here were not very pleasant." The tea had helped to clear her head from the liquor and calm her nerves. She was feeling more in control of herself. Which was always important where Papa was concerned.

"'Tis their job to be unpleasant toward suspected murderers."

Her chin rose in the air. "They told me I was not permitted to leave Bath."

Papa rubbed his temples. "I shall have my local solicitor call on me in the morning to see if he can recommend a barrister."

Lady Amy's eyes grew wide. "You think I will need a legal representative?"

"Of course you do, young lady. You broke your engagement with Mr. St. Vincent. He shows up here—God only knows why—and ends up dead with a very large knife stuck in his chest. I doubt if the Bath police would believe a maid or a footman was overcome with the need to do away with the man."

"Excuse my interruption, my lord, but there was other evidence the detectives uncovered while they were here."

When Papa only nodded in his direction, William continued. "Lady Amy had gone into the garden to see if Mr. St. Vincent was there when she didn't find him in the library, so her shoes were wet from the grass. One of the detectives noted that Mr. St. Vincent was stabbed in the garden and left a trail of blood to the library, where he collapsed."

Papa shook his head. "Well done, my girl. Well done."

Amy closed her eyes and sighed.

"May I ask a question, my lord?" William asked.

"Go on," her father said.

"May I be present when the barrister calls? I heard the exchange between the detectives and Lady Amy, and as she was a bit distraught during the questioning, I might be able to remember things that will help."

"Or hurt," Lady Amy said.

"My lord, the coroner has arrived." Stevens entered the drawing room, still looking a bit out of sorts.

"Fine. Lead them to the library." Lady Margaret walked over to Amy and extended her hand. "Come, my dear, you best get some sleep. I will have Cook fix a tisane for you."

Amy took her aunt's hand and rose. She felt the result of all the evening's events and wanted more than anything to gain her bed. Hopefully, Papa would not notice how wobbly on her feet she was.

"My lady, I left the book you wished to borrow in the library. Perhaps it is best if I bring it home with me."

"What book is this?" Papa asked.

"*Unsolved Gruesome and Ghastly Murders of London* by Melvin Fulsom." William's voice lowered at the end when Papa's brows threatened to fly off the top of his head.

"Lord Wethington, I think it is probably best if you took the book home once we are able to enter the room. In fact, how much would it cost me to have you burn the thing?"

★ ★ ★

After a disturbed night's sleep, Amy was summoned from her bedchamber by Lacey, who still looked a bit pale. "Milady, Lord Winchester has requested your presence in the drawing room."

"Thank you, Lacey."

The maid twisted her hands in her apron. "Oh, milady, do you suppose they will hang you?"

The little bit of breakfast Amy had managed to swallow earlier made a reappearance at the back of her throat. "Of course not, Lacey. I did nothing wrong."

Taking a deep breath, she rose from the seat by the window, where she pretended to read a book to get her mind off the events of the prior evening. She'd tossed and turned all night, unable to forget the sight of St. Vincent staring up at her with blank eyes, his body stiff and pale.

Whatever had he come to see her about, anyway? She'd made it clear their betrothal was at an end. Was it possible the reason for his visit had something to do with his murder? She rubbed her palms up and down her arms, feeling as though she would never be warm again.

Grabbing a thick plaid woolen shawl that Aunt Margaret had brought her from her last visit to Scotland, she scooped Persephone into her arms and made her way downstairs. The knocker on the door sounded as she reached the bottom step. Stevens opened the door and stepped back to admit William.

Not quite sure why, Amy felt a bit calmer at the sight of him. He bowed to her after handing off his gloves, hat, and coat to the butler. "Has the barrister yet arrived?"

"I don't know. I was just summoned to the drawing room."

Papa and another man both rose as she and William stepped through the doorway.

"Ah, here is my daughter now." Papa came from around his chair and took her hand in his to draw her forward. "This is Lady Amy." He nodded in William's direction. "And the young man I told you about who happened upon the scene last night. Lord Wethington."

At least he hadn't called him *boy* again.

Both men shook hands.

"Amy, Mr. Nelson-Graves is a barrister and has agreed to assist us in this matter." He turned toward William. "He has been highly recommended by my solicitor, Mr. David Hearns."

Ever the hostess, Amy gestured to the chairs forming a slight semicircle around the low table near the fireplace. "Shall we be seated? I will send for refreshments."

They managed small talk about the weather, politics, and the arrival of spring while they waited for the tea cart. Amy wished they could just get to it. The horrid detectives from the police the night before had never mentioned what time they would be arriving for their return visit.

The housekeeper entered the room, followed by a footman pushing the tea cart. With Amy feeling as unsettled as she did, she asked Mrs. Brady to pour so she would not scald one of the men with hot tea to add to her crimes. She continued to smooth her palm over a very contented Persephone. The movement was a comfort to her and a joy to her beloved dog.

The latch on the drawing room door clicked softly as the servants left, and the group grew silent. Mr. Nelson-Graves cleared his throat. "Perhaps it would be best if you told me, in your own words, Lady Amy, how the events of last night progressed." He placed his teacup in the saucer and picked up a pad of paper and a pencil.

Her stomach churned, and she looked to William for support. Prior to now, her friendship with him had been lengthy, but confined to not much more than a few dances at the Assembly Rooms and debates at the book club. However, she felt connected to him. Most likely that happened when two people stood side by side and gaped at a bloody murdered man at their feet.

William nodded at her, and she took a deep breath. "A few days ago, I summoned Mr. St. Vincent to my home for the purpose of advising him that I intended to call an end to our betrothal."

"And why was that?"

Amy glanced over at Papa, hoping she had misunderstood this question. "Why was what, Mr. Nelson-Graves?" She took a delicate sip of tea, hoping she looked very innocent. Perhaps that would work when the detectives arrived.

The barrister looked up from his notes. "Why did you break your engagement?"

"I felt that we no longer suited."

Papa snorted and jumped up. He strode across the room and poured himself a brandy. He held the bottle up. "Lord Wethington?"

"No, thank you, my lord. The tea is fine."

Papa returned to his seat. "Not for me. Don't care how early in the day it is. I don't like my daughter being under suspicion of murder." He waved at Nelson-Graves, who had stopped writing to observe Papa. "Continue."

The barrister looked at her. "And how did Mr. St. Vincent take this news?"

Papa leaned back, swirling the brandy around in his glass, his eyes never leaving her. Although he had harangued her into accepting Mr. St. Vincent, he'd said many times that he only wanted what he thought was best for her. Not unlike other women of her station. Marriage, a home of her own to manage, and children to raise.

He'd told her years before that since he'd not been successful with his sister, he would not make the same mistake twice. Hence his determination to push Amy headlong into marital bliss.

Truth be told, marriage was not something she had anything against, except she wanted more from a lifelong commitment than merely convenience. Her ideal marriage partner was just that. A partner. Certainly not someone who would expect to rule her life and oversee her every move. "I'm afraid my interview with Mr. St. Vincent did not go well."

"Did he become abusive?"

"No. Not at all. Frankly, it was all over quite quickly. However, he made it obvious that he was not pleased. The conversation was short. I gave him his ring back and he left." She was still dithering on whether to reveal the anonymous note, the details contained in the missive, and her interview with the contact who had confirmed the information.

She took a sip of tea and continued. "For some unknown reason, he arrived again at my home last evening and requested an audience."

"Had he sent word ahead of time?"

Amy shook her head. "No. I was not expecting him."

"Go on."

"When I entered the library, he was nowhere to be seen. After checking the drawing room to determine if he was there, I returned to the library, and then noticed the French doors to the patio were open, so I thought perhaps he had stepped outside for a breath of fresh air.

"However, I went as far into the garden as I could with the lack of light and then returned to the library. After taking only a few steps into the room, I stumbled over something and fell to my hands and knees. It turned out to be Mr. St. Vincent's body." She shuddered.

"Dead?"

"Yes. Very dead."

When he'd finished with his note-taking, Mr. Nelson-Graves looked up at William. "And how do you figure into this, my lord?"

William cleared his throat. "I had arrived to bring a book to Lady Amy that she had asked to borrow. As I entered the home, I heard a scream and hurried to the library, from where the sound had come. I found Lady Amy staring at the dead man—who I later learned was Mr. St. Vincent."

"And Mr. St. Vincent had a knife stuck in him?"

"Yes."

The door opened and Stevens stepped into the room. "My lord, the men from the Bath police department have arrived."

Mr. Nelson-Graves tucked away his notepad with his scrawled notes and pulled out a clean pad. "Lady Amy, I advise you to look to me when the detectives ask you questions. I will nod if you should answer and interrupt if I feel you are incriminating yourself."

Amy broke into a sweat. Incriminating herself? Good lord, this was real. Not one of her books that she plotted and took such joy in writing, but a real murder. And she was a genuine suspect. Truthfully, if she were not a member of the aristocracy, she would most likely right now be finding herself in prison. Just the thought of such a dreadful place raised gooseflesh on her arms.

The two men from the previous evening entered the room, and Amy's mouth dried up. She shifted in her seat so she was closer to William, which Papa took note of with raised eyebrows. William reached out and patted her hand.

After the men had been seated and declined an offer of tea, the one who had introduced himself the night before as Detective Ralph Carson leaned forward. "Are you ready to confess now, Lady Amy?"

CHAPTER 5

All the blood drained from Amy's face, and her heart began to pound. Sitting on her lap, Persephone must have sensed her fear, because she growled in the detective's direction. "I beg your pardon, Mr. Carson?" Surely she hadn't heard him correctly.

Mr. Nelson-Graves shifted in his seat, glaring at the detective. "I request that you not harass my client by asking such provocative questions. If you care to make reasonable inquiries, I will be happy to instruct Lady Amy which ones to answer. On the other hand, we will call an end to this session entirely if you do not abide by the rules of common decency."

Carson smirked. "I take it you are the barrister?"

"Yes. My name is Mr. Nelson-Graves, a barrister from London. I have been retained by Lord Winchester on behalf of his daughter, Lady Amy."

Amy offered the horrible detective a tight smile. "Would you care for some tea? I can send for another cart to be brought in." *And then pour the hot beverage over your head.*

Ignoring her offer, Detective Marsh studied her carefully. "Perhaps my partner was a bit premature in his questioning."

"Sir, perhaps before you begin questioning my daughter in *my* home, or make premature, ridiculous assumptions, I would know who you are." Lord Winchester spoke softly, with all the power and dignity of his station. He reclined in the comfortable winged chair, his arms resting casually on the armrests, his gold-and-ruby ring with the family crest passed down from centuries of Winchester ancestors catching the light coming through the window.

Carson blanched and wiped the smirk from his face. "I apologize, my lord. I am Detective Ralph Carson, and this is my partner, Detective Edwin Marsh, from the Bath police."

After a few moments' pause, Papa dipped his head slightly at their introduction, and everyone turned their attention to the barrister, who cleared his throat.

"I must warn you that Lady Amy will answer no questions I feel are inappropriate, self-incriminating, or unnecessary. Furthermore, I want it noted that I find your initial question to be crass and unfounded."

Although Detective Carson flinched at the barrister's terse words, he glanced briefly at Papa and said, "Hardly unfounded, Mr. Nelson-Graves. Lady Amy was discovered in the library last evening with a dead man at her feet." Carson leaned in closer to the barrister. "The man in question was her fiancé."

"Ex-fiancé," Amy whispered.

Carson waved a dismissive hand in her direction. "No matter. The point is, she broke their engagement and he showed up, possibly to discuss the situation, and ended up dead."

"And why do you assume my client is the guilty party? What is your proof?"

"Her shoes were wet."

Nelson-Graves continued to stare at the man. "And?"

Detective Marsh jumped in. "According to what we have ascertained from our investigation last evening, Mr. St. Vincent apparently left the room through the French doors and descended to the garden. There he was attacked with the knife, stumbled his way back up the stairs to the patio, through the doors, into the library, where he collapsed. The grass was damp and so were Lady Amy's shoes. It follows that she was in the garden also."

The barrister raised his eyebrows. "My good man, did you not consider that she went into the garden to see if Mr. St. Vincent was there?"

Ignoring his question, Carson turned to Lady Amy. "I would have you answer a few questions."

Lady Amy looked over at Mr. Nelson-Graves, who nodded at her.

Detective Carson leaned forward, his focus on Lady Amy. She began to perspire, and somewhere in the back of her mind she told herself to remember this so she could show true emotion the next time she wrote an interrogation with a suspect. She unclenched her hands when Persephone let her know she was grasping the poor dog like a lifeline.

"Let's start at the beginning again. Why did you end your engagement with Mr. St. Vincent?"

"I felt we no longer suited."

"Why is that?"

Lady Amy hesitated. "Personal reasons."

"A reason, perhaps, to kill him?"

Nelson-Graves frowned at the detective. "Do not answer that question, Lady Amy."

Detective Carson continued while Marsh scribbled answers. "Why would Mr. St. Vincent return after you already broke your engagement?"

"Reading others' minds has never been one of my talents, sir, so I could not tell you why he would return."

"Did he come back for his ring, perhaps?"

"No. I had already returned it."

Detective Carson studied her carefully. "Were you aware of the fact that the deceased was involved in the opium trade?"

It seemed she didn't have to hold on to that information to save St. Vincent's reputation after all. "It had come to my attention, yes."

Papa shifted in his seat and sat forward. She didn't look at his face but imagined his surprise.

"Is that the reason you ended your engagement?" Carson fired the question so fast while Marsh continued to scribble that she was beginning to feel a bit dizzy.

"Yes."

Carson allowed her to take a sip of her tea, where she noted her hand shook, and then continued with his questioning. Obviously feeling the tension in her mistress, Persephone jumped from her lap and trotted close to the fireplace, where she proceeded to walk in a circle and then collapse on the floor, ignoring the humans in the room. "How did you find out about St. Vincent's opium connection?"

"I received a note with the information."

Marsh jumped in. "From whom?"

Amy patted the perspiration on her upper lip with a napkin. "I don't know. It was unsigned."

"Where is the note?"

"I lost it," she blurted. She'd never been good at lying, so she hoped glancing down at her tea would hide the untruth in her eyes. She'd kept the note and had every intention of keeping it until she decided it would be more beneficial in the police's hands. Right now she wanted whatever she could get to help her solve this mystery on her own. These two men were so sure of her guilt that she didn't trust them to uncover the truth.

"Now let us talk about the night he was killed," Marsh continued.

Her breathing increased, but she stiffened her shoulders, ready to take on the detectives. "Very well."

"Describe for us exactly what happened from the time you learned he was here to speak with you."

Lady Amy turned to the barrister, who nodded.

"I was summoned from my bedchamber by our parlormaid, Lacey. I had been expecting Lord Wethington, who was loaning me a book. However, when I mentioned that, my maid informed me Lord Wethington was not my caller, but Mr. St. Vincent. I told her to put him in the library and when his lordship arrived to put him in the drawing room." She glanced over at William, who gave her an encouraging smile.

"Tell us, step by step, what happened once you left your bedchamber." Both Mr. Nelson-Graves and Detective Marsh held pencils poised over notepads. She felt as though she stood at the front of a classroom, ready to read her essay to the class while the teacher stood at the ready, prepared to write her comments—and in Amy's case, mostly criticism.

Once more she recited the events that led to her finding St. Vincent in the library. She was already weary of telling the story, but she knew that over the next few weeks she would have to do so many more times.

Once her narrative was finished, Detective Carson turned his attention to William. "Please tell us what happened when you heard Lady Amy scream."

"I followed the sound down the corridor with the man at the door on my heels. We entered the room to see her ladyship staring at something on the floor. It was not dark in the room, but a bit dim, so I turned on a few gas lamps on my way to her and looked down.

"Mr. St. Vincent was lying on his back, his eyes open and a knife in his chest."

The detective reached into a satchel resting next to him and withdrew a large knife. "Is this the knife?"

Amy closed her eyes at the sight of the bloody knife, all the tea she'd consumed ready to make a reappearance.

"I believe so," William said.

"Wait one minute." Mr. Nelson-Graves stood and walked to the detective, looking closely at the weapon. "I want Winchester's cook to look at that knife."

The detective glowered. "Very well."

Papa walked to the brocade bell pull by the door and yanked it four times. "I suggest we take a minute to give my daughter a respite while we wait for our cook to arrive."

Amy took a deep breath and relaxed. Fool, her. Even with her background on writing murder mysteries, she hadn't thought to ask Cook if the knife belonged to them. But then again, the coroner had taken it, along with the body, and she had not been in any frame of mind to think of that while they waited for the police to arrive.

"You summoned me, milord?" Cook entered the drawing room, glancing at the somber-looking group and immediately tensed.

"Yes. The detectives from the Bath police wish to ask you a question." Papa spoke in a calming tone, which appeared to put Cook a bit more at ease.

Detective Carson held up the knife. "Do you recognize this knife?"

Cook stepped back, her eyes wide as she looked from Papa to the detective and shook her head. "No. I have never seen that knife before. It is not one of ours."

"You are certain?" Carson looked annoyed.

"Yes, sir. Not one of ours."

After a quick curtsy, Cook left the room, mumbling to herself, and the questioning continued for what Amy felt was hours. They went over and over the same information until she wanted to scream. They had her retrace her steps for them. Then had William do the same. From her own research, she knew it was a way for the police to trip up a suspect. Ask the same question to see if the answers were different in any way.

Finally the two detectives stood. "We are finished for today."

Amy was embarrassed to realize her underarms were wet and she probably smelled. All she wanted to do was take a nice long bath, followed by lunch and a nap.

"Detective Marsh," Mr. Nelson-Graves said. "I assume there is no reason for my client to remain under suspicion. She has answered all of your questions."

"Not so. She might have answered all our questions, but she is still the main suspect. She had reason, place, and time. No one saw her enter the library to note how long she was there before she screamed. Her shoes were wet, and one of your staff mentioned she had blood on her hands when he arrived at the scene."

"We have established she went to the garden to seek Mr. St. Vincent, so her shoes would be wet. She fell on the body, so her hands would have blood on them. The cook has already stated the murder weapon did not belong to this household." Mr. Nelson-Graves drew himself up. "I demand you continue your search for the actual murderer."

"I suggest you conduct your legal representation and we will continue with our investigation. Do not be concerned, my good man. We shall carry on with a thorough search." He turned toward Amy and pointed his finger at her. "Once again, I remind you not to leave Bath."

Amy bristled under their command and stood to walk to the window as Persephone raced from the fireplace, her nap apparently finished, and jumped into her arms. She snuggled with the beloved dog as Detective Marsh looked toward Papa.

"In all fairness, I must advise you that one of our men obtained a list of your staff members and conducted a search in our files."

Papa's brows rose, and he nodded at the detective. "Yes?"

"It seems your gardener, Mr. Albright, served time in prison for murder."

"Has he been arrested?" Papa sputtered. Papa never sputtered.

Marsh shrugged. "No. He has not been located. However, he is your employee. Did you not know his background before he was hired?"

Everyone in the room swung their attention to Amy.

CHAPTER 6

"Who hired the gardener?" Papa glared at Amy, his face flushed bright red as the two detectives left the room. "I don't remember engaging anyone for this house."

Amy raised her chin, ready to do combat. Papa was correct. Since he was rarely, if ever, present in their Bath townhouse, she and Aunt Margaret had done all the hiring. "I hired him."

"Did you check references?"

Botheration. She probably hadn't. In fact, if memory served, Aunt Margaret was in London having new wardrobe items made when the necessity to hire a gardener had arisen, and Amy had asked one of the staff members—who no longer worked for them—to recommend someone. She'd been in the middle of a book that was giving her a great deal of trouble, and all her concentration had been taken up with that.

"Of course. What sort of an employer do you think I am?"

"The kind who finds out one of their employees is a murderer. Right after a murder is committed on the premises." Papa stomped over to the sidebar and picked up the bottle of brandy to pour himself another drink. He looked over at Mr. Nelson-Graves, who was shoving papers into his satchel. "Are you headed back to London?"

"Yes. I squeezed this visit in by putting off another appointment. I must hurry to make the new time arranged."

"Wait and I will take the rail to London with you."

Papa downed the drink just as Aunt Margaret entered the room. She sailed across the room and took the brandy bottle out of Papa's hand. "Much too early, brother. Is the interview over?"

He looked longingly at the bottle. "Yes. It is. Were you aware of the fact that your gardener, Mr. Albright, spent time in prison for murder?"

Aunt Margaret sucked in a deep breath and covered her chest with her hand. She turned to Amy. "Murder?" For once her placid demeanor escaped her.

Amy nodded. "Apparently."

"Did you check his references?" Papa asked that question of Aunt Margaret.

"Of course," Aunt Margaret said quickly. She probably didn't even remember that she had been out of town when Amy hired Mr. Albright. Since the man had his own rooms miles away, it hadn't seemed like such a poor decision at the time to trust him with a few flowers and shrubs. He wasn't likely to make off with the family silver. Or flowerpots.

No. Maybe just murder a guest.

Papa turned to William. "I have a number of matters in London that need my immediate attention. I did not expect to have to travel here to assist in a murder."

Well, botheration. Perhaps the next time someone was contemplating murder in their library, he would ask the victim to wait until it was a convenient time for Papa.

"Will you assist my daughter in locating this gardener and see that he is fired—if he is not arrested first for murder?" Papa continued.

Annoyed that her father felt it was necessary to ask William to "assist," which in his mind meant take over, she swallowed the words she wished to say. But then again, if she and Aunt

Margaret had someone working for them with a murder in his background, Papa probably felt they did need the guidance of a man.

William nodded at her father. "Please do not concern yourself, my lord. I will do what I can to assist."

"And once you find this man, notify the police of his whereabouts. That might clear this whole thing up quickly." Papa nodded toward William and turned to Amy before leaving the room with Mr. Nelson-Graves. "Stay out of trouble, daughter. Send a message if the police return with the absurd idea of arresting you." He gave her a quick kiss on the cheek, his usual departing gesture, except this time he pulled her in for a hug also.

Amy made her way over to the sofa near the fireplace and sat, petting Persephone as the little dog licked his rear end. Whatever would she do if the police *did* return to arrest her? She could always climb out a window, but with nowhere to go, that seemed like a foolish idea.

Her aunt sat next to her and took her hand. "My dear, I believe while this nasty business is going on, you should conduct your life as usual. Keep your social engagements and don't answer any foolish questions. If rumors begin—which they most certainly will—it is important that you are seen as a victim of a crime against a friend and not a suspect."

"Thank you, Aunt Margaret. That is precisely what I will do." She batted Persephone's tongue away from her ministrations.

"Even though the detectives seem to be focused on you, if they had sufficient proof, they would not have walked out of here without you in handcuffs."

Although Aunt Margaret meant well, her words flooded Amy's insides with fear, but also with determination to not stand by while she was under suspicion. She nodded. "Thank you. I am sure they will find the culprit soon."

"Very good, niece. Remember how politicians deal with these type of things. Until they are carted off and tossed behind bars yelling and screaming, they always proclaim their innocence, even when the evidence is overwhelming."

Wonderful. Now Aunt was comparing her to some unsavory public servant with dirt on his hands and illegally gotten money in his bank account.

"I am off this evening to a musicale at Mr. Berry's home." Aunt Margaret had a very active social life and was liked by many. Amy never stopped wondering why someone as poised, pretty, and amicable as her aunt had never married.

She often pondered whether there was a broken heart in Aunt Margaret's history. Then she chastised herself for assuming, like everyone else in the world, that there had to be a *reason* Aunt Margaret had never married. Perhaps she simply didn't want to.

"Do you wish to join me?"

Amy shook her head. "Thank you, but I believe I will remain at home this evening. I feel the beginnings of a megrim and think an early night is a good idea."

Aunt Margaret patted her hand and stood. "If you change your mind, let me know." With a kiss to the top of Amy's head, her aunt left the room.

"This is certainly a mess you find yourself in, Amy." William regarded her from where he stood in front of the window. "If there is anything I can do to help, please ask."

She grinned and walked across the room to stand right in front of him. Persephone growled. Amy backed up. Sometimes the dog could be a bit unsociable. "I plan to solve the murder myself."

His brows rose. "Excuse me? I believe I just heard you say you planned to solve the murder yourself."

"That would be correct." She nuzzled the soft fur on her dog. "*I* intend to find the real killer."

William sighed and smiled at her like she was a child suggesting she could fly. "First of all, what do you know about murders, and how will you discover anything the police cannot?"

Amy smirked and placed Persephone on the floor. The dog ran in circles around William's feet several times, barking wildly, stopped, licked her bottom, then walked off, her chin in the air. "If I tell you something, you must promise to never repeat the information. Do you agree?"

William raised one eyebrow and leaned against the windowsill, his arms crossed. The sun coming through the glass behind him cast a shadow over his face. She wanted to see his expression when she told him. "Let's sit over there"—she waved her arm—"on the sofa."

He shook his head and grinned. "Lead the way, my lady."

Once they were settled side by side on the sofa, she said, "I am very familiar with police activity, my lord." She lowered her voice, even though the room contained only her and William.

"Indeed? All the reading you've done? Is that why you wanted to borrow my book?"

"Noooo." She dragged the word out and picked the dog hairs from her skirt. "I am familiar with killers because I write about murders all the time. I am the mystery writer E. D. Burton."

He hesitated for a moment, then grinned. "And I am Mr. Arthur Conan Doyle, so we make a fine team."

She shook her head. "I am not lying, William. I *am* the mystery writer E. D. Burton."

Almost a full minute of silence passed as William stared at her before he offered a slight, somewhat unsure-of-himself smile. "Well done, Amy. You almost had me believing that."

"It's true."

He shook his head. "E. D. Burton is a very talented and popular mystery writer."

Amy dipped her head. "Thank you for the compliment."

"Although this is all quite amusing, I must state again that, surely, you jest. E. D. Burton is most definitely a man. A very talented man. No woman could write such things."

While she enjoyed his praise of her books, it was a tad insulting that he could not stretch his imagination far enough to believe a woman could write mysteries. At least this woman, anyway. In fact, she was becoming more than a bit annoyed. If he had told her he was truly Arthur Conan Doyle, she would not have interrogated him in such a manner. It stung that men had such an opinion of women.

"No, I do not jest, and yes, a woman could write such things. Because I do."

She reached down and scooped up Persephone, who had graced them with her presence once again. She settled comfortably on Amy's lap and then proceeded to stare up at William.

"Let me understand this. You are E. D. Burton, whose books we've read and discussed at the Mystery Book Club."

She nodded, unable to keep the grin from her face at his discombobulation.

William jumped up and ran his fingers through his hair, turning in a circle. He pinched the bridge of his nose, stopped, and looked at her, his hands on his hips. "E. D. Burton?"

There was really no need to once again claim her alternate identity. Honestly, the man was becoming almost boorish in his refusal to believe her. She just sat and stared at him.

"Why?" He almost choked on the word. "Why would a sweet young woman such as yourself write horror stories?"

He thought she was sweet? How very nice. She almost forgave him for his stubbornness.

Almost.

"Do you wish to know why I write them, or why it has been a secret? And why am I telling you this now?"

"Yes." He waved his hand around as if directing an orchestra. "All of the above."

She gave herself a minute to consider. She'd never really thought too much about her desire to tell stories, except that ever since she'd been a young girl she'd always seemed to have a story in her head. For as odd as that sounded.

"I write them because I can. And I must. That is the only explanation I can give you, the only one that makes sense. To me, at least. When I began writing seriously, Papa was appalled. I made the mistake of letting him read my first manuscript, and he was a bit overwhelmed by some of the details in the murder scenes."

"Indeed. I remember wondering if the club should even read a couple of those books because of the tender sensibilities of the ladies."

"I have no tender sensibilities."

"Clearly."

Not sure if she'd just been insulted, she continued. "Anyway, when I told him I had received a contract for the book, he ordered—which didn't work too well with me—then *asked* nicely if I would use a pseudonym."

"And E. D. Burton was born?"

She grinned. "Yes."

"I am afraid that I don't know whether I am also appalled or impressed."

"Impressed would be nice."

He stared off into the distance at the portraits of her dead and unknown ancestors gracing the west wall of the drawing room. The ones Papa couldn't abide looking at in his London townhouse library so had sent here.

She could see the emotions playing over William's face. Stubborn disbelief, denial, then finally acceptance. Apparently, something she'd said had convinced him. "Aside from that—I now bow to your superior knowledge in solving murders—you are the one under suspicion for Mr. St. Vincent's murder. What do you intend to do?"

She tilted her head and looked at him. Sometimes it appeared the man was a dunderhead. "To find the true killer." She hopped up, dumping the dog to the floor once again. "You were here for the meeting just now. You know as well as I do that Detective Carson and his cohort have already decided I am the murderer and they won't spend a great deal of time looking for the true culprit. Instead, they will investigate *me* and try to build a case on the fact that St. Vincent had been my betrothed. I broke the engagement, and now he is dead. If we don't do something ourselves, I could end up swinging from the end of a rope." She gripped her neck and blanched.

"*We*? When did '*I* will solve the murder' become *we*?"

She raised her chin, adopting her best lofty demeanor. "If you have no regard for my future well-being, will you at least consider that if I am charged with this crime, the true killer would go free? Possibly to murder again."

"Yes. There is that."

"Precisely. I shall begin with the clue the detective threw out as he was leaving. He said they had not caught up with Mr. Albright. I can find out where he keeps his rooms. If he's left Bath in a hurry, he might not have had time to take everything with him. We can search his rooms and look for clues."

William groaned. "Search his rooms? Don't you think the police have already done that?"

"First of all, I am not entirely sure they will do that. As I said, to my way of thinking, they will spend the bulk of their time trying to prove me the killer. The murder only happened yesterday, and they have been so focused on me, searching Mr. Albright's rooms might not be a priority. Also, if he is not there to let them in, they cannot officially search his rooms without cause. The fact that he served time for murder and is employed here doesn't denote sufficient cause to believe he murdered Mr. St. Vincent. We might very well find our own clues before they do."

"We? There is that frightening word again."

She raised her chin. "Will you help me or not?"

"The devil take it. If I don't help you, I would never get another full night's sleep just imagining all the trouble you will get yourself into on your own."

She sat very still as he weighed the situation. The William she knew from the book club was a very shrewd and calculating man. He didn't jump into things and always examined everything from all angles before he made a decision. After a few minutes, he said, "Very well. I will assist you. However, you are to take no risks on your own."

She grinned at him. "Of course not!"

"E. D. Burton?"

Amy rolled her eyes.

CHAPTER 7

"Amy!" The sound of Eloise's high-pitched voice, which she generally made use of when she was excited, echoed throughout the house. Grinning at her friend's less-than-ladylike entry, Amy left the drawing room, where she had been attempting to lose herself in a book, and met Eloise as she hurried past a very surprised Lacey, who had apparently answered the door.

Eloise threw herself into Amy's arms and hugged her. "Why did you not summon me this morning? I just heard from one of Father's employees that a man was murdered here, in your house, yesterday." All her words were rushed together, in a very typical Eloise manner.

"Come, let's sit down." Amy took her friend by the arm and they walked to the settee.

Eloise took both of Amy's hands and stared at her. "Well?"

Amy took a deep breath. "Actually, the murder victim was Mr. St. Vincent."

Eloise drew back, her eyes wide. "Your fiancé?"

"Ex-fiancé."

After several moments of silence, Eloise said, "When did he become your *ex-fiancé*?"

"There is so much I haven't had the chance to tell you."

"So it seems. You never said a word about it Thursday at the book club meeting, nor Saturday when we met for lunch."

Amy picked up the hurt in Eloise's voice. As best friends, nothing so important should happen between them that the other didn't know about immediately. She'd been so tied in knots since the arrival of the note about St. Vincent's activities that she hadn't discussed the situation with anyone. Not even Aunt Margaret, with whom she shared just about everything.

"I apologize, Eloise. The whole thing was so very strange."

Eloise tapped her foot. "I'm waiting."

Amy stood and wandered the room, gathering her thoughts. Eloise twisted to watch her as she roamed the area. "I received a note—unsigned—stating that Mr. St Vincent was involved in the opium trade."

Eloise joined her as Amy reached the window and leaned against the sill.

"That's not good."

"No," Amy agreed.

"I can see why you would break your engagement, but surely it wasn't worth killing him over?"

Amy rolled her eyes. "Please. Must you be so dramatic? He returned a few days later—yesterday, in fact—for what purpose I don't know, because he was dead before I saw him."

Eloise studied her in stunned silence. "Tea. I need tea." She walked to the bell pull and tugged. "Once we have tea, you must start at the beginning and tell me *everything*."

★ ★ ★

Late that evening Amy sat at the desk in her office next to her bedchamber, where she scribbled away, three lamps arranged in a semicircle surrounding her pad of paper to provide enough light. She usually did not write at night and preferred the light of day to flood her office and keep her thoughts flowing.

But to engage her mind while she waited for William to arrive to embark on their assignation, she continued working on her current novel. However, being the main suspect in a murder herself took some of the fun out of her writing. It brought to mind Mr. Tolstoy's book *War and Peace*.

One of the characters, whose name she could never remember since they had so many different variations of their names, played at the game of war. He had maps and strategies and movements during the Napoleonic wars. It had encompassed his entire world for weeks. Then he received an envelope with his name on it, ordering him to do his duty to his country. He promptly lost all interest in the pretend war. Now it had become real for him.

Her typewriter sat alongside her, but she only used it when she was certain which words she wanted on the paper. Once a letter or word was typed onto the paper, it was too difficult to remove it. No crossing out words like she did when handwriting her books.

The method she employed was to write the entire book by hand, then transfer it to her typewriter one chapter at a time when she was satisfied. Her publisher had bought the machine for her from a newspaper supplier, and she was still struggling to learn the contraption.

She tapped her fountain pen against her lips, considering what to write next. She was at the part where the murderer had kidnapped the daughter of her main character. Not knowing much about children, she was finding it hard to put on paper how a small child would behave if snatched away from her mother.

She sighed and threw down her pen, wincing as ink splattered the wall next to her desk. She rubbed her eyes, unable to concentrate.

"Lord Wethington has called." Lacey tapped lightly on the door.

"Thank you, Lacey. I will be right down." She quickly added, "The drawing room, please."

She didn't think she could ever enter the library again. She shuddered just thinking about the room where she'd found a dead St. Vincent staring up at her.

With a quick glance in the mirror over her dressing table, she patted the sides of her head, smoothing her hair, and left the room.

"I did not think you meant it when you said you would clothe yourself like a man." William's brows rose as he regarded Amy in her attire as she entered the drawing room. She glanced down at the trousers hugging her legs, suspenders, shirt, vest, and jacket barely buttoned over her generous bosom.

"We debated this nigh on an hour already. If we are to break into Mr. Albright's rooms, wearing trousers is the best option. We might have to climb through a window."

William continued to study her, his concern clearly written on this face. "I know we've spoken of this already, but I must reiterate that if you are seen by anyone who knows you, out late at night, without a chaperone, dressed in trousers, your reputation would be ruined."

She waved him off. "My reputation would hardly hold up if I am in prison or swinging from a rope." She gulped and pushed that picture from her mind. "That is precisely why no one will recognize me. A young woman would not be out and about at night, unchaperoned, and dressed like this. Besides, due to my age, I am on the borderline with the necessity of a chaperone, anyway. When one is absolutely necessary, Aunt Margaret fills in."

"Does she know about this?"

Amy looked aghast. "Aunt Margaret? Of course not!"

William pinched the bridge of his nose. "I'm still not convinced that stealing into a man's rooms at night is the best occupation for a young, gently reared woman. I should be doing this myself."

Amy quelled the desire to stomp her foot like a child. "Please stop. I write murder mysteries, remember? In my research, I have done a great many things that would cause most young ladies of my station to swoon."

"That is enough." He held up his hand. "Those are things I do not wish to be privy to, I assure you." He opened the door and waved her through. "I believe your father needs to take you in hand."

She shook her head and picked up the derby hat sitting on the table by the front door and plopped it on her head. Excitement built as she considered actually doing something to help herself rather than waiting for the police to do their job. They thought she was guilty, she knew she wasn't, so therefore she had the advantage. They could spend their time chasing after clues to prove her guilt, while she could uncover the real murderer.

They'd gone only a few steps when Amy came to a sudden stop. "Wait. I forgot Persephone." Before he could comment on that, she turned and hurried back into the house, returning within a few minutes, the dog in her arms.

"Why are you bringing that thing with us?"

Amy sucked in a deep breath. "How dare you! Persephone is not a 'thing.' She is my beloved pet." She ran her hands over the dog's back. "She would be mad at me if I left her behind."

"Is that right? How do you know if a dog is mad at you?"

"She won't talk to me."

He stared at her openmouthed for a minute and then pointed at the animal. "She has no tail."

Amy snuggled the dog against her. "Which makes her special."

Mumbling under his breath, he took Amy by the elbow to escort her down the steps. The dog regarded him from her perch in her mistress's arms. "She just smirked at me, you know."

As they made their way to the carriage William had arrived in, Amy continued to enlighten him on the wonders of her beloved dog. "Pomeranians are very intelligent dogs. They can be trained very quickly and can learn tricks and games. They are actually descended from large working dogs in the Arctic."

William glanced at Persephone and snorted.

Amy settled in her seat and raised her chin at his derision. "Our own Queen adopted a small Pomeranian only two years ago. So obviously, Persephone comes from royal stock." When he did not seem impressed by that fact, she added, "Did you know that in 1767, Queen Charlotte brought two Pomeranians to England? Phoebe and Mercury—those was their names— were even painted by the very well known artist Sir Thomas Gainsborough, although the dogs in that painting were much larger."

After a few moments, he dipped his head. "I am duly impressed."

Amy huffed at his blatant lie as the carriage moved forward. It would transport them to the less-than-desirable area where Mr. Albright's rooms were located. Not as bad as some neighborhoods she'd passed through in London, but not much better. Which was just as well, since they would attract very little attention, as those of the lower classes believed it was better for their health to mind their own business.

Once they were well under way, William leaned back on the comfortable seat and crossed his arms over his chest. "As intriguing as your outfit is, I don't think anyone would be fooled into believing you are a man. You are much too . . ."

"Too what?"

"Womanly. I would hate to have to resort to fisticuffs to protect your honor."

Despite his lack of love for her dog, she couldn't help but feel a bit flattered. First he'd thought her "sweet" and now "womanly." It had been a long time since she'd regarded William in any way other than as a friend, but now she found herself taking a second look at the man. He truly was good-looking, smart, and considering what they were up to tonight, both adventurous and willing to help a lady.

Amy leaned forward. "There is something I learned in my research. Most people see what they expect to see. When we stroll along together, everyone will assume we are two men, and that is what they will see."

William looked out the window, his glance darting back to her legs. "Not if they look closely."

She thought back to the first time she'd met William. Despite Papa's blustering and with Aunt Margaret's help, Amy had just manipulated her way out of a London Season, in which she had no interest. She had just started writing and did not want to travel to London to be dressed up in frills and folderol and paraded before "acceptable" gentlemen in hopes of securing a husband.

William was strolling along George Street as Amy exited a millinery shop, carrying more bundles than she should have been, one of them blocking part of her view. As always, she was in a hurry and walked right into William as she made to cross the street.

Every package she carried tumbled to the ground, the wind picking up the one with a new pair of kid gloves in it. "Oh, get my gloves!" she shouted at William, and waved to where the small box had landed in the middle of the street.

"Of course," William said, dodging carriages and horses and arriving at the small package just as a coach wheel smashed the item flat. He picked up the ruined box, covered with mud and flattened like a pancake, with two fingers and walked it back to where she stood.

"Your package, my lady." He made a gallant bow, and she burst out laughing. That had been the beginning of their friendship, which had strengthened when they both joined the Mystery Book Club of Bath.

William often attended the dances at the Bath Assembly Rooms and had danced with her a few times. Over the ensuing years, she'd learned that he was five years older than her, the only son of Viscount Wethington, with one sister who lived in France. He enjoyed riding, hunting, and other manly pursuits, and the one time she'd asked about his views on marriage, he had shut her out so quickly she had never brought up the subject again.

Amy set a snoring Persephone alongside her, pulled a small notepad and pencil from her jacket pocket, and flipped through a few pages. "I've been thinking about why the detectives were so quick to assume I killed Mr. St. Vincent."

"Having a dead man in your library who had not arrived in that condition is not enough?"

"Not funny, William." She continued. "As you have so rightly pointed out—many times—a lady of my station is considered delicate, with weak sensibilities. Why would I, all of a sudden, grab a knife and plunge it into the man? That is a serious line to cross, and it makes no sense. At least if I were writing a book about it, I would be sure to close that loophole. Also, in my books I always have more than one suspect."

"Perhaps our tax-funded protectors of the law like to see things the simple way. A man who was once engaged to a lovely young woman ends up dead at her feet with no one else at home except the lady in question and her staff. Case closed."

"Aha! And why did she have a knife?"

"Because she knew St. Vincent was there for no good."

"Who keeps knives in their library?"

"She could have stopped by the kitchen on her way."

"So it was premeditated? Why?"

William threw his hands up. "I don't know; you are the murder-mystery author here. You tell me."

Amy smirked. "Precisely. As an author, I have done a lot of research and have probably investigated more murders than the police. Therefore, I will solve the crime before they do."

"And that, my dear lady, is why you have engaged in a veiled attempt to pretend to be a man as we ride into the more unsavory part of Bath."

After an extremely bumpy ride, the carriage came to a rolling stop. William flicked the curtain aside and took in their surroundings. Amy looked out the window at the busy street, with ladies of the evening, drunkards, and pickpockets all mingled together. As she watched, a lad no more than eight years old ran into a man stumbling along. When the man fell to the ground, the boy quickly searched his pockets and ran off.

The number of people out and about could be good or bad. Good because she and William might possibly meld into the crowd, bad because they might have to climb through a window to get into the gardener's rooms and someone might see them. Although, given the lives these people led, she doubted if anyone would care too much.

"I told the driver to leave us off a few buildings before Albright's room." William dropped the curtain, blocking her view of the goings-on outside. "What I suggest is first I simply go to his door and knock. He might just be there. I can always ask for someone else and apologize for my intrusion."

"And if he is there, we can wait until we see him leave."

"Yes. Otherwise, I will survey the inside and outside of the building to see the best way to break in." He rotated his neck. "I cannot believe I just said that." Sliding forward on the seat, he said, "This won't take long."

Amy patted Persephone on the head as William stepped from the carriage and strode away. Before they left the house, she'd wrapped the dog in a warm blanket she'd made into a sort of coat for her pet. Her darling Persephone would be comfortable while they did their necessary work.

Less than ten minutes later, William returned. "He's not at home. I spoke with the landlady as I was leaving, and she said she hasn't seen him in a couple days." He pulled up the collar of his jacket. "Much colder out there than I thought."

"Where in the building is his room located?"

"First floor, one flight up. But the lock on the door doesn't look too sturdy. I think I might be able to get us inside without making a fuss."

Anxious to get the search under way, Amy moved forward as William stepped back out of the coach. He glanced at her dog. "She won't be barking and causing a ruckus, will she? The last thing we want is to call attention to ourselves."

"Not at all. She is very well behaved. She will merely sleep while we are gone."

"Then why bring her?"

"I told you. If I didn't, she would be mad at me."

"And then wouldn't talk to you." He ran his palm down his face, then reached out to help her from the carriage. Before she could stop his movement, he must have realized it would look rather odd for a gentleman to be helping another gentleman out of the carriage unless the man was in his dotage. He dropped his arm and stepped back, allowing her to descend the two steps to the ground.

Amy looked around, unable to hide her smile. This was quite thrilling.

"Stick close to me. Even though you think you can fool others into believing you are a man, in the event you are mistaken, I have a pistol with me."

"You do?" A tingle of excitement settled in her stomach. "I should buy a gun myself."

He sucked in a deep breath and his eyes widened. "No. No, no, no."

They began to walk toward Mr. Albright's building. "My goodness, you made your point. Why not?"

"Because without proper training, you would probably shoot a hole in your foot."

"I will receive proper training. How hard can it be? I had no trouble learning how to use my typewriter."

"Your what?"

"Typewriter." She stopped and looked up at Mr. Albright's building. "It's a machine like a printing press. Except much smaller. You roll a piece of paper into it and tap on letter keys to write things."

"What's wrong with a pen and paper?"

"Nothing, but a typewriter saves time. Or that is what it will do eventually. Right now I'm a bit slow trying to pick out the letters. And you have to be careful because it's not easy to get rid of a letter or word once it's on the paper."

He pushed open the entrance door to Albright's building. "Just like it's not easy to get rid of a hole in your foot once you shoot it."

Honestly, the man was so annoying. As grateful as she was to have his company and assistance, he was beginning to act the protective male, and she found it somewhat irritating. Papa and her brother had learned a while back to allow her the freedom she needed to write her books and do the necessary research.

She'd given Papa her word that she would not do anything to place herself in danger, and since she had the annoying William at her side, she felt as though she wasn't going back on her promise with their venture that evening.

The sound of a baby crying, the smell of urine, and walls with patches of peeling paint marked the residence as a poor building in a poor neighborhood. A rat scurried across the entrance hall. Amy squealed and grabbed William's arm. Behind the closed door of one flat, the sound of raised voices, and then a crash reminded her they were in a dangerous part of the city where so many led desperate lives.

They made their way up the stairs with no need to remain quiet, since the tenants were making plenty of their own noise. The walked up to number seven, the room Mr. Albright had identified as his own when he'd been hired. At least she'd had the presence of mind to ask that much of the man.

William shook the doorknob. It was apparent from the way the door rattled that the lock was anything but sturdy. "Move back," he said.

With a hard shove of his shoulder, he slammed against the door and it popped open. Amy looked around, but none of the other doors opened to see what the noise was. Most likely the other tenants were all too busy dealing with their own misery to concern themselves with anyone else's.

They closed the door and looked around at the shadowy space. Mr. Albright's room was no larger than their gardener's shed. There was very little light from the street, but William produced two candles and a flint from his inside jacket pocket. They quickly made their way through the room, looking under the bed, beneath the mattress, and in his wardrobe, where they found one pair of trousers and two shirts, all work-worn.

A drawer in an old wooden desk leaning against the wall, appearing as though it would collapse in a mild storm, revealed a pencil, a few coins, a small pad of paper, a razor, toothbrush, and a small pouch of tobacco. The man had obviously left in a hurry.

Since the space was so small, there wasn't much to search. Amy stood with her hands on her hips and turned in a circle to view the room. "I don't know what I had expected to find, but at least more than the little bit that is here."

"What did you think? That Mr. Albright kept a journal of his life that would reveal he was Mr. St. Vincent's killer?" William spoke over his shoulder as he looked at the ceiling, stopping underneath the old-fashioned chandelier. "Come here."

Amy wandered over to where he stood. "What?"

"I'm going to lift you up, and I want you to feel around inside the candle cups. I can't really tell from here with only the light from the candle, but it appears there is something in one of them."

"Most likely a candle."

William shook his head. "No." He turned to her. "Here, let me lift you up."

Although it was quite improper for him to take her in his arms to lift her, curiosity won out over propriety. He placed his hands alongside her waist and lifted. Goodness, she was no slender, lightweight woman, but he lifted her as though she weighed no more than a child.

She was a bit unsteady in this position, but she grabbed one of the cups and held on.

"Can you feel anything?"

"Not yet."

Her fingertip hit something, and with a bit more stretching, she was able to wrap her hand around an object. "I have something in my hand. Let me down."

Slowly he lowered her, and she held up what looked like a cloth pouch. She maneuvered her fingers and felt an object inside.

William took the pouch from her hand and tucked it into his pocket. "We won't be able to see much here in the dark. We'll take it with us. Nothing else has turned up, and very few people put things in their lamps unless it's something they don't want anyone else to find. I suggest we leave and examine the article away from here."

Amy stopped breathing and looked quickly at William when there was a knock on the door.

William raised his finger to his lips and took her by the hand, then led her across the room to climb into the wardrobe. She thanked her cleverness again for dressing in trousers. Trying to squeeze herself into the space in her normal attire would have been quite an endeavor.

The knock sounded again, and then a rattling of the doorknob. "Mr. Albright?"

William leaned close to Amy's ear. "That's the landlady."

"Mr. Albright? Someone was looking for you before. And your rent is past due."

The pounding of Amy's heart was so loud, she cast a glance at William; certain he heard it. After a few minutes, the landlady said, "If your rent isn't paid by tomorrow, I'll have to let out your room to someone else."

They both breathed a sigh of relief at the sound of footsteps and grumbling leading away from the door. After a few minutes, William shifted. "I think it's safe to leave now."

They climbed from the wardrobe and hurried across the room. William opened the door, peeked out, and waved her forward. They made their way down the stairs and out of the building. They practically ran the short distance from the building to the carriage, where William took the seat facing backward. A true gentleman.

Once settled, he tapped on the ceiling of the vehicle, and it began to move.

"What is in the pouch?" Amy asked.

He withdrew it from his pocket and pushed the sides of it apart. He pulled out an odd-looking porcelain object.

Amy took it from his hand and looked it over. "What is this?"

"An opium pipe."

CHAPTER 8

"Well then, it appears Mr. Albright not only served time for murder but also indulges in opium, which is a connection to Mr. St. Vincent."

William moved the pipe this way and that, examining it in the light from the lantern anchored on the carriage wall next to him.

"What I find confusing is why he is not still in prison. Generally those convicted of murder never see the light of day." Amy shifted on the seat across from him as the coach rolled along, removing them from the dangerous neighborhood. She patted a snoring Persephone and mindlessly ran her palm over the dog's soft fur.

"That would be a good point to investigate. Had he escaped, perhaps?"

Amy shook her head. "No. The police would have mentioned that he was an escapee when they told us about him. I feel as though they've tossed down the gauntlet for me to do my own investigation."

"No. No." He shook his head. "They would not do that. I am sure the last thing they want is a woman wandering around Bath talking to strangers about murder."

"I have done that numerous times in my research."

"Amy, this is not research but real life." He leaned forward, his forearms resting on his thighs. "There is a murderer out there who will not be happy to know you are second-guessing the police. If it becomes known that their main suspect is conducting her own investigation, your life could be in danger."

A light drizzle began as the coach made its way through the bumpy and dark streets of Bath. William rested his head on the soft Morocco leather squab and studied her. "Tell me a little bit more about how you came to write murder mysteries, of all things. I would think a young lady's interests would lie more in romance stories, something like Miss Austen wrote."

"I tried to write romance. I even started doing so in the schoolroom before I attended boarding school. My governess encouraged me to write stories, and it soon became a part of my daily life."

"As other young girls keep a journal."

She laughed. "Except my stories were not like what other girls wrote in their journals." She tapped the side of her head. "You see, I have a logical mind."

"And we all know there is nothing at all logical about romance." His murmured words, along with his cocked eyebrow and slightly turned up lips, did strange things to her insides again. "Is it your contention that possessing a logical mind lured you from romance and toward murder and other ghastly themes?"

She shrugged. "I lost interest in writing romance, and after my governess pointed out many times that whenever she presented me with a problem I could usually solve it by using logical steps, I thought solving mysteries might be more fun."

"Ah, not the way a woman's mind should work."

Amy drew herself up, narrowing her eyes at William, who was looking quite smug in the light from the carriage lantern. "And where is that written, my lord? Are women not as intelligent as men? Do they not have the same right as men to use the brain God gave them?"

He stared at her openmouthed. "You are a suffragette!"

"Of course I am," she sniffed. "You are aware that I am a believer in women's rights. Did you think a woman who has no problem dressing as a man or going into unsavory places to do research and then writes about murder would *not* be a suffragette?"

"That is an excellent point. I have no problem bowing to your superiority in this matter. With your nonfeminine logical brain and experience with murder and all the mayhem it causes, where do we go next?"

Amy dipped her head in deference. "You are above all other men, my lord." She edged farther up on her seat, her facial expression quite serious. "Until we can locate Mr. Albright, we must turn our attention to others who had a reason to dislike St. Vincent so much they were willing to put a knife into his chest."

"And also knew where to find him to do that."

A slow smile teased her lips. "Yes. A very good point, my lord. I shall add that to my notes when I return home. I believe I will make a detective out of you yet."

"Thank you, no. I prefer my murders to be between the pages of a book that I read seated in a comfortable chair in my library at night, with a warm fire in front of me and a brandy at my fingertips."

"So very dull." Actually, she was finding a totally different side to William that she'd never seen before. Protective, inquisitive, and willing to take a risk to help a friend. Maybe not so very dull, after all.

"One thing we have not considered is who will inherit St. Vincent's estate."

Amy's eyes popped wide open. "Of course! How could I ever have let that slip from my mind?"

William offered her his now familiar crooked smile. "Perhaps investigating a murder where you are the main suspect has rattled your normally logical mind? In any event, St. Vincent has a nephew, Mr. Francis Harris. I don't know the man well—the last I heard he was out of the country—but it would not hurt for me to poke around a few of the gentlemen's clubs to see if he has returned now that his uncle is dead. From what I know, Harris is the only heir to St. Vincent's estate." William grabbed on to the strap alongside him as the carriage hit a large gap in the road that tossed her from her seat to the floor.

"Ouch."

He leaned down and helped her up. "Are you hurt?"

She rubbed her sore bottom but didn't want to mention what part of her had taken the brunt of the fall. "I am fine. Thank you."

Once she was settled again, taking note that Persephone had slept through the whole ordeal, she said, "How did you know who St. Vincent's heir was?"

"It pays to have friends in various situations and employments. That is all I can say."

Annoyed at his elusive answer, she said, "Speaking of Mr. St. Vincent's estate, it might not hurt to gather whatever information we can about his financial state. He seemed quite irate when I ended the betrothal. Since ours was hardly a romantic connection, I must admit I was quite taken aback when he became so angry."

William cleared his throat, which Amy knew he did when he was about to say something provocative at the book club. "I hope you don't mind if I ask about your betrothal. I am aware that it is a personal matter, but something about it might shed some light on his murder."

"Yes. I agree. There could most definitely be some link."

He seemed to relax when she didn't refuse or order Persephone to attack him. "Very well. How did the betrothal come about? And I know you received a note about his activities—which would be another good line to follow—but was that the only reason you decided to rid yourself of the man?"

She gazed out at the darkness as they made their way back to her townhouse. A steady rain had started up, causing the traffic to slow down. Recalling the uncomfortable conversation with her papa, she pushed aside the hurt and began her story. "Papa had been quite anxious to see me married, and as he put it, 'settled.' I honestly believe he thought a husband would 'take me in hand' and stop me from writing or doing other things of which he did not approve. I had refused a so-called 'Season' in London for two years before he forced me—threatening to cut off my allowance—into traveling to London to make my bow to the Queen. After three miserable months of balls, musicales, dinner parties, and soirees, no one appealed to me, and I am quite happy with my life just as it is."

"Then why the engagement?" His softly spoken words in the cozy darkness with the rain dripping down the window encouraged her to continue.

"In a moment of weakness, he convinced me that Mr. St. Vincent, who had approached him with an offer for my hand—which is so very old-fashioned, by the way—would make a fine husband. I knew Mr. St. Vincent and had spent some time with him at a garden party, attended the theater when he was present, and danced a few times with him at the Assembly. While I found him to be a pleasant man, I never thought much about him as a husband."

She took in a deep breath. "However, during our conversation, Papa referred to me as a 'spinster' and said how unhappy I would be in my old age. As I said, it was a weak moment for me. I agreed to the arrangement, but I must admit, almost from the day we became engaged, I thought about a way to get out of it."

"How very unkind of him to say that. I know he is your father, but I fail to see you as an unfortunate spinster, someone who would be unhappy in the coming years. You have a full life with your writing and social life. That being said, marriage is a very serious commitment. One should not take it lightly. *Till death do us part* is a frightening prospect."

She wondered at the somberness of his statement and if perhaps it was the result of some pain he'd suffered in the past. Before she could dwell too long on that, William nodded and continued. "Based on what you've told me, I understand what you mean about St. Vincent being unnecessarily upset by your request to end the engagement. I shall contact the man who handles my business affairs, Mr. Harding. He might have information available to him which would cast some light on the matter."

Amy straightened in her seat and scowled. "Now just a moment, my lord. *You* are going to gather information at the gentlemen's clubs and *you* will speak with your man of business. That sounds too much like leaving me out of the investigation."

William grinned as he nodded to her. "Not at all, my lady. I am sure your 'logical' brain will think of many things to do to continue searching for the killer. Just be sure to stay out of trouble if I am not with you." He glared at her. "And no guns."

★   ★   ★

The next afternoon, Amy sat in front of her mirror, her chin resting on her fist. She stared at her reflection and sighed. One thing she disliked more than anything was making social calls, which many women of her station did on a regular basis. Sitting around drinking gallons of tea while sharing gossip was not a productive way to spend her time. About once a month, she did force herself to endure the torture, and considering she would, no doubt, be the latest subject of the gossip, it would serve her well to make a few calls that afternoon. Face her enemies, as it were. She'd always thought that the best defense was a good offense.

Today Aunt Margaret and Eloise would join her, since while Amy despised afternoon calls, Aunt Margaret loved them. Another way they were so very different.

Eloise was also not fond of making the dreaded calls but had sent a note around, in answer to Amy's plea earlier in the day to join her, saying that she would certainly support her friend.

"Are you ready, Amy?" Her aunt entered Amy's bedchamber while pulling on white kid gloves. Aunt Margaret's bedchamber was down the hall from Amy's, and she could hear her bird, Othello, chatting away. He was currently reciting "The Phoenix and the Turtle."

Dismissing the bird, she admitted she would never be ready for the torment she was about to endure, but for the sake of the investigation, she would submit. She never knew from where her next clue would come, and showing herself in society would limit the rumors. Amy slid a hatpin into the silly confection she called a hat to anchor it to her head. "Yes. I am ready, Aunt. Where are we off to today?"

"Two places, actually. It is past time I made a visit to Mrs. Morton—"

Amy groaned.

Aunt Margaret's brows rose. "And after her, we should call on Lady Marlberry. The poor dear slipped and injured her hip. The doctor has confined her to the house for a while."

Amy followed her aunt from the room, down the stairs to the door. "I don't mind Lady Marlberry at all. She is quite sweet, but Mrs. Morton is not one of my favorite people. She is a member of our book club, and I will need to suffer her presence this evening, as it is at our weekly meeting. She takes every opportunity to insult me with innuendos. I can just imagine what she will have to say about Mr. St. Vincent's death."

"Which is precisely why you need to present yourself today."

Eloise awaited them in the front hall, looking as miserable as Amy felt. She was truly the best of friends.

Mrs. Morton's house was in one of the best sections of Bath on Dunsford Place. Her husband, a very pleasant man, made his money in stocks and railroads and had risen from near poverty to the elite of Bath society. It was rumored that Mrs. Morton had been a scullery maid before she married Mr. Morton, who had himself been a clerk. He apparently had quite a head for business, however, and after receiving a small inheritance, he'd spent the following ten years turning it into a fortune.

His wife had taken on airs once they had received their first investment check and never turned back. That was one of many reasons Amy disliked the woman. That and her way of asking questions or making statements that could be taken differently than the words spoken.

Amy's stomach fluttered at the sound of lively chatter, which led them to the room where they were announced.

If a mouse had decided to eat a biscuit at that moment, the munching would easily have been heard by the seven women in the room. Stunned silence greeted the three entering.

Mrs. Morton rose, her hand plastered against her chest. "Oh, my dear, dear, Lady Amy. How very, very horrible for you." She floated across the room, her obvious delight at having the notorious woman whose ex-fiancé had been murdered right in her drawing room simply too much for her to hide. "You must be devastated. I cannot imagine how you were even able to rise from your bed."

Since it was not considered good *ton* to smack one's hostess over the head with one's reticule, Amy merely smiled and allowed herself to be swept into Mrs. Morton's arms and hugged until she thought she would faint from lack of air.

She took in a deep breath when the woman finally released her and studied her carefully. "How are you holding up, my dear?" Then Mrs. Morton took to fluttering a handkerchief that had miraculously appeared in her hand. She patted the corners of her eyes. "I am so very, very sorry to hear of your troubles."

"That is quite enough, Isabel." Aunt Margaret scowled. "May we at least be seated and offered some tea?"

"Yes, yes, of course." Mrs. Morton ushered them to the settee closest to her, glaring at Miss Davies, who currently occupied that seat. Miss Davies quickly removed herself to another chair. Aunt Margaret and Eloise were then forced to sit farther down in the room, leaving Amy to deal with Mrs. Morton by herself.

"Here, my dear. Just sit yourself down and I will see that you have a strong cup of tea."

"Isabel, for heaven's sakes, the girl is fine," Aunt Margaret snapped, then swept her eyes around the room, glaring at all the goggle-eyed guests. "In fact, my niece had already broken her engagement with Mr. St. Vincent before he died."

"You mean was murdered," Lady Ambrose said, whipping her flowered fan so hard the curls alongside her hair bounced.

"Well, yes. He was murdered. But there is no reason to assume Lady Amy is heartbroken or in need of consoling."

"Is it true you found his body?" Miss Everhart, a young miss barely out of the schoolroom, pushed her spectacles back up her nose, then gripped her throat, her eyes huge. Everyone else leaned forward as well, the anticipation on their faces alarming. And William seemed to think women were too delicate to write about murder? Amy was willing to bet just about every woman in this room had read one of her books.

Amy accepted a cup of tea from the maid and took a sip. "Yes. I was unfortunate enough to find his body."

Gasps ricocheted around the room. "Oh, how very unpleasant." Lady Ambrose gave her fan another flutter.

Aunt Margaret looked over at Amy and shook her head slightly. Amy wasn't sure if her aunt was commiserating with her or silently warning her not to toss her teacup at Lady Ambrose's head.

"These are wonderful biscuits, Mrs. Morton," Eloise said from across the room. "Do you think your cook would share the recipe?"

"Have the police found his murderer?" The delicate, sweet, simpering Miss Everhart totally ignored Eloise and was at it again, dripping with avid curiosity.

Suddenly everyone in the room was extremely interested in their teacups. *Uh-oh.* Apparently word of her being the main suspect had spread far and wide. Well, she wouldn't give them the satisfaction of again tossing pitying looks her way combined with fake shock and suppressed glee at her dilemma.

She raised her chin and looked Miss Everhart in the eye. "No. As a matter of fact, they have not." She took another sip of tea and turned toward Miss Davies. "Miss Davies, I must say that is a lovely dress you are wearing. That color suits you quite well."

Unfortunately, the group was still not about to surrender. Miss Davies barely got her thanks out before Mrs. Morton said, "Lady Amy, dear, surely you must have some idea of at whom the police are looking."

"I read in this morning's paper that the investigation is continuing, and no one has been arrested." Amy wanted to kiss Mrs. Welling, who had remained silent up to that point.

"*Yet*," Mrs. Morton said, waving her finger at Mrs. Welling. "Not yet."

"I wonder how poor Miss Hemphill is holding up." Lady Ambrose *tsk*ed and took a bite from her tart. Considering how her bulk tested the seams of her dress, 'twould perhaps have been better if the woman had left the array of treats alone.

"Miss Hemphill?" Aunt Margaret asked, glancing over at Eloise, who looked as surprised as Amy felt.

"Oh, yes, my dear." Lady Ambrose waved her hand. "But that is not news. Just about everyone knew she expected Mr. St. Vincent to make her an offer of marriage before she set off for London a couple of months ago. I understand she has recently returned"—she glanced in Amy's direction, then away—"but found the man had already betrothed himself to Lady Amy in her absence."

St. Vincent had been expected to make an offer to Miss Hemphill? How the devil had Amy not known that? She looked over at Aunt Margaret, then Eloise, who both gave her a slight shrug. Hopefully one of her cohorts would not let the story die there.

"Did you say Miss Hemphill was expecting an offer from Mr. St. Vincent?" Her saving grace came from Miss Everhart, who apparently was as ignorant as Amy about this expected proposal.

"Oh, indeed. They were courting for a few months, and then, according to Miss Hemphill's brother, she unexpectedly took a trip to London. She is a member of our sewing group that meets every Tuesday at my house to sew clothing for impoverished infants. We were all quite taken by surprise at her abrupt departure." Lady Ambrose practically drooled when she offered that piece of information.

"Lady Carlisle and Mrs. Miles." The butler's low voice interrupted the question Miss Everhart was about to ask to announce two new guests.

The two women, whom Amy knew from the book club, entered the drawing room, giving her an excuse to depart. She was not prepared to continue answering questions about Mr. St. Vincent's death. If she remained here much longer, the story would grow until someone swore they had seen her plunge a knife into the man's chest.

She stood and smoothed out her skirts. "I must leave your company, I'm afraid. I have an appointment this afternoon." Amy moved toward Eloise and took her arm. She looked over at Aunt Margaret. "Shall I send the carriage back for you?"

"No." Her aunt placed her teacup on the table next to her, barely finding room for it with all the ornaments and picture frames there. "I promised Lady Marlberry I would call."

"Oh, do give the lovely lady my regards," Mrs. Morton gushed.

"I will."

When good-byes and the necessary kisses at the air alongside cheeks were finally over and done with, Amy, Eloise, and Aunt Margaret left the house. Fresh air had never smelled so good. Of course, the misty air wasn't exactly fresh, but any air was better than the poisonous variety she'd been breathing for the past half hour.

"You did quite well," Aunt Margaret said as they entered the carriage.

Eloise settled alongside her, across from Aunt Margaret. "They are a bunch of blabbering, gossipy women." She patted Amy's hand. "You aunt is correct. You did quite well."

"Actually, it wasn't nearly as bad as I had anticipated. But at least I have made an appearance in public, so hopefully some of the more outlandish gossip will cease."

The carriage started forward, and Aunt Margaret grinned at her. "Not at all, my dear. They will feast on this until long after Mr. St. Vincent's murderer is caught and hanged."

"Which, of course, won't be you," Eloise quickly pointed out.

CHAPTER 9

Amy had always looked forward to her Mystery Book Club meetings. The best times, of course, had been when they'd been reading one of her books—and no one knew the author was in the room. It had been hard sometimes when one of the members would go on about how certain they were that this or that was what the author meant when Amy knew them to be completely wrong.

She'd giggled through some explanations of a murder that were incorrect and huffed a bit when one of the members offered a criticism of her writing. For the most part, though, her fellow book club members praised her books.

Tonight, however, she was filled with trepidation at the prospect of being the center of attention, not for her writing but because of Mr. St. Vincent's murder. There could be nothing more fascinating for a group of mystery book fans than to dissect an actual murder of a person who, while not actually from their group, nevertheless had a close relationship to one of its members. And had been found dead in her house.

After the uncomfortable call she had made that afternoon, Amy reminded herself that she could handle whatever came her way. Once the initial condolences and other nonsense were out of the way, she might hear a few opinions from these well-informed members on who may have wished to see Mr. St. Vincent dead.

With her head held high, Amy passed through the store, a sense of calm coming over her upon seeing all the books before her. She loved books, had always loved books, and could not have been happier with her budding career as an author.

She entered the back room of the establishment, a fixed smile on her face, prepared for the deluge of questions. She breathed a sigh of relief when the first person she spotted was William. He immediately broke from the group he was speaking with to greet her. "Good evening, Lady Amy."

"Good evening to you as well, Lord Wethington."

He took her by the hand, giving it a slight squeeze as he led her to the group he'd just left. Mr. Colbert, Mr. Davidson, Lord Temple, and Miss Sterling immediately viewed her with sympathy. "I am so sorry for your loss, Lady Amy," Miss Sterling said.

Botheration. How very annoying this was. "Thank you, Miss Sterling. I appreciate your words; however, Mr. St. Vincent and I had parted ways before his . . . death."

"Indeed?" She looked to the others in the group, a smirk on her face. "How very odd that he was murdered after you—"

"Mr. Davidson, what sort of a return did you find with that investment you told me about a month or so ago?" William jumped right in, and she blessed him for his kindheartedness. Miss Sterling, however, looked miffed, and Amy knew that despite William's intervention, the questioning about St. Vincent had certainly not ended.

Eloise arrived on time for once and joined the small group. She also gave Amy's hand a slight squeeze and murmured, "Has it been bad?"

Amy shook her head no as Mr. Davidson rambled on for a few minutes about his investment. She avoided looking at Miss Sterling, afraid the woman would ask more questions.

"Lady Amy." Amy turned as Lady Carlisle hurried toward her. "I'm so glad you decided to join us tonight instead of wallowing in grief at home."

Eloise moaned as Amy gritted her teeth. Wallowing in grief, indeed. "Good evening, Lady Carlisle. Thank you for your kind words"—*please, God, forgive me for that lie*—"but since Mr. St. Vincent and I were no longer betrothed, while I am regretful for his death, I don't consider myself grieving."

Lady Carlisle patted her hand and leaned in toward her, then gripped her arm as if to steady herself.

"Are you unwell, my lady?"

She shifted and righted herself. "No. I am quite well, thank you. I am just concerned that all this nastiness would wear you down. But I know you are a very strong woman." She patted her hand again just as Mr. Colbert called the meeting to order.

Eloise and Amy took seats on the sofa as everyone settled in. Eloise leaned toward her as she adjusted her skirts. "Maybe there won't be any more questions."

"I'm not so sure. With all the looks being cast in my direction, I'm afraid I will be the center of attention." She sighed. "Why did he have to get murdered in my house?"

"Yes," Eloise said, "Most inconvenient." She paused, then leaned in farther. "Have you considered yet why he called on you?"

"I have no idea. I made my position clear when I broke the engagement. I also wonder if his reason for being there had anything to do with his death."

"And," Eloise whispered, "how did he come to be murdered in your garden? Was he followed to your house?" Amy shrugged. So many questions with so few answers were giving her a fine headache. Best to suffer through the meeting and speak with William to see if he had any new ideas when it was over.

The group quieted and looked at Mr. Colbert, the group leader, with expectation. William raised his hand. "May I speak, Mr. Colbert?"

"Of course, Lord Wethington."

William stood and turned to address the group. "As lovers of mystery novels, we are more interested than most in the unexpected death of one of our townsmen. Like the rest of you, I am also aware that one of our members—Lady Amy—had a *previous* connection to Mr. St. Vincent."

He glanced at her and took a deep breath. "Since I was at her home to deliver a book she had asked to borrow when Mr. St. Vincent's body was discovered, and during the subsequent interviews by the police, I can say with confidence that the detectives assigned to the matter are doing everything they can to uncover the person who perpetrated this despicable crime. I believe I speak for Lady Amy when I ask all of you to put aside this matter and go on with our book discussion as usual."

"Bravo, Lord Wethington," Eloise mumbled.

Amy's eyes filled with tears at William's graciousness. She scanned the somewhat disgruntled faces of a few members who had undoubtedly planned to question her once the meeting ended. When William sat, she mouthed, "Thank you."

He gave her a slight wink.

The meeting went forward as usual after William's speech. Truth be known, her mind wasn't truly focused on the discussion of *A Study in Scarlet*, which continued from the prior meeting. The book club's usual method was to discuss a book until everyone was satisfied that their opinion had been heard. Then they picked a new book to read and discuss. Some books took two or more weeks; some discussions were wrapped up in one meeting.

She was anxious for the meeting to end so she could tell William what she'd learned about Miss Hemphill that afternoon. She'd added her to her list of suspects, along with Mr. Albright. If William had gathered information while visiting his clubs, they might even have someone else to consider.

★ ★ ★

"Lady Amy, a word, please?" William walked up behind her as Mrs. Miles tried her best to drag out information about Amy's broken engagement. For goodness' sake, the woman was quite persistent. Her son, Mr. Richard Miles, looked, if anything, bored.

Amy turned. "Yes, Lord Wethington?" Thank goodness he had interrupted. She was afraid she would have said something disagreeable to Mrs. Miles if her interrogation had gone on any longer.

"There is a matter of importance I must discuss with you.'"

"Oh, of course, my lord." She turned to Mrs. Miles with what she hoped was a regretful expression. "I am so sorry to cut our visit short, Mrs. Miles, but I look forward to seeing you next week."

"Oh, my dear. Perhaps we can take tea sometime soon." The woman was like a rabid dog with a meaty bone in its jaws.

"Mother, it appears Lady Amy does not wish to continue this discussion. I believe you have asked just about any question possible about her engagement, the unengagement, the book she borrowed from his lordship, Mr. St. Vincent's visit, the police interview, and how she is holding up. I also do not believe her ladyship would be interested in visiting for tea to continue the discussion." Mr. Miles looked fondly at his mother, but his tone was one of annoyance.

"Do you think so, Richard?"

"I do." He took her by the arm and nodded to Amy and William. "Good evening." He moved his mother toward the door, and suddenly Mrs. Miles turned into a bumbling old woman who depended on her son for guidance. The quick change in her demeanor was startling. Amy had never paid much attention to the relationship between mother and son and had assumed Mr. Miles attended the meetings only to escort his mother. He rarely offered opinions during the discussions, and Amy had heard him mention to another member one time that he seldom read the books being discussed.

She shrugged and turned to William. "It would probably be a good idea for us to meet somewhere tomorrow. I find, after the deluge of questions and innuendos I dealt with tonight, I look forward to a warm cup of tea, a hot bath, and my bed." That seemed to be her list of desires quite a bit these days.

He cleared his throat. "I agree. I shall escort you to your carriage and we can discuss a time."

They bade farewell to those who had remained behind to enjoy the late supper she and William would normally have attended as well. Eloise had left as soon as the meeting ended, offering her apologies for abandoning Amy. The poor girl did look unwell and feared she had caught a chill.

Rain had begun to fall while they were inside, and the dampness had her shivering. Hopefully, she wouldn't catch a chill herself. She needed to be healthy to solve the murder.

William looked up at the sky, then noticed her trembling. "Wait inside the store, and I will summon your carriage."

She smiled. Ever the gentleman.

It took only about ten minutes for him to return, carrying an umbrella he must have taken from his own carriage, which was now behind hers. She linked her arm in his, and they huddled under the umbrella to avoid the rain that had suddenly turned into a downpour.

He helped her into the carriage, holding the umbrella over his head. "What time would suit you tomorrow?"

"Ten o'clock? Perhaps you can call for me and we can take a stroll in the Pump Room at the Baths." She looked at the wind whipping against the carriage and the water dripping from the umbrella and smiled. "If the weather has improved."

"I assume you do not wish to speak in your house?"

Amy nodded. "Yes. I prefer not to, since Mr. St. Vincent was killed in *my* garden. I do have to be careful. Even though I trust all my employees, one can never be too careful."

"A wise decision. If we are unable to venture out to the Baths tomorrow, I will await your missive with a new time and day." With those words, he backed up, closed the door, and slapped the side of her carriage as a signal for the driver to begin the journey home.

★   ★   ★

Amy poured over her notes the following day as she waited for William to arrive for their trip to the Baths. The sun had awakened her earlier, making their trip possible. The Pump Room could be quite crowded this time of year, and if such was the case today, they could stroll the outside of the building, along the path surrounding the Roman Baths. They could even talk quietly at the Abbey nearby if they found no other private place.

Earlier, as she gazed out the window while getting ready for the day, she had been amazed at how clean and fresh everything appeared after a rainstorm. As far as she could see from her room, all the buildings looked scrubbed clean, the grass had a deeper green color, and new buds had sprouted almost overnight on the trees, which had just recently shaken off the shroud of winter.

Despite the trouble that hounded her, she couldn't help but feel hopeful with all the signs of spring and new beginning surrounding her. This was the time of year she generally took a break from writing to just enjoy the warmer weather and allow the cobwebs in her brain to clear.

This year there would be no respite while she investigated a murder. Not a fanciful one for a book this time, but a real one that had her front and center as the main suspect. Her current novel was almost finished and would soon be sent off to her editor. She was currently transcribing the manuscript from her written version to the typewriter.

The previous evening she'd soaked in the bath, dreaming of the long vacation she would take when this matter was cleared up. Somewhere exotic. Perhaps the Orient. Or maybe even one of the islands in the South Pacific that were rumored to have naked people inhabiting them. As she lazily dripped water over her leg from the flannel, she'd wondered if she would be daring enough to go naked were she to travel there. What it would feel like to have the sun and soft wind on her bared body.

"Milady, your young man has arrived." Lacey interrupted her unseemly thoughts. The maid regarded her. "Are you unwell? You are a bit flushed."

Amy jumped up, feeling as guilty as a young girl facing Cook with two stolen biscuits behind her back. "Yes. I am fine." She waved her hand, wishing—nay, praying—the redness in her cheeks would fade before she had to face William. "Please tell Lord Wethington I will be down directly." As Lacey turned to leave the room, Amy added, "And he is *not* my young man."

She found William in the drawing room, flipping through a book. "Good morning."

He looked up, a bright smile covering his lips, his eyes taking her in with pleasure. "Are you feeling unwell, Amy?" He frowned and closed the book as he walked toward her.

"No," she snapped. She raised her chin. "Are we ready?"

He blinked twice at her abruptness. "Yes. Of course. Shall we go?"

"I apologize, William. I should not have snapped at you. 'Tis a small matter that had me a bit disconcerted, but all is well now."

"Good."

She sailed past him out of the drawing room, not waiting for his escort as she made her way from the front door to his carriage. She waited, not too patiently, until he caught up to her. "My goodness, you are in a hurry today."

Thankful that she seemed to have recovered her normal demeanor, she nodded. "Yes, I have interesting things to tell you."

He joined her in the carriage and tapped on the ceiling to alert the driver. "For privacy, we could just ride around the city and share information and make notes."

Amy shook her head. "No. Even though I am not of an age to need a companion, I don't want to do anything that would be reported back to Papa and have him insist on hiring someone to trail me like some barely-out-of-the-schoolroom debutante."

"Very well. 'Tis such a pleasant day, a stroll around the Baths area will be lovely."

"What do you have there?" She gestured toward the tome he'd been flipping through when she joined him in the drawing room.

He grinned and held it up for her to view. "It's the book that brought me to your house the night St. Vincent was murdered."

"Oh, wonderful. How did you get it?"

"The police sent word that they were finished with your library and had brought the book to the station since they knew it belonged to me. I had just retrieved it before I arrived at your house."

William moved to her side of the carriage and opened the book to point out a few things. They talked a bit about the contents on the short ride from Amy's townhouse to the center of the city, where the Roman Baths and Bath Abbey were the main focus of tourists.

She had taken the baths herself a few times, but most of the regular visitors were Londoners who came for the healing waters and to enjoy a smaller Season of *ton* activities during the summer.

The Baths had been built by the Romans as a place for public bathing. In 60 AD when it was first built, it had been known as *Aquae Sulis*, Latin for *the waters of Sulis*. The structure itself was very Romanesque, with pillars surrounding a large pool in the center. More recently, carvings of Roman emperors and the governors of Roman Britain had been placed on the terrace that overlooked the Great Bath.

She and William left the book in the carriage, and arm in arm they strolled around the Roman Bath part of the area, then made their way to the Pump Room. It was a beautiful space, with high windows allowing a tremendous amount of light into the room. They got into the line to receive a glass of the horrible-tasting water and then moved to the square in front of Bath Abbey, where they settled on a bench, just two more people in the throngs that traveled to the city from other places.

Amy turned to him and withdrew her notes from her reticule. "I visited Mrs. Morton for afternoon tea yesterday with Eloise and Aunt Margaret, and naturally I was the center of attention and many questions were tossed in my direction."

"I admire your bravery, Amy. I would much rather face pistols at dawn then confront a roomful of curious, gossiping women."

"Aunt Margaret thought it would be beneficial for me to be seen so the rumor would not start that I was under arrest, awaiting execution for St. Vincent's death." She shuddered at the thought, then continued. "However, one thing I did discover is that Miss Hemphill—I'm not sure if you know her?"

William shook his head no.

"Well, I have met her once or twice. A pleasant woman, slightly older than me. Lady Ambrose, one of Mrs. Morton's callers, took a great deal of delight in informing me—and everyone else—that Miss Hemphill and Mr. St. Vincent had been courting a few months ago. It seems she then unexpectedly left for London. It was during the time she was gone that he began to court me and eventually made his own trip to London to approach Papa with an offer for my hand."

William cupped his chin with his thumb and index finger and studied her. "Do you suppose that means something?"

"I'm not sure, but from what I learned, she had been somewhat assured that an offer from Mr. St. Vincent would be forthcoming. Then she up and left Bath, only to return recently to hear that her suitor had become betrothed to me."

William looked off into the distance for a while, then turned to Amy. "Do you suppose she was so angered by his betrayal that she murdered him?"

"'Tis possible, is it not? A woman scorned and all that."

"Yes. Very possible." He glanced at the notes in her lap. "I assume she has been added to your list of suspects?"

"Yes."

William stood and offered her his hand. "Let us take a stroll, and I will tell you my story. Which I am sure will end with us adding another to our growing list."

CHAPTER 10

"Another suspect?" Amy was only too happy to include another name to her short list.

"Perhaps." He steered her away from an approaching couple. "It might be best if we take some refreshment at one of the tea shops on Broad Street. We might find a nice quiet corner where we can talk, and you can take notes."

"Excellent idea."

They chatted about the weather, how the town was growing, and which shops were worthwhile and which shops were only for those who came from out of town. Nothing said was in any way provocative, and they appeared to be no more than any other couple enjoying the lovely day.

After they were settled in the tea shop at a table near the back of the store, with the fragrant scent of tea emanating from a blue-and-white teapot and an array of small sandwiches in front of them, William began the conversation. "As I knew previously, Mr. Francis Harris, St. Vincent's nephew, stands to inherit whatever it is your fiancé left behind."

"Ex-fiancé."

He stared straight into her eyes. "He'd been out of the country for some time and took up residence about two weeks before St. Vincent's death. Just one week before, the two of them almost came to fisticuffs outside St. Vincent's townhouse."

Amy leaned back and let out a deep breath. "How very interesting."

"Indeed." He popped the rest of his sandwich into his mouth.

"What else did you discover? I can tell from your expression that you know more."

William wiped his mouth with his napkin and tossed it alongside his plate. After sliding the plate to the side, he leaned on his forearms. "From what I was told by a club member who witnessed the exchange, Mr. St. Vincent had planned to cut off the allowance he'd been providing his nephew."

Amy frowned. "I wonder what would have precipitated him doing that?"

"Do you know if St. Vincent was wealthy?"

"Papa was the one to hold the meeting with St. Vincent when they worked out the marriage contract. He would know about St. Vincent's finances." She let out a frustrated breath. "I should have asked to see the contract, but I felt so pressured by Papa at the time that the thought never occurred to me." She shook her head. "It sounds as though Mr. Harris had a reason to pop off his uncle. He would gain the business."

William choked on his tea. "Pop off?"

Amy grinned. "Murder-mystery-author talk."

"I wonder if the police know about Mr. Harris?" William tapped his fingertip on the table, a habit she'd noticed that indicated he was thinking hard. "The problem is, I am not sure how much of an investigation they are conducting."

"That is why, instead of turning this information over to the police, we need to follow up on it ourselves." She saluted him with her teacup.

★ ★ ★

Two days later, it being Sunday, Amy left the morning service at St. Swithin's church to see William waiting for her at the bottom of the stairs. He gave her and Aunt Margaret a bow. "Good morning, ladies. Did you enjoy the service?"

"What I heard of it. I'm afraid I was out late last evening and had to depend on Amy to nudge me when I began to doze off." Aunt Margaret grinned. "Will you join us for luncheon, my lord?"

"I am glad your niece was able to perform that service for you. And yes, I would be honored to join you for luncheon." He extended his elbows, and the ladies took his escort to their carriage. It was another pleasant spring day. Budding flowers grew along the pathway from the church doors to where the carriages awaited their passengers.

As their carriage drew up to the front of their townhouse, two men stood at the door, speaking with the butler, Stevens. It took Amy only a few seconds to recognize Detective Carson and Detective Marsh from the Bath police. Good heavens, didn't they have better things to do on a Sunday morning than annoy her?

"Oh, dear," Aunt Margaret said. She turned to Amy. "Maybe they found the killer and want to let us know."

"Or they are still focused on me and want to harass me some more. We are not postponing luncheon." Amy gritted her teeth at the men's poor manners to show up, unexpected, on an early Sunday afternoon. *Don't they go to church?*

Amy and Aunt Margaret stepped out of their carriage as William walked up to them from his vehicle. "Looks like you have visitors." He gestured with his head in the direction of the front door.

"Yes. Unexpected and uninvited." Amy hoped her terse words reached the detectives' ears.

William took her arm as they climbed the steps, Aunt Margaret in front of them. "I don't believe the police think they need to be expected. Or invited," he murmured in her ear.

"My goodness, Detectives, early afternoon on a Sunday? We are just now arriving home from church." Aunt Margaret regarded them with all the dignity of her station.

"I'm afraid there are things that must be discussed with Lady Amy," Carson said, not looking the least bit apologetic.

Very well. If they could be impolite, she could also. Just as she was about to tell them they could wait in the drawing room while she, Aunt Margaret, and William had their lunch, her aunt said, "We were about to have luncheon. If we all retire to the drawing room, I will have Cook send in tea and sandwiches to hold us over."

"We don't require any refreshments, my lady." Marsh sneered.

"But we do," Aunt Margaret snapped. "Therefore, you may wait in the drawing room—sans refreshments—while we enjoy our lunch." She swept past them, leaving both men gaping after her. Amy grinned. She truly did love her Aunt Margaret.

Although the three of them pretended everything was normal while they enjoyed the delicious white soup, baked salmon with lemon caper sauce, potatoes, and new peas, a cloud hung over the three of them as they ate their meal.

Amy found she could not eat as much as she normally did, wondering what could have brought the detectives out on a Sunday to question her. If they had good news, certainly they would have shared it rather than sit for almost an hour while she and her companions had their luncheon.

Eventually, Aunt Margaret took a deep breath and tossed her napkin down. "We might as well hear what those horrid men have to say."

William rose and drew back Aunt Margaret's chair, then Amy's. The three of them made their way to the drawing room, where Detective Carson paced and Detective Marsh stared into space. He rose as they entered the room.

"Please take a seat." Aunt Margaret waved in the direction of a group of chairs surrounding a small table, then settled herself on the settee and patted the space alongside her for Amy to sit. William continued to stand, resting his elbow on the fireplace mantle.

"I apologize for calling on a Sunday, but something just came up, and we need to get a few things straight."

Amy nodded, since she assumed it was her with whom they wished to speak.

Detective Marsh looked down at his notes. "One of our detectives went to your gardener's flat yesterday to see if the man had returned from wherever he had gone, or in the alternative, to search his rooms with the landlady's permission."

Amy refused to look in William's direction, afraid their break-in would be obvious to the detective. Instead, she raised her chin. "Yes?"

Detective Carson rubbed his index finger alongside his nose and looked up at her with a fake confused expression that would never have fooled anyone beyond three years of age. "What our man didn't understand was that the lock on Mr. Albright's door had been broken. It looked as though someone had thrust something, possibly himself"—he stopped and looked up at William—"and entered the rooms."

Amy refused to comment, since no question had been asked. William also remained silent.

"What is it you wish to say, Detective? Is there a question there? Because if so, I did not hear it." Aunt Margaret, ignorant of Amy and William's foray to Albright's apartment, was the perfect person to question the detectives. No guilt there.

Carson leaned forward and glared at Amy. "Did you and your cohort here"—he jerked his thumb in William's direction—"break into Mr. Albright's rooms?"

Amy drew herself up. "Of course not." Hopefully the flush on her face would appear to be indignation and not guilt. From Detective Carson's raised eyebrows, it seemed he chose guilt.

"I would like to ask you, Detective," William said from where he stood at the fireplace, "what has the police department done in the way of finding Mr. St. Vincent's killer? Since the murder is almost a week old, and you are just now considering searching Mr. Albright's rooms, it seems to me the investigation is not as thorough as I believe it should be."

Now it was Detective Marsh's turn to flush red. "We are doing a thorough investigation, Lord Wethington, I can assure you. However, these things take time."

"Would you care to share with us what you have uncovered so far?"

"No. That is police information and business."

William was not to be thwarted. "Seeing that you all but accused Lady Amy of the deed the night the body was discovered, I think it is her business to know exactly what it is you are doing."

"That is not how the police work, my lord. Lady Amy is still the only person who had opportunity and reason. While we are not in a position to actually charge her with murder, no one else has been discovered who might be involved."

Since Amy and William had added two more people to their list, along with Mr. Albright, the police were clearly not doing their job. She'd been right all along. They were focused on her and would spend their time trying to prove she was guilty rather than looking for the actual killer.

"If that is all, Detectives, I bid you good day." Aunt Margaret stood and smoothed out her skirts. "My niece has refuted your claim that she broke into Mr. Albright's rooms. If that is all you have to ask after interrupting our day, then Stevens will show you out."

The detectives rose to their feet. "That is all we have right now, but I will say this." Marsh looked back and forth between Amy and William. "Interfering in a police investigation is a crime. If someone—and I'm not making an accusation here—did break into the flat of an individual under consideration for murder, and took anything they found out of those rooms, that person, or persons, would be breaking the law and subject to criminal charges."

"Good day, Detectives." Aunt Margaret walked to the drawing room door. "Stevens, please see the detectives out."

Both men lumbered from the room.

Amy closed her eyes and took a deep breath. Once the sound of the front door closing reached them, Aunt Margaret placed her hands on her hips and glared at her and William. "Whatever were you two thinking, breaking into that man's flat?"

★　★　★

Tuesday morning, Amy tapped lightly on Eloise's bedroom door. Eloise's maid had answered the front door and, knowing Amy as well as she did, just allowed her to find her own way to Eloise's room.

"Come in." The scratchy, deep voice did not sound like Eloise.

Amy opened the door. Eloise was in bed, her eyes red and a handkerchief crushed in her hands. She took one look at Amy and sneezed.

"Oh, dear. I guess you are still unwell." Amy settled herself in the chair next to Eloise's bed.

"Yes, and getting caught in the rain the other night on the way home from the book club meeting did not help. Is there any news on St. Vincent's murder?" Sneeze, sneeze, sneeze. Blow nose. "Sorry."

Amy waved her off. "It is my opinion that the police are so focused on me that they are spending their time trying to find proof of my guilt rather than looking for other suspects."

Eloise laughed, then coughed for a full minute. "Sorry," she murmured.

"That's all right, Eloise. I know you're ill. You don't have to continue to apologize." It did occur to Amy, though, that she had best make this visit short, since she didn't want to catch Eloise's cold.

"What I came to tell you is William—Lord Wethington—and I are conducting our own investigation of the murder." She grinned at Eloise's surprised expression.

"In truth?"

"Yes."

Another sneeze and hacking cough. Amy backed up the chair she sat on.

"Sorry."

Amy took a deep breath. "We broke into my gardener's flat the other night. I was going to tell you all about it after the book club meeting, but you left early."

"Why?" More coughing. One very loud sneeze.

Amy held up her hand. "Do. Not. Apologize." She took a deep breath. "I think it best if I tell you more about this when you are feeling better."

Eloise collapsed back onto her propped-up pillows. "As much as I hate not hearing the entire story, I believe you are correct. In fact, when you leave, can you ask Gertrude—"

"The one at the door?"

"Yes. Have her bring me a tisane from Cook. I need to sleep."

Amy hopped up and backed away from the bed as Eloise began another rousing session of sneezing and coughing. "I'll just . . . let myself out."

Eloise waved her off, and Amy made a quick exit. She found the maid and asked for the tisane. Three times on the way home she felt her forehead to see if she was fevered.

*   *   *

That afternoon Amy picked up the small satchel of sewing supplies she'd put together to attend Lady Ambrose's sewing circle. Hopefully, Miss Hemphill would be there and Amy could get more information on the proposal St. Vincent was supposed to have made to her. Of course, it was quite probable the woman would stick Amy with a very long and sharp needle for taking her man, but with the detectives wandering in circles, she needed to put an end to this matter once and for all.

"Sewing circle, Amy?" Aunt Margaret grinned as Amy placed the satchel on the settee in the drawing room, where her aunt was enjoying an afternoon tea and a book.

"Is that one of my books?"

Aunt Margaret shook her head. "No, dear. I've told you before, I cannot read about all that blood and such." She shuddered. "I don't know how you can write it. It would keep me awake nights."

Amy shrugged into her pelisse and drew on her gloves. "I intend to get more information from Miss Hemphill on this marriage proposal she was expecting from Mr. St. Vincent." Amy had kept her aunt up-to-date with the investigation she and William were conducting after having admitted to her on Sunday that they had indeed broken into Mr. Albright's rooms.

While Aunt was not pleased with the danger involved in their trying to solve the murder themselves, she agreed it appeared highly unlikely the police would do anything more than bumble around until they simply arrested Amy for the crime.

"Are you taking Persephone with you?"

"No. She appears a bit ill today. Her nose sounds congested, and she's very lazy." Amy paused and studied the dog, who was snoring away in the corner. "Do you think it possible for me to have contracted Eloise's cold and passed it along to Persephone?"

"Are you ill?"

Amy shook her head. "No."

"Then I doubt you could pass along an illness you do not yourself possess." Her aunt had the strangest way of saying things. "If you don't take her with you, aren't you afraid she won't talk to you?" Aunt Margaret nodded toward Persephone.

"Yes. I know how silly it sounds, but my darling pet does have a way of letting me know she is displeased with me. Besides, if I am interested in conversation, I can always ask Othello to spout some poetry for me."

"Have a good time sewing. I would go with you, but I don't know what I despise more, Lady Ambrose or sewing." She settled back into her chair and picked up her book. "Good luck."

★   ★   ★

Five women were sitting in a group, chatting away and moving their needles in and out of colorful pieces of cloth, when Amy was announced by Mrs. Ambrose's butler. Raised eyebrows and pursed lips greeted her as she entered the room and took a seat near the hostess.

Miss Hemphill was not in the room.

"Welcome to our little group, Lady Amy." Lady Ambrose fluttered. She actually fluttered as she welcomed Amy. No doubt she had secured a coup de foudre by having the very notorious Lady Amy attend her sewing circle so soon after her erstwhile fiancé had met his end in her library.

"Thank you. I am delighted to be part of such a noble project." 'Twas indeed a noble project, but if Miss Hemphill did not join them, there would be very little delight on her part.

"I am so glad to see you out and about, Lady Amy. So many women would take to their beds after a tragedy such as what your fiancé endured—"

"Ex-fiancé."

"But then, some women don't have the delicate sensibilities that I possess." Mrs. Richmond, an older woman with a pointed nose, a perpetual scowl, and an unpleasant demeanor to match it all attempted to look sympathetic.

The woman's ploy did not work. Her joy at Amy's predicament, and her insinuation that Amy was without delicate sensibilities—which was undoubtedly correct—were simply too hard to hide.

"Actually, Mrs. Richmond, Mr. St. Vincent was not my fiancé when he died. We had already gone our separate ways."

"Indeed? I did not know that." Miss Penelope O'Neill, sitting next to her sister, Gertrude, both of them dressed identically again, put the cloth she was working on down on her lap. "Why was he at your house, then?"

Amy sighed. Some women danced around a question; others came right out with it. Miss O'Neill was one of the more forthright ones. "That shall forever remain an unanswered question, Miss O'Neill, since I did not speak with him before he was . . . killed."

Three women sucked in their breath. *Botheration.* They knew the man had been murdered. Amy reached for her cup of tea and took a sip before pulling out the items from her satchel.

Silence, broken only by the sound of teacups placed in their saucers and mumbles of "Would you care for a tart?" descended on the group as the ladies all lowered their heads and took a great deal of interest in their sewing. Apparently Amy's presence had a silencing effect on the group. Hopefully there would be no more questions. She wasn't there to provide answers but to discover some. If it hadn't been for her need to solve this case before she was arrested, she would never have put herself in a position where she could be picked apart like carrion.

She'd barely stabbed the cloth in her hands with her needle when Lady Ambrose's butler appeared at the door to the drawing room again. "Miss Hemphill, my lady."

Miss Eva Hemphill walked through the door. Her hair was in disarray and her clothing looked wrinkled, as if she'd slept in the outfit. She was pale and appeared quite fatigued. The newly arrived guest took a few steps into the room, took one look at Amy, and slid to the floor in a dead faint.

Chapter 11

Amy watched slack-jawed as Miss Hemphill collapsed, and several women dropped their sewing to rush in her direction. Had the woman really swooned when she looked at her? There could be any number of reasons for her to be lying in a heap on the floor. Perhaps she had missed her breakfast, or she was beginning to suffer from an ague, or she had tripped on something when she entered the room.

Or she thought she had come face to face with her ex-lover's killer.

Amy quickly reminded herself that Miss Hemphill had made their list of *most likely to have brought an end to Mr. St. Vincent's life.* Maybe she had fainted because she thought Amy knew she had killed Mr. St. Vincent. Or suspected as much, at any rate.

"Oh, dear. Whatever happened?" Miss Hemphill struggled to sit up, looked around at the group, and grew even paler when her eyes settled on Amy. There was absolutely no mistaking the anger and hatred in the woman's eyes. Enough to make Amy back up a bit in her chair, wondering if Miss Hemphill was about to lunge across the room and tear the hair right out of her head.

As quickly as that anger had surfaced, it disappeared, and she even offered Amy a slight smile. Miss Hemphill climbed to her feet with Lady Ambrose's assistance and stumbled her way to a chair, where she sat and sighed deeply. For heaven's sake, were they to be troubled by all this drama the entire afternoon?

Rather than start up any new dramatics, Amy put her head down and grew busy with her sewing as the other women fussed over Miss Hemphill, sending for fresh tea and running for cool cloths and a pillow for her head. All the time, however, Amy's mind was in a whirl about what had just happened. Two things were certain: Miss Hemphill had swooned when she spotted Amy, and her eyes had been filled with hatred when she first awakened and looked at her again.

Someone with that much anger would be quite capable of plunging a knife into a man's chest. Miss Hemphill went from another name on their list to the very top. No matter how hard it would be, she must talk to the woman today. Maybe once everyone had tea and things settled down, she could ask a few questions that would not seem out of the ordinary but might help things along with the murder investigation.

Amy's logical mind began to sort out the known facts and assemble them into an equation. Miss Hemphill had expected to receive an offer from Mr. St. Vincent. Sometime after that, she'd left for London. Mr. St. Vincent began to court Amy and traveled to London himself to see Amy's father. She and St. Vincent became engaged. A mere few weeks later, Amy received a letter from an anonymous correspondent telling her about St. Vincent's unsavory dealings. She ended her relationship with the man. Miss Hemphill turned back up in Bath and Mr. St. Vincent turned up dead.

Miss Hemphill sent the note!

It was so obvious, Amy almost shouted with joy. Of course she had sent the note. Who else would care if Amy knew St. Vincent was trading in drugs? If Lady Amy learned about his nefarious business, there was a good chance she would call an end to their engagement. And Mr. St. Vincent would be free to marry Miss Hemphill.

Except he didn't marry her.

He had called on Amy instead.

And ended up with a knife in his chest.

Another fact: it was well known that her ex-fiancé owned a shipping company, which was where, Amy assumed, he had been able to bring opium into the country to sell to unfortunate individuals. Hopefully, with William investigating St. Vincent's financial information, he might gain facts and figures about his business as well.

"My goodness, Lady Amy, you certainly have a fervor for making garments for the poor."

Amy's head snapped up as she regarded Miss Gertrude O'Neill, who grinned as she looked down at the two garments Amy had already sewn while she worked out steps in her head. In fact, a cup of cold tea sat in front of her that she'd ignored since it had been placed there, and somewhere in the back of her mind she knew the ladies had all been conversing while she ruminated on murder.

"I apologize. I'm afraid I was distracted by a problem we are having with a member of our staff, and I have impolitely ignored all of you." She took a sip of the tea and grimaced at the temperature.

"We were discussing the dance at the Assembly next Saturday evening. I assume, since you are not in mourning for your fiancé, that you will attend?" Lady Graham's semi-insulting question had her daughter, Lady Susan, blushing.

"Ex-fiancé."

The Assembly dance would be a good opportunity for Amy to look over members of her various circles to determine if there were others to be added to their list of suspects. Plus, she might gain information about St. Vincent's nephew. "Yes. I believe I will be attending." She looked the woman in the eyes and raised her chin. "And yes, you are correct, Lady Graham. Since Mr. St. Vincent and I had parted ways before his unfortunate death, I am not in mourning."

A quick glance in Miss Hemphill's direction proved Amy had been correct. The hatred pouring forth from the woman's entire body was an unsettling and very dangerous thing. Amy would be sure to ask William to attend the Assembly with her.

The next couple of hours passed without Amy ever having the chance to speak with Miss Hemphill. But given the nasty looks the woman had given her all afternoon—when she thought no one was noticing—convinced her that a conversation with the woman would not happen anyway.

Finally tired of all the sewing and gossiping, Amy packed her supplies in her satchel. "I believe I will leave you ladies now. As I mentioned earlier, we have a staff problem which needs my attention."

Lady Ambrose rose and grabbed Amy by the shoulders. "Thank you so much for coming today. We can always use another pair of hands." Surprised at the woman's honest words, Amy was even more startled when Lady Ambrose leaned in and kissed the air alongside her cheek and took the opportunity to whisper, "Be careful."

Stunned, Amy merely nodded and took her leave.

Be careful?

★   ★   ★

As Amy did not see William for the rest of the week, by Saturday she was more anxious than ever to speak with him about her visit to the sewing circle. He'd sent a note around Thursday morning saying he would not be attending the book club meeting but asked that she do him the honor of attending the

Assembly Saturday evening with him. If she was amenable, he would pick her up at eight o'clock.

He offered no reason for his absence from the club meeting, which left her hoping he was busy uncovering information to help in their search for the killer.

Amy had spent her time finishing up her book and pondering Miss Hemphill. It had been a rainy, dreary week, and she and Aunt Margaret left the house a few times to shop and have tea on Broad Street. Eloise was still not up to snuff, so rather than risk becoming sick herself, Amy passed on visiting her friend, but sent along notes of fond wishes for a full recovery soon.

Since her aunt knew Amy and William were investigating St. Vincent's murder, she now felt comfortable keeping her up-to-date on the happenings, even though Aunt Margaret made no secret of her disapproval.

Surprisingly, Aunt Margaret had made a few suggestions that actually made sense. Perhaps Amy was not the only one in the family with a logical mind. Or perhaps a criminal mind.

"Have you considered the path these illegal drugs take?" Her aunt swirled a hefty teaspoon of sugar into her tea as they enjoyed the end of their dinner before they both were to dress for the Assembly dance.

Amy nodded. "I am assuming, since Mr. St. Vincent owned the shipping company founded by his great-grandfather, most likely the drugs came from there."

"Yes, perhaps they did. But on the other hand, there would have to have been someone to accept the drugs from the ship and then distribute them. I don't see your fiancé—"

"Ex-fiancé."

"—dirtying his hands by actually dealing with that part of it. I'm thinking there was another man who accepted the drugs, packaged them for individual sale, and then perhaps turned it over to other distributors, to sell. This person would receive a cut of the profits for his part in the chain."

"A very good point, Aunt Margaret." Amy thought for a minute. "If what you say is correct, then the man who was taking a cut of the profits might have reason to do away with St. Vincent. After all, he was accepting the drugs. Why not just sell them himself? Or perhaps demand a larger cut."

"Except Mr. St. Vincent owned the shipping company. He was the one bringing the opium into the country. That would still be necessary. Would whoever inherited it be willing to continue the practice?"

They both remained quiet as they pondered this new idea.

Aunt Margaret checked her timepiece and slid her chair back. "It is time to prepare for the Assembly."

They were both ready and waiting in the drawing room when William arrived to escort them to the dance. Why was it, now that they were spending more time together, she noticed how handsome and well dressed the man was each time he appeared at her doorstep? This was the same old William she'd known for years.

As they rode in Wethington's carriage through the town to the Assembly Rooms on Bennett Street, she went over in her mind the discussion she and Aunt Margaret had just had about the drug distribution. That was something else to bring to William's attention.

She glanced out the window as they approached the Assembly Rooms. Pleasant weather would be wonderful for a spring evening ride; however, they were instead burdened with another downpour that had already wet her gown, even though she'd worn a long coat and huddled under the large umbrella William had used to cover the three of them from the house to the carriage.

At least the rain had slowed a bit by the time they arrived at their destination in the heart of the city. While the Assembly

Rooms had been built almost two hundred years before, new upper rooms had been added and opened with a grand ball in the late eighteenth century. They had become the basis of fashionable society, with Miss Austen and Mr. Dickens as well as nobility frequenting the place.

The building, made of Bath stone, was U-shaped, with four main function rooms: a ballroom, the tearoom, the card room, and the octagon. It was richly decorated with fine art and crystal chandeliers and remained one of Amy's favorite places to gather with her friends and enjoy an evening of dancing.

A footman assisted her and Aunt Margaret with their heavy woolen coats, while William removed his own outerwear. Amy and Aunt Margaret slipped into the retiring room, just off the main room, to fix their hair and make sure they were presentable.

The music started up just as they entered the ballroom. William stood against the wall, chatting with several members from the book club. No doubt catching up on what he had missed at the meeting.

The room's pale-blue walls with white wooden trim made the area seem larger and brighter when the numerous chandeliers were lit. The well-worn wooden floor was already crowded with couples dancing a quadrille. Ladies wore their best gowns, and gentlemen attempted to outdo each other with well-trimmed jackets and colorful ascots.

"Good evening, Lady Amy, Lady Margaret." Mr. Colbert beamed at them. He was always such a cheerful man. Mr. Miles and Mr. Davidson followed suit. Lady Carlisle and Miss Sterling smiled and gave a slight dip.

"Good evening, everyone," Amy and Aunt Margaret said at once.

Now that two meetings of the Mystery Book Club had passed since St. Vincent's death, it appeared she was no longer the main subject of gossip. The group had not stopped speaking abruptly when she approached them.

About ten minutes had passed in pleasant conversation when the musicians began a waltz. "May I request this dance, Lady Amy?" William spoke rather quickly, no doubt anxious to have time alone with her so they could discuss the subject first and foremost in their minds.

"Yes, thank you, my lord." She took his extended arm, and they walked to the center of the room.

William swung her into his arms, and they began the steps. "I have a bit of information for you," he said as he turned the two of them to keep from crashing into another couple. She leaned her head back to look into his eyes, surprised, up close, at how much taller he was than she had realized. So many things about William had previously escaped her notice.

"Where have you been all week?" Goodness, she sounded like a harpy, demanding to know where he was. "I'm sorry, I did not mean for it to come out that way."

Instead of showing annoyance, he merely smiled that crooked smile of his that made him look like a little boy. "I apologize for my absence. I had a difficult situation to handle—nothing dealing with our investigation. But I do have information on Mr. St. Vincent's finances as well as his nephew, Mr. Harris."

"And I have information on Miss Hemphill. But why don't you go first?"

William moved them to the edge of the dance floor so they could waltz at a slower pace and not interfere with the other couples. "First off, I met Mr. Harris at my club the other night. I must admit, he's a likable chap, not too good at cards, but there was something seemingly 'off' about him. Not that he bragged about it, but based on a few things he said, we were correct to assume that Mr. Harris was St. Vincent's heir, both to his business and everything else."

"That could be a reason to hasten someone's death."

"Just so. However, as I told you earlier, the argument over-heard in front of St. Vincent's townhouse was due to Mr. St. Vincent cutting off Harris's allowance."

"Were you able to find out why?"

"Not from the individual who was privy to the argument, but rather from interesting information Mr. Harding uncov-ered." The music ended, and Amy was amazed to see how many more people had entered the room while they were dancing.

"Walk with me to the refreshment table." William took her by the elbow, and they made their way through the throng.

Amy leaned in close to his ear. "What did your man of business learn?"

William shook his head and stepped up to the table, retriev-ing two glasses of lemonade. He handed one to her and took her other hand in his. "Let's go for a stroll."

Since the room had grown so crowded, it soon became apparent that a stroll would not be possible. Amy was also frustrated as they were continuously stopped by friends and acquaintances, some who wanted to discuss St. Vincent's death and others who just wanted to chat.

"I believe we must continue our conversation another time." William looked as frustrated as she felt. "Perhaps I can call on you tomorrow afternoon?"

"A very good idea. Why don't you join us for luncheon after church again? Even though Aunt Margaret is now aware of our determination to find the killer and has even come up with a good point I will share with you, she prefers not to know too much about what we are doing. She is concerned for my safety. So, we will have to discuss matters after lunch. Maybe take a ride to Royal Victoria Park and stroll among all the spring flowers, if the weather allows."

William studied her with tightened lips. "I must agree with Lady Margaret. I've warned you before that if the killer becomes aware of your snooping into the murder, you could very well be in danger."

"I am not going to sit by while the detectives assigned to this case do nothing but look for ways to close their case against me. Once I am in jail, there will be nothing I can do to help myself." She shook her head. "Dangerous or not, I have to do whatever I can to find out who killed Mr. St. Vincent."

William grinned. "I didn't really think your aunt's comments, nor my agreeing with her, were going to stop you." He looked up over her shoulder and stiffened.

"What?" Amy turned, but being of short stature, she couldn't see beyond the gold buttons on the jackets of the two men in front of her.

"Mr. Harris. He just entered the room."

"How very interesting." Amy moved sideways until she got a clear view of the door. "Is that him? With the dark-burgundy jacket and gold ascot?"

"Yes." William darted a glance toward Amy.

"What?"

"He just spotted me and is coming this way."

Within minutes, William broke into a smile and extended his hand. "Mr. Harris, good to see you."

The nephew slapped William on the back and turned to Amy. "And who is this lovely creature?"

"Lady Amy Lovell, may I present to you Mr. Francis Harris."

"Indeed? Lady Amy? I see now why my uncle was willing to surrender his bachelorhood." He took Amy's extended hand and kissed it. She quelled the urge to wipe it on her gown.

"A pleasure, Mr. Harris." Once again apologizing to God for the little white lie, she eased her hand behind her and rubbed the back of it on the tablecloth covering the area holding the drinks and other refreshments.

There was indeed something "off" about Mr. St. Vincent's nephew. It was not in his looks, which were quite pleasant. Where Mr. St. Vincent had dark hair and brown eyes, Mr. Harris's hair was more of a light brown, with hazel eyes. He stood about equal in height with William and filled out his clothing quite well.

Something in his eyes troubled her, though. He reminded her of someone who was keeping a secret from everyone else and thought it to be quite a joke. "Are you staying long in Bath, Mr. Harris?"

"Please, call me Francis. I always think of my father as Mr. Harris."

She had no intention of calling him Francis or anything else, since she did not plan to spend much time with the man. To her dismay, the musicians started up another waltz and Harris turned to her. "May I have the honor of this dance, Lady Amy?"

Sometimes she wished good manners had not been so instilled into her by her governesses. She would have loved more than anything to refuse and resume her walk with William. But then again, perhaps as a woman she could gain information from him that William had been unable to unearth. "Yes, of course, Mr. Harris."

He took her hand and led her to the dance floor. 'Twas not as crowded as it had been earlier when she and William had danced, so there was more room to move around. Mr. Harris proved to be quite an accomplished dancer, and despite her initial reluctance to accept his request for a dance, she found herself relaxing.

"I find I am very much in your debt, Lady Amy." His smile did not wipe away the uneasiness she felt at his comment and the hairs that rose at the back of her neck.

"And why is that, Mr. Harris?" she asked with a suddenly dry mouth.

"Why, for my uncle, of course." He moved them in a graceful turn and studied her for a moment. "I have you to thank for killing him."

CHAPTER 12

Amy came to an abrupt halt and stared at Mr. Harris. The couple to their rear crashed into them, the man mumbling something insulting as they skirted around. The woman turned and glared at them.

"Although I find it in extremely bad taste, I assume you are attempting some sort of a joke?"

The horrid man continued to grin as he nudged her to continue with the dance. "Not at all. Uncle was found dead in your library with no one else about. You had broken the engagement a few days before. What else am I to assume? So, I thank you. As soon as the will is read, I will be a wealthy man."

Had it not been the height of rudeness, Amy would have kneed Mr. Harris right where it would hurt the most. In fact, her body shook with the need to wreak some sort of violence upon the man. She was so flabbergasted she couldn't even speak. It was as if her mind was frozen while her body continued to move with the music.

"I should like to take you for a ride sometime. Again, I must remark on how easily Uncle had fallen under your spell after swearing for years he would never marry. A beautiful woman will win every time." He lowered his voice. "And let's face facts, Lady Amy. If we are to enjoy each other's company, it must be soon, since the police will probably arrest you shortly."

Mr. Harris's smirk was all the motivation she needed. Seething with anger, she shook her head and pushed at his chest so he was forced to release her.

"What is wrong?" The cur had the nerve to look surprised.

She could hold it in no longer. She drew her arm back and slammed her fist into his face. Not the delicate slap or light tap to which most women would resort. Amy put everything into that punch, to the point that her arm ached.

Mr. Harris reared back, stumbled, and landed on his arse. Had she her newly acquired Kodak at hand, she would have taken a picture of the stunned expression on his face to enjoy for the rest of her days.

All the couples in the area stopped and stared at her with horror and Harris with a puzzled expression. Her breath was coming so hard and so fast, she was afraid she would pass out again. Black dots continued to swim in front of her eyes, and a loud buzzing commenced in her ears.

A warm, secure arm wrapped around her waist. "Time to leave, my dear." William walked her forward, even though she swore her legs wouldn't move. They made their way through the now silent room, the guests parting like the Red Sea, to the exit, where William grabbed their coats from the man at the door.

"Aunt Margaret!" Amy finally recovered herself enough to know they had left her aunt behind.

"Right here, dear." Aunt Margaret's comforting voice and strong arm wrapped around her shoulders as William led them both from the building.

He snapped open his large umbrella and covered them all while they waited in silence for his carriage to be brought around. Thankfully, the presence of William and Aunt Margaret had steadied her, and she no longer felt as though she would faint. But the anger soon returned in full force, and she had to fight the need to return to the Assembly Rooms and use her knee to leave an even stronger message with Mr. Harris.

Strands of music reached their ears, so the dance had continued. William helped her and Aunt Margaret into the carriage and climbed in after them.

Amy had begun to shake, and William pulled a woolen blanket from under his seat and handed it to Aunt Margaret, who covered her with it. She felt as though she would never be truly warm again.

I have you to thank for killing him.

"Oh, that horrid, horrid man! He is despicable, contemptible, odious, repugnant—" She turned to Aunt Margaret. "I cannot think of enough wretched words to describe him."

"Dear, I think you need to calm yourself. Then tell us whatever it was he said that set you off into such a rage."

Amy drew in a deep breath. "I have never struck anyone in my life." She rubbed her knuckles, which reminded her of how hard she had hit the man. "I am a lady." She laid her head on the soft leather squab and closed her eyes. "And now I am ruined."

★　★　★

The next afternoon Amy left her room, having been summoned by Papa, who had arrived from London. Her eyes were red from lack of sleep the night before. On the ride home from the Assembly Rooms, she'd told Aunt Margaret and William what Harris had said. It had taken all of Amy and her aunt's persuasive skills to keep William from returning to the Assembly and adding his own form of displeasure to Mr. Harris's body.

A hot bath and one of Cook's tisanes had not relaxed her enough to sleep. She'd tossed and turned and sent word to Aunt at the crack of dawn that she would miss church services. Perhaps it was a coward's way, but she could not face those at church who had witnessed her fall from grace the night before.

William had said when he left them off after the dance that he would call that afternoon so they could continue their discussion. That was the summons she had been waiting for, and Amy was quite surprised when Lacey said it was Papa awaiting her.

"Good afternoon, Papa." Amy walked into her father's office next to his bedchamber, where he sat behind his desk. She bent and kissed his cheek. "I assume all is well?"

"As well as it could be with my daughter under suspicion of murder." He tempered his words with a warm smile. "How are you doing, my dear?"

"Fine." No point in upsetting Papa with all the information she and William had gained over the past several days or informing him of the nasty Mr. Harris and the right hook she'd delivered to his chin. Fathers tended to dislike knowing their gently reared daughters could hold their own in the boxing ring.

She rounded the large, highly polished cherrywood desk that had been in Papa's office ever since she could remember and took a seat across from him.

"I have come to Bath to discuss a few things with you." Papa leaned back in his chair and tapped the armrest with his fingertip. "Please rest assured that I have not abandoned you. All of this could not have happened at a worse time."

"So you've said," Amy mumbled.

He scowled at her. "However, I've been corresponding with the police, and it appears they are at an impasse. What I concluded from their last missive is they are no closer to solving St. Vincent's murder than they were the night it happened."

Amy jumped up, too unsettled to sit. "That is because they are not looking at anyone else except me. They are spending all their time digging for proof that I am the guilty party."

"Sit down, daughter. I agree, which is why I have engaged a private investigator to delve into the matter. Sir Roger Holstein will be contacting you shortly to go over a few items."

Amy's eyes widened in horror. Things were going along nicely with her and William conducting their own investigation, since they never stumbled over the detectives, who were searching in the wrong place. If they had an investigator following their footsteps, he would just get in their way.

"Papa, I don't think that's a good idea."

His brows rose. "And why is that? To have someone on your side, as it were, is a good thing. He will go places the police have refused to go and find a few people who had a reason to kill Mr. St. Vincent."

Botheration and blast it! Things had been running rather smoothly, and now another person would arrive to stir the pot. It was bad enough with Aunt Margaret questioning her every move without having some hired nodcock getting in their way. Amy cleared her throat. "Um, perhaps with my background in murders, I can do a bit to help find the true killer."

Papa hopped up and slammed his hand on the desk, causing Amy to jump a few inches in the chair. "Absolutely not! It is too dangerous for you to be snooping around. Whoever killed your fiancé—"

"Ex-fiancé."

"—will be quite comfortable as long as the police are only considering you. It would become outright dangerous for you to be involved." He sat back down and straightened his jacket. "I will hear no more about you entering this foray. And remember, young lady, as much as it distresses me, you are an author of mysteries, and that is a far cry from actually solving a real crime." He glowered at her. "And it is in your best interests to put that all aside anyway and concentrate instead on getting a husband!" His voice rose on the last four words.

Well, then.

A slight tinge of red covered Papa's cheeks. "I concede that perhaps Mr. St. Vincent was not the best candidate for a husband, and I regret my part in encouraging you to accept his offer."

Encouraging? He had practically placed his foot on her back to push her in that direction, but one didn't point out such things to one's father.

He continued. "But that doesn't mean we should abandon the idea altogether. What about young Wethington, who always seems to be hanging about when I arrive?"

She stared at him aghast. "Papa, please. Lord Wethington and I are friends. We belong to the same book club and enjoy similar activities. Nothing more than that."

Her father pointed his finger at her. "A good reason to consider matrimony. Many successful marriages have begun with less than that."

Attempting to dispute his comments about a husband would be useless. He never listened during those arguments anyway. If he didn't want to hear any more about her investigation, that was fine, but that didn't mean she would stop what she was doing. She and William already had three people on their suspect list, as well as information on St. Vincent's financial condition that William had yet to share with her.

Perhaps she was not a professional investigator, but it appeared she was doing a much better job than the police.

Papa shifted in his chair and attempted to look remorseful for his outburst. "If you have been poking around, you will turn over whatever information you possess to Sir Holstein when he visits with you."

When she just stared at him, he added, "I mean it, Amy."

Since she hadn't asked for her word to hand over her information, it was best to nod to appease him before he did. Although women were not considered as honorable as men, she never gave her word and went back on it. Before Papa could ask, she jumped up. "Is that all, Papa? I am expecting Lord Wethington shortly. We are going for a stroll through Royal Victoria Park."

Papa's face lit up. "Indeed? You see, I was correct about the lad, and I'm pleased to hear that. Lord Wethington is a fine man and would make an excellent husband."

Amy groaned. "Papa! Again, we are just friends. I've told you before I have no desire or need for a husband."

He waved his hand in dismissal. "Nonsense. Every woman needs a husband."

"Aunt Margaret?"

Papa scowled. "Do not remind me of my stubborn sister. If I had my way, she would have been married years ago, with several children taking up her time and attention."

Glad to have his scrutiny diverted from her and in Aunt Margaret's direction, Amy took the opportunity to escape. "Perhaps that is so." She began to back away toward the door. "If you will excuse me, I must prepare for his lordship's arrival." As she reached for the door latch, she stopped as a horrible thought crossed her mind. "Um, Papa. Are you staying long?"

"No. I shall be off first thing in the morning. I am extremely unhappy about leaving you to your own devices with a killer about the place. However, I have too many matters in London that cannot wait on my attendance."

Giddy with relief, Amy had turned to leave the room when Papa said, "However, as soon as I can free up your brother's time, he will arrive to look after you."

Her stomach sank at those words as she hurried up the stairs to fetch her bonnet and gloves. Having her brother about was almost as bad as Papa looking over her shoulder. She pushed that thought aside as she noticed the sun shining brightly. A great day for a stroll and a discussion of murder.

She no sooner had herself ready for the day than she heard the sound of carriage wheels outside the house. A quick peek out her bedroom window, which faced the street, confirmed it was William, and she hurried downstairs before Papa could accost him and begin an interrogation. She might be able to slip a lie past Papa, but she doubted William would try.

William had only placed one foot in the entranceway when she grabbed his arm. "So nice to see you, my lord. It's lovely outside, is it not?" She shoved him through the door and practically dragged him down the steps.

Once they reached his carriage, he pulled his arm back. "Whatever is the matter with you, Amy?" He pulled on the cuffs of his jacket and opened the door to the carriage.

"Nothing. I'm just anxious for us to share our news."

He settled in the seat across from her and smirked. "This doesn't have anything to do with the Winchester carriage I caught a glimpse of when I rode up to your house, does it?"

She sighed. "Yes. Papa sent word to have the carriage dispatched to the rail station to meet him. He arrived to see how I was bearing up with the murder hanging over my head. But worse than trying to convince Papa I am doing well and not attempting to solve the mystery myself—"

William snorted.

"—he has arranged for a private investigator to join the search! That is terrible."

"Why? Maybe it would be better to let the bloke take over so you can remain out of it and safe."

Amy drew herself up and glared at him. "I will not remove myself from the search. First of all, we have put a lot of time and effort into this. Second, this man will be starting at the beginning and we are so far ahead of him. Third, this is my neck headed toward the noose if we don't undercover the culprit." She wrapped her arms around her body and shuddered. "Frankly, after Mr. Harris being so sure I murdered his uncle, I'm afraid the police will arrive at any time and haul me off to prison."

"Mr. Harris is an idiot," William snapped. "Please put that blackguard from your mind. My theory is he does not think you murdered Mr. St. Vincent at all. A reminder: he is on our list of suspects. If anything, I believe he attempted to trick you into revealing how much you knew. He attempted to shock you, and it worked."

"Dreadful man."

"Agreed." The carriage turned from Royal Avenue onto Marlborough Lane. William knocked on the ceiling to alert the driver to stop. "This is a good spot to walk. I will have my man return for us in about an hour."

Amy gathered her things and took William's hand after he stepped out of the carriage. He spoke with the driver, and once the man was on his way, William took her arm in his and they began their walk.

It was truly a pleasant day. The newly awakened spring flowers and rare bright sunlight raised her spirits considerably. She took in a deep breath and smiled, her confidence rising. They would solve this and go back to their normal lives.

"I believe you were going to tell me about Miss Hemphill." William directed them toward a pathway on the left.

"Yes. A most interesting and very strange thing occurred. I attended Lady Ambrose's sewing circle Tuesday last, since I had learned that Miss Hemphill was a member of the group, and I had hoped to speak with her."

"I believe that is the woman who had been courted by St. Vincent and then disappeared to London?"

"Yes. And she returned shortly before he was killed."

His nod encouraged her to continue.

"The very strange thing that happened was her reaction to me. You see, I arrived at Lady Ambrose's house before Miss

Hemphill. I was sitting in the room when she entered behind the butler. She took one look at me and fainted dead away on the floor."

His head whipped around to stare at her. "You don't say? How very odd."

"That is precisely what I thought. But she quickly recovered herself and continued to cast hateful and alarming glances in my direction the entire time I was there."

William chuckled. "I hope you didn't think she would be full of kind thoughts about you. From what you told me before, she was expecting to become engaged to Mr. St. Vincent and then returned from her trip to find you had snagged him while she was gone."

Amy huffed. "I hardly *snagged* him. He and Papa worked everything out, and I was coerced into the betrothal."

"With Miss Hemphill absent when this all took place, I can imagine what she thought when she returned. But in any case, a collapse at the sight of your mere presence does seem a bit over the top."

"That's what I thought. She avoided me for the rest of the time I was there, and finally, realizing I would never get any information from her, I left."

"So she remains on your suspect list?"

"Definitely. One other thing. Every time our eyes met while we were both there, the amount of hatred I saw there actually frightened me. I believe Miss Hemphill is someone who could harm another person if provoked."

"Interesting. Well, she is on the list. I think it would be a good idea to get as much information about her as we can. For example, why did she disappear to London?"

"And, remember, Mr. St. Vincent also took a trip to London during that time period. That was when he met with my father."

William walked alongside her for a few minutes, staring at the ground, obviously pondering what she'd just told him. Then he looked over at her. "What is it your aunt had to say about our investigation?"

"Thank you, I had almost forgotten about that. One thing we have not considered up to this point is the distribution of the drugs St. Vincent was importing." She stopped and bent to pick a flower that had been trampled by careless strollers. She sniffed the bloom and held on to it. "Although St. Vincent owns a shipping company, there would still have to be someone who accepted the drugs and then repackaged them for sale to individuals."

"Of course. I doubt he would dirty his hands with such doings. So there is a middleman who might have a reason to see Mr. St. Vincent dead. That does make a lot of sense. I have no idea how we would uncover this person, but that is definitely something we should add to our list."

"Agreed."

Their walk took them to a bench, where they sat and simply enjoyed the lovely spring air. After a few minutes, William said, "There is something I need to share with you about Mr. St. Vincent."

"What is that?"

William leaned forward, placing his forearms on his thighs and turned his head to look at her. "According to Mr. Harding, when St. Vincent approached your father with the offer of marriage, his business was on the verge of bankruptcy."

CHAPTER 13

"Bankruptcy?" Amy couldn't have been more surprised if William had told her St. Vincent had survived the knife attack and this entire murder was a figment of her imagination.

"That is correct. Also, he had borrowed significantly on his personal holdings to keep the business propped up. It seems he'd suffered a loss when one of his ships went down. However, my man said although that was an unfortunate event, it should not have put him in the precarious situation he was in when he died." He shrugged and sat up, placing his arm across the back of the bench. "Shipping is a risky business. While I know you are indeed a prize catch on the marriage mart, I believe Mr. St. Vincent was more interested in your dowry than suddenly enamored with you."

"Should I be insulted?"

"No. You are the prize, not him." William stood and took her arm again.

"Well, thank you for that." They began their stroll again. "What I don't understand is how Papa could have missed St. Vincent's nebulous financial state, along with the fact that he was selling opium."

"The man was devious. The only reason my man uncovered his true financial state was because he has another client who suffered the same loss, so he had a basis from which to start.

That gave him the idea to delve further into St. Vincent's financial circumstances and come up with how close he was to ruin."

Amy frowned and picked up her skirt, deftly stepping around a small pile of dog leavings on the pathway. "That is probably why he was so upset when I ended the engagement."

"And most likely why he returned, hoping to convince you to reconsider."

"Poor Miss Hemphill." She looked up at William. "I don't know her very well, but she doesn't appear to come from a well-off family. Her dowry was most likely not enough to salvage Mr. St. Vincent's business."

They had strolled along for about another five minutes when Amy burst out laughing.

"What?" William smiled, even though he clearly didn't understand what was so funny.

"That horrible Mr. Harris believes he will be a wealthy man when the will is read. Instead, he will inherit a bankrupt business."

"Serves him right."

"Especially if he was the one who killed Mr. St. Vincent, only to inherit the ruined business." Amy continued to smile at the awful man's predicament.

"I believe we shall keep Mr. Harris on our list of suspects. If he contends that he will be wealthy, he obviously doesn't know about his uncle's financial state. I wonder why it's taken so long for the will to be read?"

"I have no idea. Generally it's done after the funeral, but there is always the chance that some other reason has held it up. Maybe his solicitor is in London, or perhaps traveling and unaware of the man's death."

She began to giggle. "I know it's unkind to enjoy what the man is about to hear, but Mr. Harris was so horrid to me, I can't help it."

William patted her hand. "Well deserved, my dear." He gazed off into the distance and frowned. "Is that not Lady Carlisle?"

Amy studied the lady walking toward them. It was indeed Lady Carlisle. She was strolling with Mrs. Miles and her son. The two women had their heads down and were in a deep conversation, while Mr. Miles looked as though he would prefer to be anywhere other than where he was. A situation she had often observed at the book club meetings as well. It was nice of him to take his mother places, but the sour look would surely take the joy out of the outings.

"Good afternoon, Lady Carlisle, Mrs. Miles, Mr. Miles." William's voice drew their attention.

"Oh, Lord Wethington, Lady Amy, how nice to see you." Lady Carlisle studied them with interest and speculation. Of course, it would be a surprise to members of the book club to see her and William taking a stroll together, since they had never before been more than acquaintances.

"I see you are enjoying a stroll on this lovely day," Amy said.

"It is lovely out, is it not?" Mrs. Miles offered a smile in complete opposition to her son's scowl. They chatted for a few minutes and then went their separate ways. "Did you notice how fatigued Lady Carlisle has appeared the last few times we have seen her?" Amy asked.

"Not particularly, but I was busy watching Mr. Miles act like strolling with his mother and Lady Carlisle was the worst thing he would do this week."

"Yes. He does confuse me. I know he accompanies his mother everywhere, which is quite nice of him, but on the other hand, he doesn't mind showing how much he dislikes it." Amy shrugged. "I find him to be an odd sort, actually."

They walked for a few minutes; then William said, "My mind keeps returning to Miss Hemphill and her overly dramatic reaction to your presence at Lady Ambrose's sewing circle. We know she expected Mr. St. Vincent to propose to her, but might there be more to her story?"

A sudden realization struck Amy. She shook her head. "So much has been going on. I nearly forgot to tell you."

William placed his hand on hers. "It's quite all right. As you say, a lot has been going on. What is it?"

"You were there when I told the police I had received an anonymous note informing me of Mr. St. Vincent's dealings in the drug trade."

He nodded. "I remember."

She stopped their momentum and stared into his eyes. "I firmly believe Miss Hemphill wrote that note."

William studied her for a minute, obviously deep in thought. Then he nodded and moved them forward again. "It fits."

"Perfectly. She knew I would not abide marrying a man who did such a thing, and by sending me that note, it was practically guaranteed I would end our engagement, leaving him free to marry her."

"Except we now know he would not have married her anyway, since he needed money, and you stated it is your belief that Miss Hemphill does not come with a large amount of blunt."

William turned them back toward the park entrance, where they had left his carriage. Nothing more was said about either Miss Hemphill or St. Vincent. Amy was almost relieved. This matter had taken over her entire life to the point that she wasn't even able to plan her next story. Something that had never happened to her before.

Deciding a short nap would restore her, she looked forward to her return home and enjoyed the ride back to her house, gazing out the window as they made their way through Bath.

"Shall I see you at the book club meeting on Thursday?" William shifted as the carriage came to a stop and opened the door.

"Yes. I plan to attend. Right now all I can think about is putting all of this from my mind."

"I agree that would be a good idea." He helped her out of the vehicle, and they had started up the steps when Amy's head whipped around. "Goodness gracious!" She slipped free of William's arm and picked up her skirts, racing around to the back of the house.

"Amy! Where are you going?"

There was no time to answer him, and she continued on, the sound of William's feet slamming against the patio stones right behind her.

"Why are we running?" He had caught up to her as they both maintained their pace.

"Mr. Albright," she panted. She'd seen him in the garden as they had started up the front steps. It appeared he had seen her as well and ducked behind the gardener's shed. There weren't a lot of places he could hide.

"There." William pointed to Mr. Albright climbing the fence behind the shed. William sped up and reached the fence just as Mr. Albright landed on the other side. He continued to run, but William climbed over, and in less than a minute he had the man by his collar.

Amy reached the fence, holding her side, which pained her something fierce. "Hold him." She barely got the words out. *Darn this corset.*

William was dragging Mr. Albright back toward the fence, who was shouting and demanding to be let go.

"William, if you walk him two houses down toward the south, there is an alleyway. Bring him to my house." Still out of breath, she walked slowly through the yard and climbed the steps.

"My goodness. Whatever is going on?" Aunt Margaret stood at the front door, frowning and looking Amy up and down. "I heard a great deal of shouting and then you yelling at someone."

"Mr. Albright."

"He is here?"

"Yes. I saw him in the yard when William and I were leaving his carriage. He ran off, but William managed to catch him. He is bringing him to the house."

Aunt Margaret placed her hand on Lacey's shoulder. The parlormaid stood wide-eyed, gaping at Amy as she climbed the stairs. She probably looked a mess following her race after Mr. Albright.

"Everything is fine, Lacey. You may return to your duties."

"I heard a lot of shouting, milady. Is everyone well?"

"Yes. Just fine. Please go to the kitchen and ask Cook to send in tea to the drawing room."

Giving Amy a curious look, Lacey made a slight bob and hurried down the corridor.

With their voices still raised, William and Mr. Albright entered the house, William dragging Mr. Albright by his coat collar rather than the man moving forward of his own accord.

"Take him to the drawing room, William," Amy said.

She, Aunt Margaret, and the two men entered the room. William gave Mr. Albright a shove and pointed to the red-and-white-striped chair next to the hearth. "Sit there."

Both men attempted to catch their breath as Amy and Aunt Margaret took seats across from Mr. Albright. He looked uneasy, but in truth did not look as terrified as he surely would have if he had been guilty of Mr. St. Vincent's murder. No matter what, though, he had disappeared after her ex-fiancé's death, had hidden an opium pipe in his room, and had run just now when they had spotted him.

Something was wrong for sure.

Hands behind his back, William paced in front of Mr. Albright; then he stopped and glared at him. "Did you kill Mr. St. Vincent?"

"No, milord."

Honestly, did William believe the man would just confess right here? Amy used a softer tone than William had. "You served time in prison for murder."

Mr. Albright gave her a curt nod.

"Why did you disappear after Mr. St. Vincent was killed?" William must have taken a cue from Amy's tonality and had lowered his voice.

Albright slammed his hands down on the armrests of the chair, his face flushed a bright red. "Of course I disappeared. For the same reason you are questioning me now. Because I spent time in prison for murder, I would be the first person the police would look at."

William crossed his arms over his chest, standing tall, forcing Mr. Albright to lean back to look into William's face. "Actually, that is not correct, Mr. Albright. The first person they looked at was Lady Amy, since St. Vincent was her fiancé and he had come to see her."

"Ex-fiancé."

Mr. Albright scoffed. "Her ladyship would never kill anyone."

Amy smiled at his confident words, although that didn't get them any closer to the actual killer. She leaned forward. "Mr. Albright, although I appreciate your faith in my innocence, we do have a couple of questions. If you were sent to prison for murder, how is it you were let out? I have never heard of anyone convicted of murder leaving prison except in a coffin."

If her gardener was surprised at her blunt words, he didn't show it. "Because I wasn't guilty. The man who murdered the bloke confessed before they got the chance to hang me." Mr. Albright looked anything but smug when he said those words. He looked like a man who had been accused of all sorts of things he had never done and had managed to suffer through them all.

William continued with the questioning. "We have determined that Mr. St. Vincent was supplying opium to people who are dependent on it. We found an opium pipe in your flat a couple of weeks ago."

"You're the nodcock who took it? I thought it was the police."

"Why were you hiding it in your room?"

Appearing a bit more relaxed since no one had mentioned summoning the police, Mr. Albright leaned back and rested his foot on his knee. "For the same reason I moved on as soon as I found out the jackanapes had turned up dead in the house. Once the police found my opium pipe, then connected it to my short stint for murder, they would be dragging me off to prison. Not going there." He shook his head. "Never again."

Lacey arrived in the room pushing a tea cart, and Aunt Margaret directed her to roll it next to her. The next few minutes were taken up with tea being fixed and passed around. William took one sip of the tea and looked over at Mr. Albright. "Would you prefer a stronger drink?"

Looking quite relieved, the gardener answered, "Don't mind if I do, your lordship."

William strode across the room and poured two glasses of brandy. He returned and handed one to Mr. Albright. "Lady Amy learned that Mr. St. Vincent was importing opium. Is he the one from whom you got your drug?"

"Nay. I seen the cove hanging around here a few times when he was cozying up to her ladyship. He ain't the gent what sells me my dope."

Amy placed her teacup carefully in the saucer. "Do you know the name of the man who does sell you the opium?"

Mr. Albright shook his head. "In that business, it ain't smart to ask too many questions."

"Can you tell us what he looked like?" William asked.

The man thought for a minute. "Hard to say, actually. Nothing special about him. Medium height, dark hair, not fat, but not thin."

Well, that certainly hadn't helped. He'd described just about fifty percent of the men in Bath.

Aunt Margaret had remained quiet up until then but smiled warmly at Mr. Albright. "Why did you return here today after being gone for so long?"

He shrugged. "I had a few of my things stored in the shed. Thought things had cooled enough that I could slip in and out."

"Opium?" William guessed.

"Yeah, a bit of that too."

Amy had been excited when they caught Mr. Albright, thinking he would possess information that would help them with the investigation. She had even hoped he might confess to the crime and they could put it all behind them.

But after speaking with him for the past several minutes, she had serious doubts that Mr. Albright had killed Mr. St. Vincent. Another thought crossed her mind. "Are you currently employed, Mr. Albright?"

"No, your ladyship. My landlady just tossed my things out the door last week, and I've been sleeping at my sister's house. But there's about fifteen of us there."

Amy looked over at Aunt Margaret. Despite Mr. Albright's running off, Amy didn't want to get involved in hiring a new man, since their efforts so far hadn't turned up anyone acceptable.

Of course, neither she nor Aunt Margaret had spent a great deal of time actually searching for a new gardener.

"If you will excuse us for a moment, Mr. Albright, Lady Amy and I will return shortly." Aunt Margaret stood and beckoned to Amy, who followed her out of the room.

"Are you considering the same thing I am?" Amy whispered, since they stood right outside the drawing room door.

"Yes. Mr. Albright has always been a good gardener. We haven't been successful thus far in replacing him." Aunt Margaret grinned. "Not that we've been looking."

"And the garden is beginning to look frightful," Amy added.

"Then I think we agree. We shall extend an offer to Mr. Albright to continue with his work here. However, I think it best if we don't inform your father. He worries about these ridiculous things."

Amy smiled. She had no doubt things would come crashing down on their heads if Papa knew Mr. Albright was back at work. She had so liked the man before all this trouble started. He'd successfully grown several of her favorite flowers and brought her some of them in a bundle at least once a week.

"What about the opium? Do you think he is addicted? I understand those who are can become quite unpleasant when denied the drug."

When Aunt Margaret raised her brows at Amy's words, she added, "I know this because I've done research for my books." Amy crossed her arms over her middle, studying the spot on the table near the door that Lacey had missed when she dusted that morning. "I hate to send the man back to a room with fifteen people."

Aunt Margaret nodded. "There is only one way to discover if he is addicted." With a swish of her skirts, she returned to the drawing room.

"Mr. Albright." Aunt Margaret took her seat once again across from him.

William and Mr. Albright had been conversing when the ladies entered the room and appeared to be quite relaxed. Aunt Margaret's authoritative tone had the gardener sitting up straight.

"Yes, milady?" He looked hopeful, but a bit of distrust had entered his eyes. The poor man had been through a great deal, what with being falsely imprisoned for a murder he hadn't committed, and had probably learned over the years to treat every potential act of kindness with suspicion.

"Are you addicted to opium?" Her words cracked in the room like a bolt of lightning.

Mr. Albright sat up even straighter and looked Aunt Margaret in the eye. "No, milady. I seen what it can do to those who are, so I've never reached for my pipe too often."

She studied him for a minute as if to discern if he was being truthful. After a few moments, during which it seemed everyone in the room held their breath, Aunt Margaret said, "If we allow you to return to your job, will you give me your word that you will not indulge in the drug? Never?"

He didn't hesitate. "Yes, milady. I would be very grateful to have m'job back. And I promise I will never touch the stuff again."

Aunt Margaret nodded. "Very well. I believe you are a man of honor, and now that you have given me your word, I trust you will be the best worker any employer ever retained."

Mr. Albright's face turned a bright red. "Milady, no one has ever before in my life referred to me as a man of honor. You can be sure I will indeed be the best gardener you ever had." He let out a huge breath and smiled at the three of them.

"Milady, a missive was just delivered by a young boy." Lacey entered the drawing room and handed Amy a folded piece of paper. "He is waiting for your answer."

Amy looked over at William, then opened the note.

Dear Lady Amy,

I ask permission to call upon you tomorrow afternoon at two o'clock. Upon recommendation from Lord Carlisle, your father has retained me to assist in the matter of the death of your fiancé, Mr. Ronald St. Vincent. If you could arrange for Lord Wethington to also be in attendance it would be greatly appreciated.

Sir Roger Holstein

"Ex-fiancé," she muttered.

CHAPTER 14

The next afternoon Amy sat in the drawing room running her palms over Persephone's soft fur. The dog let out soft-pitched moans at Amy's ministrations while she gazed out the window, waiting for Sir Holstein and William to arrive. The interview with the private investigator Papa had retained might be a bit strained.

If he was as good as he should be to solve a murder, he would be able to trip her and William up and get information from them they might not want to share. Now that she and William had a few suspects and had done a great deal of work on the investigation, she wanted to see it through to the end herself. The murder-mystery writer in her did not want to share the information they'd gathered.

Plus, if Papa learned from the investigator that she was conducting her own search for the killer, he would most likely order her to London. Even though the police had told her not to leave Bath, if Papa assured them she would be under his guardianship—*prisoner, more like*—they would most likely let her go. Marquesses had standing in society, and few people would be brave enough to naysay one.

She had warned William after she received the note the day before to be careful about what he said when the investigator began questioning them. He had tried at first to convince her that it might be wise to allow Sir Holstein to take over, but she'd refused. He said he was concerned for her safety. Indeed! Men always said that when they wanted you to do something you did not wish to do. One day things would be different. She hated how women were treated like children.

The curious part of her—the part that loved writing books that needed a murder solved—would never allow someone to take over an investigation she had begun. In fact, she had toyed with the idea of making the sleuth in her next book a woman. When she mentioned that to her publisher, he had said it wouldn't sell. She would not give up on the idea, though.

After a lively debate, William had finally agreed to keep their investigation to themselves, and hopefully he would honor her wishes.

"Milady, Lord Wethington has arrived." Lacey entered the room with William right behind her.

"Good afternoon, Lady Amy." He bowed slightly and took the seat alongside her on the settee.

Persephone looked up at William, growled, then jumped from Amy's lap and pranced from the settee, her chin high and her nonexistent tail in the air. She settled next to the fireplace and, with a soft groan and a deep sigh, closed her eyes.

William watched the dog, then shook his head. "That is a very strange animal. I don't believe she knows she has no tail."

"Shh. Don't say that. I don't want to hurt her feelings."

William stared at her as if she'd just grown another head. "She doesn't understand what we say."

"Yes. She does. Watch." She called to the dog.

Persephone ignored her.

She called again.

Still no response.

Amy looked over at William, who was smirking. "She is getting a bit deaf."

"Uh-huh."

"Persephone!"

The dog slowly opened one eye, stood, shook herself, and promptly left the room.

William cleared his throat. "Now that we have determined that I did not insult your dog, I must ask. Are you prepared for this interview?"

"Yes. I plan to be as helpful as I can be without giving Sir Holstein the information we have uncovered in our investigation. Let him follow his own trail. If I refused to at least appear as though I am helping, Papa would be here in Bath posthaste to escort me back to London."

"Do you dislike London so much, then?"

"No. In fact, I love to visit there, call on friends, spend time at the museums, attend the theater and opera, do some shopping, but after a couple of weeks I grow very weary of all the people, noise, smells, and confusion. And, if I am relocated to London, you can be sure for all intents and purposes I will be under house arrest."

"Let us compare notes before Sir Holstein arrives," William said as he withdrew a notepad from his jacket. He flipped a few pages. "So far we have cleared Mr. Albright." He looked up at her. "I think we agree he had no reason to kill Mr. St. Vincent, since his sins—occasional opium use and a past murder charge— have all been brought out into the open. He was too anxious to hang around and continue his employment to possibly be the killer."

"I agree. But that reminds me, I must have Aunt Margaret write to Papa and tell him Mr. Albright has been found and is innocent of any charges. We are still debating whether to mention that we have reemployed him."

"Why your aunt?"

"Because she's been dealing with Papa more years than I have. She has a way of calming him when she knows he will become riled by what she is about to tell him."

William shook his head and laughed. "To get back to our notes. Yes, I agree, Mr. Albright can be scratched off our list." He looked down at his notes again. "Then there is Mr. Harris."

"He is firmly on my suspect list. His glee at Mr. St. Vincent's death and joy at becoming, he thinks, a wealthy man troubles me. Also, there is that argument you were told uncle and nephew had outside St. Vincent's townhouse the week before he was murdered."

"And don't forget how he tried to rattle you by claiming you killed St. Vincent. I believe he was hoping you would blurt something out about his connection to the deed."

"Miss Hemphill?" Amy asked.

"Another puzzle piece. She wanted to marry the man, so why kill him? You are confident she was the author of the missive you received about Mr. St. Vincent's connection to illegal drug trade, so that points the finger to her wanting the man whole and hardy."

"Yes." Amy sat for a minute, pondering that. "I think we need to give her more thought, but I am not prepared to remove her from the list yet."

William leaned back on the settee, looking quite comfortable. Only a few weeks ago, she mused, they had shared no more than a light friendship. "We have yet to uncover the middleman for St. Vincent's opium trade. There could be any number of reasons why that man would want your fiancé dead."

"Ex-fiancé."

"I need to spend some time questioning those who know the shipyard and opium trade to see if I can come up with the name of any man who should also be on the list."

They both looked up from their notes as Lacey once again entered the room, holding a small white card that she held out to Amy. "Milady, Sir Holstein requests to speak with you."

"Yes, Lacey, we are expecting him. Please show him in."

Sir Holstein was tall, slender, and of a serious mien. Which was not unexpected, given his line of work. He wore wire-rimmed glasses and carried a portfolio. While not expensive or even fashionable, his clothing was neat, clean, and pressed. A dark beard and mustache, matching his wavy hair, covered most of his face.

He bowed over Amy. "Good afternoon, my lady. Your father sends his best wishes and regards."

She smiled and nodded, not fooled by that message from Papa. He wanted to make sure she understood that Sir Holstein was here at his behest and that she was expected to fully cooperate.

Cooperate she would. Fully—not entirely.

"Please have a seat, Sir Holstein, and I will send for tea."

He sat across from her and placed his portfolio on the floor. "Tea will not be necessary, unless it is your teatime. I do not wish to interrupt your normal schedule."

"No. That is fine. It is a bit early for tea." She and William sat side by side, watching as Sir Holstein took out a pad of paper from his portfolio, withdrew a pencil, flipped a few pages, and then looked up at them expectantly.

Not sure what the man intended for her to say, she merely smiled in his direction. "My father tells me you are acquainted with Lord Carlisle."

Sir Holstein sat back. "Yes, indeed. I did some work for him, and we became friends. He's a wonderful man, very progressive in his thinking. I am honored to be invited to his home for dinner on occasion."

He looked down at the page with scrawled notes over it. "I have a bit of information here from Lord Winchester. You were engaged to one Mr. Ronald St. Vincent, the owner of a shipping company. You summoned him to your home on Friday, the eighteenth day of April, and ended your arrangement with him, to which he was not amenable." He looked up and waited for her to nod her concurrence, which she did.

"According to your father, Mr. St. Vincent arrived at your house, uninvited and unexpected, on Tuesday, the twenty-second day of April."

Again he looked up for her acknowledgment. When she nodded, he returned to his notes.

"When you were notified of his arrival, you took some time in joining him in the library, and when you entered the room, he was not there and the French doors were open."

"Yes." Amy was tired of nodding her head and decided to use her voice a bit.

"Excellent. Then you went to the garden to search for him, and upon returning, you stumbled over his body."

He switched his attention to William. "You, my lord, were in the drawing room awaiting your expected visit with Lady Amy. Upon hearing screams, you left the drawing room and entered the library, where you found Lady Amy upset, her hands covered with blood, staring at the deceased." He looked up once again at Amy. "Whereupon you fainted."

Silence filled the room, and Amy shivered at the memory of how St. Vincent had looked, staring up at nothing, the large knife in his chest. "Yes. That is the way it happened."

Sir Holstein turned his attention once more to William. "Please tell me what you saw, my lord."

William repeated the story of arriving in the library, seeing Amy staring at the floor, then fainting. He explained how he had sent a staff member to summon the police and encouraged Amy to wash the blood from her hands and face.

"How did the blood get on your hands and face, Lady Amy?"

"When I fell, my hands landed on Mr. St. Vincent's chest. Then at some point I rubbed my cheeks and transferred the blood to my face."

The investigator snapped his notepad closed. "I would like to see the library."

Amy's heart took off, and her stomach dropped to her knees. She had not been in the library since the night of the murder. "Lord Wethington will be happy to escort you."

Holstein was not having it. "I would prefer if you joined us, Lady Amy. I need to have you replay exactly what happened."

Kudos to the investigator. He was thorough.

The three of them left the room and walked down the corridor to the library. Taking a deep breath, Amy turned the latch and opened the door. The staff had done a good job of cleaning the room. A large vase of fresh flowers on Papa's desk gave the air a sweet, fragrant smell.

The French doors were locked, but two of the tall windows had been opened from the bottom, allowing the scent from the garden to drift throughout the room.

"Lady Amy, kindly walk me through your steps that night, starting when you entered the room."

Amy retraced her steps from when she had entered the library until she found St. Vincent's body, giving Sir Holstein a running narrative of her movements.

Sir Holstein turned to William. "Please, my lord. If you will pick up from the time you entered the room."

William then walked the investigator through what he'd seen that night. The man scribbled notes the entire time.

"Thank you. I would like to ask some more questions, but if you are feeling fatigued, my lady, I will be happy to return tomorrow."

Normally she would never admit to being affected by emotions and fatigue, but entering the library for the first time since the murder had rattled her. "Yes, thank you, Sir Holstein. I believe I would like to take a break."

"Very well." He bowed to them both. "I shall return tomorrow at the same time, if that is acceptable?"

"Yes. That will be fine."

The man turned on his heel and left the room, and Amy breathed a sigh of relief.

★   ★   ★

That evening Amy sat at the desk in her office next to her bedchamber and went over their notes once again, looking for something she was missing. Three people comprised her list: Miss Hemphill, Mr. Harris, and the not-as-yet-identified man who had accepted the drugs from her former fiancé and sold them. She tapped her lips with her pen and considered the names.

They all seemed plausible, but none of them had a very good reason to see St. Vincent dead. Except Mr. Harris. Money, human relationships, and power were the three main causes of murder that she'd discovered in her hours of research.

She could attribute one or more of those reasons to every name on her list. Mr. Harris: money. Miss Hemphill: human relationship. And the drug dealer could be seeking power and money as well. Killing St. Vincent meant he would become the main distributor. If, she reminded herself, the new owner of the shipping company continued with the import of opium.

However, the unknown distributor could even have been working with Mr. Harris, who would inherit the business. Again, money. Maybe the dealer wasn't getting what he thought was a fair share of the revenue.

Sliding the pen into the holder, Amy sat back and rubbed her eyes with her fists. What she needed was an early night. Aunt Margaret had gone to a musicale at one of her friend's homes.

Amy had been invited as well, but after the interview with Sir Holstein that afternoon, she had not felt very congenial.

She was about to ring for Lacey to prepare a bath for her when the maid entered her room. "Milady, a Mr. Harris has arrived and asked for a minute of your time."

Mr. Harris? The man had the impertinence to show up at her home after insulting her so horribly at the Assembly? Did he wish to engage in fisticuffs? This time she would use her knee to make her point that he was an obnoxious, uncouth, horrid man.

"Did he say what he wanted?"

"No, milady. He brought a bouquet of flowers with him."

Flowers? Whatever was that all about? Since Mr. Harris was at the top of their suspect list, she could not afford to turn him away.

Despite the voice in her head telling her not to bother, she took a quick look in the mirror over her dressing table. She glanced at her ink-stained fingers and shrugged. With all the writing she did, her fingers were never completely clean.

Mr. Harris rose when she entered the drawing room. She nodded at his bow and took the seat across from him, back straight, hands folded demurely in her lap. "Why are you here, Mr. Harris? If memory serves, we did not part in a pleasant manner at our last encounter at the Assembly Rooms."

He managed to look sheepish. "Yes, Lady Amy. I have come to offer my deepest apologies for the way I spoke to you that evening."

"If you are expecting me to say I am sorry for the punch I threw at you, it will be a long wait."

He shook his head. "No. No. I don't expect you to apologize. It was all my fault. While I don't consider this an excuse, I had a bit too much to drink that night and oftentimes have a problem controlling my tongue."

"Very well, Mr. Harris. I accept your apology." She stood, and he jumped up.

"I thought perhaps we might visit for a while." He held out the bouquet of flowers. "These are for you."

Force of habit and years of good breeding had her reaching out and taking the flowers from his hand. "Thank you." She laid them on the small cherrywood table next to the settee. As much as she wanted the man out of her house, if they chatted for a while, she might gather more information. She settled back on the settee. "Would you care for a brandy?"

His eyes lit up at what she supposed was his glee at her acquiescing to his request. He had just admitted to being a bit loose-tongued with drink, so a brandy or two might be to her benefit. She nodded in the direction of the sideboard along the wall. "You may help yourself."

With more confidence than he'd shown since she entered the room, he strode across the space and poured a brandy. "May I fetch something for you, Lady Amy?"

She needed to keep a clear head; it would not pay for her to be chatty. "No, thank you."

Once he settled back into his seat, he leaned back and rested his foot on his knee. A bit improper in the presence of a lady.

Feeling a bit uncomfortable as he studied her, she said, "I understand you only recently returned to Bath. I assume you lived here before your travels?"

"Yes. I lived here for the years of my youth, then attended school in London. I only returned on occasion to spend time with my uncle." He took a sip of his drink and leaned forward. "We were not very close, you know."

Since Amy had been engaged to his uncle and had never heard Mr. Harris's name pass his lips, she had no doubt this was the case. She wanted to ask him about the will, but it would be much better if Mr. Harris brought it up himself. Had they held the reading? Harris seemed much too cheerful to be aware of the financial state in which Mr. St. Vincent had left him.

"Are you planning on making Bath your home, then?"

He swirled the liquid in his glass and studied it for a few minutes. Then he looked up at her. "That depends."

It was time for a nudge. "Will you be running Mr. St. Vincent's shipping company now?"

He shook his head and let out a huge sigh. "That also depends on several things."

Goodness, she was tired of this cat-and-mouse game they were playing. He was much cleverer than she'd thought him to be. She cleared her throat. "Mr. Harris, I have accepted your apology, and since I see no other reason for you to visit with me, I will ask you right out why you are here. I doubt it is to deliver flowers, since the shops do that quite expediently."

He downed the rest of his drink and placed the empty glass on the table in front of him. "You are right. The time has come."

To her absolute horror, he crossed the distance between them and got down on one knee. Before she could gain her thoughts, he took her hand and said, "Will you do me the honor of marrying me, Lady Amy?"

CHAPTER 15

Amy's jaw dropped as she stared at Mr. Harris in complete astonishment. He smiled up at her as if he'd just offered her the world.

"Excuse me, Mr. Harris, although I am many years from my dotage, it appears my hearing has left me. Did you just ask me to marry you?"

"Yes."

"But I don't even know you. Why would I *marry* you?"

She hoped his explanation would be a lengthy one so she could reengage her brain. She'd been so stunned by his request, it seemed everything in her body had shut down. Staring stupidly at her, he shifted on his knees, squeezed her hand, and smiled.

His hand was sweaty.

"You are not getting any younger, Lady Amy. I imagine my uncle's proposal was your last opportunity to secure a husband. Since I am his heir, I feel it is my duty to step into his place."

Dear God in heaven, the man was mad. However, the anger that flowed through her veins was enough to wake her body up. To be certain it was not all a dream, she flicked the inside of her wrist with her fingertip. This man, this horrid cretin, had just insulted her while trying to get her to marry him.

No one had ever accused Amy of being stupid. Should she marry him, her money would be there to prop up the bankrupt business. Also, a wife could not be compelled to testify against her husband. This was all the more reason to keep Mr. Harris on their list of suspects.

The question arose, however, whether she should be a lady and thank him for his offer and then refuse, or do what she really wanted and push her foot against his chest, knock him on his arse, and leave the room.

Manners won out. "I am sorry, Mr. Harris, but while your offer is . . . interesting, I am afraid I must refuse."

He sat back on his heels, actually looking surprised. "I think you are making a mistake. As I said, there won't be many more offers coming your way at your age."

Unable to hear much more without resorting to violence, she wrenched her hand free from his and stood. "That might very well be, Mr. Harris, but since marriage is not something I pine for, I will have to take my chances and pass on your offer. Should I change my mind, perhaps some elderly gentleman looking for a nurse would be willing to take me on to save me from the horrors of spinsterhood."

He stood and brushed off his pants. "What can I say to change your mind?"

"Nothing. Now, if you will excuse me, I must give my dog a bath." She pulled her skirts close and swept past him. Speaking over her shoulder, she said, "Lacey will see you out."

She raced up the stairs to her room, closed the door, and leaned against it.

And burst out laughing.

★   ★   ★

It was Thursday, and the book club was to meet at Amy's house, as there was some sort of event at Atkinson & Tucker. Rather than cancel their meeting, Amy had offered the use of her house.

"How long does the meeting with your cohorts in crime last?" Aunt Margaret entered the drawing room, her hat clutched in her hand. "I want to be certain to stay away long enough not to walk into a discussion of dead bodies and grue-some murders."

"We are generally finished by ten o'clock." Amy moved a vase of flowers from a rectangular table near the window to the top of the piano. They would use the table for tea and small sandwiches and tarts that Cook had prepared and Lacey was in the process of laying out. "Where are you off to this evening?"

Aunt Margaret walked to the mirror in the entrance way and adjusted her hat. "Mr. Darling is hosting a card party."

Amy joined her aunt as she shrugged into her coat. "Tell me, Aunt Margaret. You know how men often call each other by their last name?"

"Yes?" Aunt's attention returned to the mirror as she smoothed back the few strands of hair that had loosened from her chignon.

Amy grinned. "Do the men in your circle of friends call Mr. Darling by his last name?"

Aunt Margaret frowned at her. "What?" Then she began to laugh. "Oh, yes. I see what you mean. You know, I have never noticed. Now if someone calls him that I will be forced to swallow my laughter." She patted Amy on the cheek. "Thank you for that, dear niece."

With a sweep of her skirt and the light scent of lavender, Aunt Margaret left the house.

No sooner had the Winchester carriage carrying Aunt Margaret pulled into the traffic than William strode up the steps, followed by a very out-of-breath Eloise. "Good evening, Amy." William offered his bow.

"Eloise, you are looking so much better." Amy gave her a warm hug.

"Yes, much, much better." Eloise rolled her eyes. "I thought I would never be allowed out of bed. Mama is very overprotective, as you know."

Eloise had a younger sister who had developed influenza a few years back, and despite healers, physicians, and numerous prayers, she had succumbed to the illness after six days with a fever. Mrs. Spencer had never gotten over losing her child and had been overly cautious with Eloise since.

Amy had not seen either Eloise or William since Mr. Harris's proposal a few days before. She linked her arms with them both and started walking. "I am so glad you arrived before the others. I have a very interesting and funny story to tell you."

"How very intriguing," William said as they all walked together to the drawing room, where they took seats across from each other.

"I had a visit Monday evening from Mr. Harris."

"Who is Mr. Harris?" Eloise asked.

Amy took a few minutes to bring Eloise up-to-date with what had been happening with the murder investigation.

"I still cannot believe you broke into someone's flat." Her eyes danced with amusement as she glanced back and forth between Amy and William.

"Yes," Amy smirked. "I cannot believe it myself."

William straightened in his seat. "Whatever did Harris come here for?"

She grinned, anticipating this reaction. "To ask me to marry him."

Eloise's mouth dropped open, and William shouted, "What?" He jumped from his seat, then sat back down again. "Why the devil would he ask you to marry him when the last time you saw him you planted him a facer?" He grinned. "Is he the sort who enjoys a woman who . . ." He flushed a bright red, which made Amy wonder what he had been about to say.

"What sort of a woman?" Eloise and Amy asked at the same time.

"Nothing. I misspoke. Tell me about his proposal."

Amy tried to talk, but her laughter was making it difficult. Every time she thought about Mr. Harris's extremely awkward and unromantic proposal, she broke into giggles again. She finally composed herself and took a deep breath. "His reason—as stated—was that I was not getting any younger, and Mr. St. Vincent's offer to marry me was most likely my last chance at marital bliss, so he was willing to step into his uncle's place."

William sat slack-jawed and stared at her. "He didn't really say that?"

"He did."

"The man is addlepated. What sort of way is that to encourage a young lady—excuse me—a lady of years, to accept an offer of marriage?" He grinned and shook his head. "Someone needs to take the man in hand. He is truly a danger to society." William leaned back in the chair. "So, when's the wedding?"

"Very funny, my lord. I thanked him for his offer and refused."

"Of course."

"Would you believe he actually looked surprised that I turned him down?"

"You? Why, you are a prize on the marriage mart." William stood and ticked off on his fingers. "You are beautiful, smart, witty, kind, talented . . ." Suddenly he seemed to realize what he was saying. His face turned a bright red again, and he sat back down.

Eloise and Amy exchanges amused glances. "Do continue, my lord," Eloise said.

He waved his hand in the air. "You understand what I mean."

"Yes. I believe we do." Amy smoothed out her skirt and tried to dismiss William's words. Surely they meant nothing.

"I'm assuming the reason he offered marriage was because Mr. St. Vincent's will has been read."

"Most likely. I thought he appeared a bit too cheerful when he arrived for the will to have already been read, but I'm assuming he counted on the fact that a pitiful example of womanhood such as I would fall at his feet in appreciation of his proposal. But that is not the only reason, I suspect."

William regarded her with raised eyebrows. Eloise leaned forward. "What?"

"A wife cannot be compelled to testify against her husband."

"Ah. Very clever, Amy." William studied her for a minute. "So if you were married to Mr. Harris, and in your investigation you uncovered proof of his involvement in his uncle's murder, you could not be forced to testify."

"Precisely. That is another reason to keep him on our list."

The sound of the door knocker drew their attention. "It appears our club members are beginning to arrive."

The both stood as Mr. Miles, Mrs. Miles, and Miss Sterling entered the room. Within minutes, Mr. Colbert, Mr. Davidson, and Lord Temple and his daughter, Lady Abigail, had all joined them.

Mrs. Miles hurried across the room and took Amy's hand. "My dear. How are you holding up?"

"I am just fine, Mrs. Miles, and how are you?" This would be the third book club meeting they'd had since St. Vincent's murder, and each time she'd told Mrs. Miles she was doing just fine. The woman thrived on drama.

Mrs. Miles patted her hand. "I'm so glad to hear that. You do seem to be dealing with everything quite well."

Not sure what the woman meant by *everything*, Amy said, "There are refreshments on the table by the window. Why don't you help yourself?"

Lady Carlisle entered the room, which completed the membership. Amy approached her newly arrived guest, who seemed a bit confused. Lady Carlisle had been hosting dinners and parties to help her husband in his quest for the position of ambassador, and it appeared to be tiring for her. "Are you unwell, Lady Carlisle?"

She smiled. "No. I am quite well. I see you have tea. I shall enjoy a cup before the meeting begins."

Amy moved from group to group while the members stood around speaking and partaking of the refreshments. Eventually Mr. Colbert called the meeting to order, and they all took seats around the room.

William selected the chair next to her and leaned in close to her ear. "I think it might be a good idea to visit with Miss Hemphill one day next week. You must think of a reason to call on her, since we need more answers. I feel as though we do not have enough information on her. It might also be helpful if you can confirm that she sent the note. I will be speaking with some of the shipyard people to see if we can get more information on the individual St. Vincent was working with."

"Sir Holstein sent around a note today that he spoke with the police and they were not very helpful."

William snorted, and Eloise, who had been listening to the exchange, shook her head.

★   ★   ★

The afternoon after the book club meeting, Lacey ushered Detective Marsh and Detective Carson into the drawing room. Amy smiled at the men and offered them a seat. They didn't smile back and sat down.

She sighed and rearranged her skirts and waited for them to begin. She'd received a note that morning from Marsh requesting an interview. It was her duty to assist in the investigation of St. Vincent's murder, but she would much rather spend her time conducting her own inquiries than answering their questions. Particularly since she was still convinced they only wanted to charge her with the murder and close the case.

"How may I assist you, Detectives?"

Detective Carson began. "It has come to our attention that you have hired a private investigator to work on this matter."

She wanted so badly to feign innocence and ask what matter he was speaking about, but annoying the man would only do her a disservice. "I have not hired anyone, Detective. I was as surprised as you were when Sir Holstein sent along a note that he wished to speak with me. It appears my father employed the man upon recommendation from Lord Carlisle, who is great friends with the investigator."

Detective Carson scowled. "It seems odd for the pompous Lord Carlisle to be friends with a lowly private investigator."

"Sir Holstein did some investigative work for Lord Carlisle some time ago and they remained friends. However, just to be clear, I do not pass judgment on friends of my friends."

He dismissed her remark with a wave of his hand. "Just as long as he doesn't get in our way. We don't appreciate having private citizens do police work."

Since that was not a question, she merely continued to look at him, waiting for his next remark. She doubted the only reason for their visit was to warn her not to allow her investigator to get in their way.

"Is there anything else, Detective?"

"Yes." Marsh opened a notebook and flipped through the pages. He looked at her with what he most likely thought was an intimidating look. "What do you know of a Miss Eva Hemphill?"

So, the woman who had anticipated marriage with St. Vincent had come to their attention. "Not much. I met her briefly at a sewing circle last week."

"Did you know she was expecting to marry your fiancé?"

"Ex-fiancé."

Carson jumped in. "Do you know why he proposed to you instead of her?"

Honestly, the man could come up with the oddest questions. "No. I can assure you I have no idea what Mr. St. Vincent was thinking. I had no knowledge of his relationship with Miss Hemphill."

"How did he come to be betrothed to you?" Carson continued the questioning while Marsh took notes.

"We spent some time together. We got along well. He seemed to be a nice sort of person. Without speaking to me first, he traveled to London, met with my father, and made his offer."

Detective Marsh smiled for the first time ever. "Do toffs still do it that way?"

Amy shook her head. "I have no idea if 'toffs' do it that way; I can only tell you what happened in my situation."

"Excuse me, Lady Amy, but you do not seem like the sort of woman who would accept an offer from a gentleman who worked it out with your father first." Detective Carson also offered his very first smile.

She raised her chin. "You are correct, Detective. However, my father was quite persuasive when he presented the offer to me. That was one of the reasons I decided to break the engagement. I do not like being coerced into anything."

Detective Marsh looked up from his notes. "You said in our first interview that you broke your engagement because the two of you did not suit. Now you said one of the reasons you ended the relationship was because it had been your father's coercion." He leaned forward. "What are the other reasons, Lady Amy?"

"As I noted before, I disapproved of his involvement with opium. Due to that and other reasons, I felt we did not suit, and I prefer to make up my own mind about such an important step as marriage."

"A reason to kill him?"

She narrowed her eyes at the man. "Really, Detective, do you honestly think I would have to kill a man to be rid of him? There are truly more civilized ways of discouraging a suitor. I invited him to my home and told him I was breaking our engagement. He left with the ring he had given me. He returned four nights later, for what reason I have no idea, and ended up dead on my library floor."

"And you had nothing to do with it?"

"I believe I have already stated, more than once, that your assumption is incorrect." No longer was she frightened by these men. They obviously had nothing to connect her to the murder except for the fact that St. Vincent had died at her house. If they had, she would be in jail right now.

The men looked at each other, Marsh closed his notebook, and they both stood. "That is all we need for now, Lady Amy."

"Detective. Before you leave. Can you tell me if you are close to finding who killed Mr. St. Vincent? I really wish to put this all behind me and resume my normal life."

Detective Marsh just stared at her for a few moments. "No. We are not."

Once they left the room, Amy wandered around, restless, unable to concentrate. Miss Hemphill had been added to the detectives' list of interested parties. That was quite intriguing. The police were doing more than she'd thought.

The next thing she and William needed to do was check further into Miss Hemphill. Find out why she had gone to

London. It could have been for a very innocuous reason, but Amy still felt there was more to Miss Hemphill than they'd discovered so far.

She checked her timepiece. It was time to prepare for the evening. William was escorting her to the theater.

They were to enjoy William Shakespeare's *Much Ado About Nothing*, one of her favorite plays. As she made her way upstairs, she thought again about William. The investigation was throwing them together quite a bit, but they were also attending other events—such as the one that night—that had nothing to do with St. Vincent's murder.

She smiled as she dressed. William's company was quite pleasant, actually. He was polite, charming, and at times he looked at her in such a way that she felt tingles inside. Which sounded quite silly, so she pushed that thought away.

Taking a final look in the mirror at the light- and dark-blue-striped gown that fit her curves quite well, along with the dark-blue gloves that covered her arms to her elbows, she smiled at her reflection. She had Lacey fasten a sapphire necklace that had belonged to her mother, and then added the ear-bobs that matched. Pleased with what she saw in the mirror, she picked up the beaded reticule and matching shawl on the chair by the door to her room and descended the stairs to await William.

She poured herself a small sherry while she waited and flipped through a book on poetry that she'd been meaning to read but had put off with her focus on murder.

"My lady, Lord Wethington has arrived." Mr. Stevens, who took over door duty in the evenings, stepped aside to allow William to enter.

"My lady, you look splendid." William's appreciative look traveled from the tip of her head—and the dark-blue feathers anchored there—to her feet, shod in delicate black slippers.

Callie Hutton

"Would you care for a drink?"

"Yes, I would." He walked to the sideboard and poured himself a brandy. "We have a bit of time before we must leave."

"The detectives visited today." Amy took a sip of her sherry.

"With good news, I hope? Like perhaps they have found the true killer?"

Amy shook her head. "No. But they did mention Miss Hemphill. They asked me if I knew she was expecting to marry St. Vincent."

"Did they ask about Sir Holstein?"

"Yes. They said the police did not like private individuals doing their work."

William laughed. "Someone has to do it. They don't seem to be moving forward."

Mr. Stevens entered the drawing room once more, his expression reminding her of someone who had just smelled something nasty. "My lady, Mr. Albright requests a word, if you please."

Amy and William glanced at each other. "Mr. Albright? How very strange. Yes, send him in, please."

They watched the man enter the room, crushing his hat in his hand. "Excuse me for interrupting you, milady, but I thought it best if I passed along some information to you."

Amy waved at the red-and-white-striped chair. "Please have a seat, Mr. Albright."

"No, milady, my clothes are dusty from the garden."

She smiled at him, trying to put him at ease. "What is it you want to tell me, Mr. Albright?"

He hesitated for a moment, then said, "Last night you had a few people here for some sort of gathering."

"Yes. My book club. We usually meet at a bookstore, but they were having an event that evening, so we met here."

The man was obviously uncomfortable, either from being in their presence or with what he was about to say.

"Is there something you wanted to say about my guests, Mr. Albright?"

"Well, ma'am. I wasn't spying on you or anything, but when I was closing up the shed for the night, I saw a few people going up the steps. One of them was the bloke what I bought my opium from."

CHAPTER 16

William sat forward in his chair. "Do you know his name?"

"Nah. He never said."

"Did he come alone, or with someone?" Amy asked.

The man didn't hesitate. "He arrived in a carriage with an older woman."

There were two couples who had arrived together. Lord Temple with his daughter, Lady Abigail, and Mr. Miles and his mother. However, Lord Temple was quite corpulent and had silver hair. Nothing like the man Mr. Albright had described earlier, and Lady Abigail could hardly be referred to as an "older woman." Amy took in a deep breath and looked over at William. "Mr. Miles?"

William studied her for a moment, then glanced up at Mr. Albright. "Are you certain, Mr. Albright? This is a very serious matter."

"I am absolutely certain. When he stepped out of his carriage, he walked under the streetlamp and even turned in my direction when he helped the old lady out of the carriage. He was the bloke what sold me the opium."

Amy lowered her sherry glass to the table. "This is quite a surprise."

"Indeed." William shook his head and downed the rest of his brandy. "Who would have thought that someone in our own circle was doing such a thing."

Realizing that Mr. Albright was still standing there, Amy smiled up at him. "Thank you very much for that information, Mr. Albright. It could be very beneficial to our investigation."

"You're welcome, ma'am. Anything I can do to help clear your name. I know you would never off a man, and I am grateful for you allowing me my job back."

"Thank you again, Mr. Albright."

He backed out of the room as if leaving the Queen's presence.

"Well, then." William stood and picked up both of their glasses and returned them to the sideboard. "It is time to leave for the theater."

Amy rose and smoothed her skirts. "I am still in a bit of shock."

They walked to the front entrance, where Mr. Stevens assisted Amy into her soft woolen black cape.

William shrugged into his coat and placed his hat on his head. They left the house, neither of them speaking. However, once the carriage was rolling away from the house, William said, "We now have a name to add to our list of suspects."

"Yes, it would seem so. As we discussed before we knew his name, I'm still not sure how his position as the link between the shipping company and the purchaser of the drug would fit with Mr. St. Vincent's murder."

"If it does at all." William spoke softly, glancing out the window as if in thought.

"What do you mean? Mr. Albright identified Mr. Miles and was quite certain about it."

He turned to look at her in the pale illumination from the lantern on the carriage wall, the dim light casting his features into shadows. "Are you aware of any connection between Mr. St. Vincent and Mr. Miles? Were they friends?"

"Mr. St. Vincent never mentioned him. He attended one—or perhaps two—book cub meetings with me, but I don't remember if he and Mr. Miles were especially friendly."

William nodded. "Just because Mr. Albright identified Mr. Miles as the man who sold him the opium doesn't prove a link between the two. There could be other sources of opium—I am sorry to say—from whom Mr. Miles could have obtained the drug."

Amy pondered that for a few minutes.

William blew out a deep breath. "However, if Mr. Miles *was* getting his drugs from your fiancé—"

"Ex fiancé."

"—many ideas come to mind that we've considered before. Perhaps he did not feel his cut of the profits was large enough. Maybe St. Vincent threatened to shut him out altogether for some reason and work with someone else."

"But how would killing him help? If St. Vincent was dead, there went the whole scheme, it would seem to me."

"Not if Miles thought he could work out a better deal with Mr. Harris."

Amy tapped her chin. "The heir."

"Correct."

She pondered that for a while. The fact that her logical, murder-solving brain had not worked that out convinced her she was much more shocked at the revelation about Mr. Miles than she'd thought.

Mr. Miles. The man who accompanied his mother every-where but didn't appear to like it. "Perhaps the reason he always looks so bored at our meetings is because he is only there to keep his contacts?"

"Blasted roads. They need to fix these ruts." William grabbed the strap hanging alongside his head. "If what you say is correct, then one, or more, of our members are addicted to opium."

"Who?" Amy grabbed the strap on her side and winced with each bounce the carriage took.

William looked toward the ceiling, which, Amy had learned from her research, people tended to do when they were thinking. "I can't imagine anyone in our club being addicted to opium."

"One thing is certain. We need to confront Mr. Miles with this information. If it is true, and it sounds like Mr. Albright has no doubt about it, Miles might cast some light on our investigation."

William shook his head. "Or he might be the killer, and we could be placing ourselves in danger."

"Then perhaps not confront him, come up with another reason to pay him a visit, and then in the course of conversation, slip in a word or two that might make him say something helpful." At least that was a method she used in her books. Keep the suspect talking until they revealed themselves. The old saying *He who speaks first loses*.

As if he'd read her mind, William said, "That might work in your books, but in real life we could be confronting a man who murdered someone in cold blood."

Amy perked up. "We shall bring a gun."

William groaned.

★   ★   ★

They decided not to send a note ahead of time but to call with the pretense of visiting with Mrs. Miles. The fact that they'd never done so before was considered and tossed aside. Older ladies always enjoyed company, and Amy doubted Mrs. Miles would question their intent.

Unfortunately, when they arrived the following Monday, Mrs. Miles was the only one at home. All Amy knew of Mr. Miles, besides that he was a bit grumpy with his mother on occasion, was that his time was occupied with gentlemanly pursuits. In other words, he did not have gainful employment of any sort. Of course, now she realized his income might very well come from the sale of drugs.

"I am so glad you came to visit." Mrs. Miles smiled at them while she fussed with her dress, belt, cuffs, collar, and hair. "I sent for tea when Gertrude told me you had arrived."

Amy wasn't sure if the woman was nervous because she was not used to company or for other reasons. Now that they were involved in this investigation, she had begun to suspect everyone's actions. "Thank you very much. Lord Wethington and I happened to be in the neighborhood, and we thought it would be pleasant to have a visit with you."

Mrs. Miles clapped her hands like a young child. "How wonderful. We shall have a lovely chat."

A maid entered the room pushing a tea cart. She set everything on the table in front of them.

"Lady Amy, would you pour, please?" Surprised that Mrs. Miles would not perform the typical hostess task herself, Amy did as the woman requested and poured tea for the three of them. She filled three plates with a selection of small sandwiches and biscuits and passed them around as well.

Amy patted her mouth with a white napkin embroidered with tiny pink and green flowers. "How are you enjoying our latest book, Mrs. Miles?"

"It is quite nice. Well, since it's a murder mystery, I don't think *nice* is quite the proper word, but I am enjoying it." She picked up a small biscuit and held it to her mouth. "I do wish we would read another of E. D. Burton's books. They are so much more . . . vivid." She popped the biscuit into her mouth and smiled.

William choked on his tea, and Amy hid her giggle. Not just because she *was* E. D. Burton, but because William had thought the ladies' sensibilities were too delicate to enjoy her books.

Apparently not.

"My dear son, Richard, enjoys Mr. Burton's books too. He always tells me that Mr. Burton is very adept at solving a murder." She leaned in close to Amy. "It is too bad you cannot have that author on your side. I know you are distressed at the murder of Mr. St. Vincent. Perhaps if you contacted Mr. Burton's publisher, he might allow you to speak with him."

"While that is a very good idea, Mrs. Miles, I don't think the author would have time to become involved in our affairs."

Mrs. Miles nodded. "You are most likely correct. Although one thinks getting involved in a murder investigation could be quite . . ." She took a sip of tea and shook her head.

William shifted in his chair. One that Amy was certain he found uncomfortable. It looked like it could barely hold his weight, and if the cushion was as stiff as the one she was sitting on, there was no comfort to be had. "Mr. Miles is always so quiet when he attends our meetings. I didn't realize he was also reading the books. I thought he only came as your escort."

"Oh, yes. He is very interested in murder. He oftentimes reads about various murders in the newspaper and tells me how he would solve it. Or how he would commit such a crime and get away with it." She actually looked proud, as though her son had been awarded a certificate in school for good deportment.

Amy was grateful she was not drinking her tea, or Mrs. Miles would have been covered in it. She refused to look at William because she doubted she could hold in her laugh at what Mrs. Miles had just said. It appeared their visit might be more beneficial with Mr. Miles *not* present.

"That is quite interesting, Mrs. Miles. Perhaps Mr. Miles should be writing murder-mystery books himself."

The woman waved her hand in dismissal. "Oh, dear me, no. He is much too busy to be writing books."

William cleared his throat and placed his cup on his saucer. "What is it your son does, Mrs. Miles? Is he employed?"

She looked confused for a minute. "Oh, dear. I'm sure he must be. He is busy all the time, away from the house, but he pays all the bills and gives me money, so I imagine he is employed somewhere."

They continued to visit for another twenty minutes, most of which was spent listening to Mrs. Miles speak of her various illnesses. Nothing further was said about Mr. Miles, so when their hostess took a much needed breath, Amy looked over at William and gave him a slight nod.

William pulled his timepiece from his vest pocket. "I'm afraid we have taken up too much of your time, Mrs. Miles."

"Oh, no. Not at all. Please don't feel as though you have to go."

Amy stood and smoothed out her skirts. "Actually, I have another appointment myself, so I am afraid we must."

"Well, please do come again. This was such fun!" Mrs. Miles stood and walked with them to the door, where William and Amy accepted their outer garments from the man stationed there.

"It has been a pleasure, Mrs. Miles." William bowed over her hand. "We look forward to seeing you at the meeting Thursday evening."

Mrs. Miles twittered. Actually twittered.

They took their leave and climbed into the waiting carriage.

★   ★   ★

Amy sat at her desk, her chin resting on her hand while she stared out the window. The visit with Mrs. Miles the day before had been quite enlightening. On the way home, she and William had discussed all they'd learned.

He planned to visit a couple of the men's clubs, since it was certain Mr. Miles would belong to one or two of them. Anyone selling opium to those who could afford it had to be in places where he would find wealthy customers.

That left Amy with nothing to do while William did his part. That was annoying. What was truly vexing was that men had clubs where they could gather but women were not allowed. Women should start their own club and not allow men to visit. Except, she realized with a sinking feeling in her stomach, most likely men would not want to enter a women's club anyway.

What if she could sneak into a men's club dressed as a man? Then she could ask questions about Harris and Miles herself!

She slumped. Stupid idea. She had no facial hair, her voice was too high, and a man's suit of clothes would not disguise her figure, as William had pointed out the night they broke into Mr. Albright's flat. Trying to resemble a man in the dark was much different than trying to pull that off where she could easily be seen.

Tired of just sitting and moping, and with no interest in continuing to plan her next book, she decided to take a nice long walk to the Roman Baths and enjoy a stroll around the Pump Room.

Since she lived only a few houses down, Amy sent a note around to Eloise to join her, then changed into her favorite light-yellow muslin with black-trimmed skirt and jacket. Her mood immediately improved. It was even warm enough that she could leave off an outer coat. She placed the matching yellow-and-black hat on her head and pulled on her black leather gloves.

She grinned at her reflection. She looked like a bumblebee. Yes, a stroll in the nice warm spring air would be just the thing. She could also ruminate on the case and see if there was something she'd forgotten.

Eloise arrived, in a hurry as usual. Her hat was askew, her hair falling down on one side, and she was out of breath. "Are we going to interview suspects?"

Amy laughed. "No. I am simply going to the Pump Room to get some air."

"Oh." Eloise sighed.

"But I will tell you all that's happened since I saw you last."

"This is so exciting!" Eloise joined her arm with Amy's. Persephone barked frantically and ran in circles as they reached the front door. Amy bent down to pet the dog. "Do you want to go for a walk, too?" She smiled at Lacey, who handed her the dog's leash. "She does not like being left behind."

"I know," Lacey said. "If you do, then she won't talk to you."

Amy clipped the leash on Persephone's collar and scooped her into her arms. "Come along, then. We shall all go for a lovely walk in the spring air."

As they strolled along, the dog sniffing everything to the right side of the pathway, then the left, Amy decided this had been a wonderful idea. The sun shone bright in a cloudless deep-blue sky. She twirled her parasol and nodded to other strollers she passed.

She filled Eloise in on what had happened in the past few days. "You know, trying to solve the mystery of Mr. St. Vincent's death cast a pall over my life that even writing about such things has never done." Amy tugged on Persephone's leash. "If one is at the center of a true murder investigation, 'tis a bit more daunting than writing about a fictitious murder."

"I would believe so. I can't imagine how frightening this must be for you."

Amy nodded. "There was one pleasant thing that came from our visit with Mrs. Miles. She told us that Mr. Miles prefers my books. It is quite difficult to allow such compliments to go unacknowledged because my writing is a secret. I long for the day when a woman will be accepted for writing anything she wants to write."

Eloise smiled. "Or doesn't have a papa who believes a woman shouldn't write such things."

"Well said." As they turned the corner, the Abbey churchyard and the Roman Baths came into view. With the official Season in full swing in London, this was the time of year many of the beau monde retired to Bath for a few days to take a respite from all the balls, soirees, musicales, and other events that kept the members of the *haut ton* busy while the young ladies sought husbands and the young men dodged the marriage-minded mamas.

From what her brother, Michael, had told her—a successful dodger of the mamas himself—there were quite a few American heiresses now involved in the Season. Apparently, a lot of the young lords who needed cash infused into their estates were taking on American wives. It was basically a mutually beneficial swap. A title for the American young lady; money for the old, crumbling estate.

They walked the cobblestone path to the front door of the Roman Baths, the little dog sniffing everything she came across. The smell had already reached them before Amy opened the door.

The Grand Pump Room, adjacent to the Roman Baths, offered refreshments as well as water from the bath's hot springs. It served as a gathering place for residents as well as visitors to the city.

Couples and groups of visitors strolled the room. There were several children present, being encouraged—not too successfully—by their parents and nannies to drink the foul-tasting water that was heralded as being good for one's system.

"Lady Amy, how lovely to see you! And Miss Spencer." They turned in unison to see Lady Ambrose and a few of the ladies from her sewing circle enjoying a stroll about the room. Mrs. Richmond and Lady Graham and her daughter, Lady Susan, all offered a slight hug and air kisses.

"Oh, my, I just love your outfit!" Lady Susan gushed. "You look just wonderful in that color."

"Thank you. Yellow always makes me feel happy."

Lady Susan latched on to Eloise while Lady Ambrose took Amy's arm and moved her forward. "It is too bad Miss Hemphill doesn't have a color to make her happy."

Amy's ears perked up. "Oh, dear. Is something the matter with Miss Hemphill?"

Lady Graham sighed. "We are afraid so, but she won't tell us what is troubling her. We have our sewing circle this afternoon, but Miss Hemphill declined our invitation to join us here at the Baths this morning." She leaned in close. "Frankly, I believe the poor girl would benefit from the waters. I am afraid she's contracted something and is not taking proper care of herself."

"The girl looks absolutely frightful," Mrs. Richmond added from behind Amy and Lady Graham. "The poor dear's nerves are so strained that she is having stomach upsets now." The woman shook her head. "I do wish she would see a doctor."

"She has not seen a doctor?" Amy asked as she tugged on Persephone's leash, since the dog seemed anxious to move faster than the women were strolling.

"No. I offered to go with her one afternoon, but she declined."

Amy's mind was in a whirl. So strained by nerves that she was physically ill? Could it be guilt that plagued the woman? Guilt because she had killed Mr. St. Vincent?

"Persephone, stop pulling." Amy bent to attempt to soothe the dog, but the little animal pulled hard enough that she tugged the leash from Amy's hand. "Stop!"

As she stood, Amy saw what had her dog so frantic. A cat darted across the room, Persephone on her tail. "Persephone, stop!" Amy ran from the group of women and shouted and waved frantically at two young boys. "Please, grab my dog."

To the sounds of the women calling Persephone, the lads tried to catch her, but they ended up on their bottoms when the cat jumped up on one of the boys and flew off his shoulder to land on a ledge. The cat licked its paws as it looked down at Persephone, who was now barking wildly.

Out of breath, Amy caught up to her dog and reached for the leash. Persephone raced off again, even though the cat was still perched on the ledge. The dog had apparently enjoyed her romp around the room and had no intention of stopping.

By now Amy had gained the attention of just about everyone in the Pump Room. Eloise had joined in the effort to catch the dog and barely missed grabbing her as the blasted animal darted in the other direction.

Amy could have sworn she heard the dog laugh.

She continued to chase the dog, several people attempting to grab Persephone as the animal raced by. Eventually the dog made a quick left turn, skidded as she attempted to gain purchase, and slammed right into the back of a man's leg. He stood with another man, both of them deep in conversation.

When Persephone crashed into him, the two startled men turned and faced Amy.

Mr. Harris and Mr. Miles.

CHAPTER 17

The two men glanced at each other, then looked back at her. "Good afternoon, Lady Amy. Such a pleasure to see you." Mr. Miles recovered first and gave her a slight bow.

Amy dipped her head. "Mr. Miles." She turned to Harris. "Good afternoon, Mr. Harris."

"Good afternoon," he mumbled. For a man who had recently proposed marriage to her, he now regarded her as something nasty on his shoe.

Eloise joined them, her face flushed, her chest heaving with breathlessness. "Hello, Mr. Miles."

Mr. Miles nodded, ignoring good manners by not introducing Mr. Harris. Persephone had run off while the four of them stood and stared awkwardly at each other. Amy cleared her throat. "I, um, need to catch my dog."

"Here she is, miss." The young boy who had landed on his bum after the cat ran up his body called to her as he led Persephone in their direction.

She took the leash from the lad and backed up, almost tripping over the dog. "I must be on my way. Have a nice afternoon." Amy grabbed Eloise's hand and dragged her along, leading them and Persephone out of the Pump Room and past the Abbey. They turned the corner before she took a deep breath and stopped for a moment. She looked at Eloise. "Mr. Harris and Mr. Miles? Together?"

"Was that the man with Mr. Miles? That is your fiancé's nephew?"

"Ex-fiancé." Amy nodded. "It is possible they knew each other and were merely having a friendly chat, but when I ran up to them, I noticed how absorbed they'd been." She began to walk slowly toward home. "Also, the fact that they both seemed uncomfortable with us seeing them together is suspicious."

"From what you've told me, both of those men are on your list of murder suspects. Odd to see them together, off alone in a corner and deep in conversation."

They continued their walk home, Eloise leaving Amy and Persephone when they came to her house. Amy and the dog continued on, surprised to see William arriving at that moment. He walked up to her, eyeing Persephone cautiously.

"Have no fear, William, I have just returned from the Pump Room, where my darling little dog escaped me and did so much running about that I don't think she has the energy to attack you."

They made their way up the stairs and entered the house, where Amy turned the leash over to Lacey. "See that she gets a treat, and she surely needs a nap."

"Causing trouble again, milady?" Lacey grinned as she bent to pet the dog.

"Yes, indeed. She is not the only one in need of a nap."

Amy's stomach gave a slight—and hopefully unheard—rumble. "Have you had luncheon yet, my lord?"

"No. I have not."

"Wonderful, because I am quite hungry. Chasing a dog all around the Pump Room will work up an appetite. Just give me a moment to let Cook know there will be two for lunch. I will meet you in the drawing room." Amy hurried down the corridor to the kitchen.

"Good afternoon, milady. What brings you to the kitchen?" The Winchester townhouse cook had been with the family since before Amy was born. She was of undetermined years, round in the middle, a perpetual smile on her face, and produced the most wonderful food one could imagine. Like her kitchen, she was always surrounded by wonderful smells of cinnamon, lemon, and fresh-baked bread.

Papa had tried several times to steal her away for his house in London, but Cook had been born and raised in Bath and refused to move to "smelly London," much to Amy's delight. Her biscuits and lemon tarts were the best Amy had ever tasted.

"I wanted to tell you we have a guest for lunch. Lord Wethington is joining me."

Cook broke into a bright smile. "Is that the lad who has been hanging about?"

Amy huffed. Cook also felt she was Amy's maternal replacement. "His lordship is hardly a 'lad,' and, yes, he has been 'hanging about.' We are working on a project together."

Cook wiped her hands on a towel and walked closer to her, lowering her voice. "You are not trying to find Mr. St. Vincent's killer, are you?"

"No." Amy shook her head. "Why would you say that?"

"Because I know your father told you not to do that, and I also know that if you are, it could be very dangerous for you. Whoever did that horrible thing to the man would not be happy to know you're snooping around."

Amy patted Cook's hand. "Don't worry, I am not in danger, I can assure you." Wishing to move the conversation away from that topic, she said, "What have you prepared for lunch?"

Cook hesitated for a moment, looking like she hadn't fallen for the switch in subjects, but then said, "Whitefish, carrots and turnips, and roasted potatoes."

"Excellent! I am quite hungry."

"'Twill be ready shortly."

Amy left the kitchen before Cook could question her further and joined William in the drawing room. "You will never guess who I saw at the Pump Room just now."

He turned from the window and crossed the room to join her on the settee. "Who?"

"Lady Ambrose and a few of the ladies from the sewing circle. They talked about how poorly Miss Hemphill has been feeling lately."

"Really? I do think we need to gather more information on her."

"Yes. I agree. I am trying to come up with a reason that would allow me to talk to her. I have a strong feeling that whatever malady she is currently feeling has to do with St. Vincent."

"Oh, I am absolutely sure of that as well." William shifted on the seat and turned toward her. "I did not meet with success in searching out Mr. Harris or Mr. Miles at the clubs I visited, both last night and this morning. I checked the roster at two of the clubs, and Mr. Miles is a member at both. Harris's name did not appear, but since he has only been in Bath a few weeks, it's possible he hasn't joined or been accepted just yet."

"But he could be there as a guest? If he was with another member?"

"Yes."

She smirked. "What about women?"

He eyed her suspiciously. "What about women?"

"Can I go to one of your clubs as your guest?" She loved the outraged expression that crossed his face. For goodness' sake, one would have thought she had asked him to escort her to a brothel. "What?"

"Women are not permitted in men's clubs," he answered stiffly.

"Why not?"

He leaned forward and spoke slowly, as if to a small child. "That is why they are called *men's clubs*. They are for men."

"What if I dressed like a man and—"

William held up his hand. "Do not continue. You will not dress as a man. I will not take you to a club. And, furthermore, you will never carry a gun."

Amy's jaw dropped. "Who mentioned a gun?"

"You did. The other day."

"Milady, luncheon is served." Lacey must have caught the last part of their conversation, given the grin on her face.

With her chin held high, Amy walked with William to the dining room. The aroma of the items Cook had mentioned had her stomach rumbling again.

Once they were settled in their seats and had served themselves, Amy took a bite of the delicious fish, closed her eyes, and gave a slight moan. Her eyes snapped open at the sound coming from William sitting across from her. "What?"

He was staring at her, his fork halfway to his mouth. He shook his head. "Nothing."

"Besides seeing Lady Ambrose and her sewing circle at the Pump Room, I also had the opportunity to observe something that I found quite interesting. I am sure you will as well."

William took a sip of water. "What is that?"

"Mr. Miles and Mr. Harris, together at the Pump Room, off in a corner, heads together in deep conversation." She added the story of Persephone running off to chase the cat and then sliding on the floor to slam into Mr. Miles's leg.

"And here I spent last night and this morning searching for either one of them, and you stumble upon them in, of all places, the Pump Room." William wiped his mouth with his napkin and placed it back on his lap.

"They were quite surprised to see me, and obviously uncomfortable the entire time I was in their presence." *Uncomfortable* would have described Mr. Miles, but Mr. Harris had looked as though he wished her gone from the planet. The man clearly did not take rejection well.

"The day after tomorrow is our book club meeting. I will be unable to attend once again, since my presence is required in London. It will be interesting to learn if Mr. Miles tries to speak to you about you running into—well, actually your dog running into—them at the Pump Room."

"That's the thing. If they were there simply as friends, just passing the time, surely they would not have looked so very uncomfortable. Almost guilty."

They pondered that thought while Lacey and another maid cleared the table and left them with a pot of tea, cheese, and fruit. Amy picked up an apple, placed it on her plate, and began to cut it into slices. "I believe I will stop by Lady Ambrose's house this afternoon for her sewing circle. If Miss Hemphill is there, I might have the opportunity to speak with her."

"If she doesn't faint at the sight of you first," William drawled.

★   ★   ★

Amy didn't see William at all that week, as he had gone to London as he'd told her to attend to business. He sent around a note on Friday that he had returned and asked to escort her to the Assembly Rooms on Saturday night.

Amy looked forward to seeing him—not for any reason other than having someone with whom to discuss the case, she told herself. As much as she enjoyed talking to Eloise about it, her friend didn't have the same dedication to solving the mystery. But then, it wasn't her neck that would feel the rope around it if Amy was found guilty.

It was time to face it: she was at an impasse. Pacing back and forth in her room as she waited for William, she ticked off the irritants. So far she'd had no success with Miss Hemphill. Then Mr. Miles had also been absent from the book club meeting, so she had learned nothing more about his meeting with Mr. Harris. The two detectives who plagued her life had sent along a note requesting an interview. Only hours later, Sir Holstein's missive had arrived with the same purpose.

The frustration had built to the point where she'd begun to think she should have gone to London with William, just to be away from Bath for a while. But that would have involved asking the detectives' permission to leave, and since she was trying to avoid them, that would have defeated her purpose.

She hoped to put all of it behind her that evening, just enjoy the dance and try to resume a bit of her happy life before Mr. St. Vincent stumbled through the French doors with a knife stuck in his chest.

A slight knock on her bedchamber door drew her attention from her meandering thoughts. "Yes?"

Aunt Margaret entered, dressed in a lovely deep-purple satin gown. The black embroidery on the neckline ran down the front of the dress and around the hemline. Long gloves with gold bracelets adorning them reached her elbows, with a matching necklace and earbobs.

"Oh my, don't you look beautiful!"

Aunt Margaret did a slight dip. "Thank you, my dear. I am attending the Assembly Rooms tonight."

"Wonderful. It's been a while since you have."

Aunt Margaret leaned back and inspected Amy. "You look lovely as well, but I think your hair could use a bit of decoration."

Amy wore a rose-colored gown with a neckline lower than usual. She patted her hair. "Yes, I was thinking about feathers or something like that."

"I have the perfect thing." Aunt Margaret held up a finger. "Wait just a minute." She hurried from the room, and Amy took the time to find her favorite dancing slippers.

"Here we are." Her aunt held up a lovely strand of pearls. "Go sit at the dressing table, and I will weave these into your hair."

Lacey had fixed Amy's hair up into a lovely topknot of sorts, with loose curls dangling from the sides of her head and at the nape. Aunt Margaret wound the beautiful pearls throughout the hairdo. She stepped back to admire her work. "There. That looks lovely."

Amy moved her head left and right to view her aunt's work. "I agree." She walked across the room and picked up her reticule and gloves. "William is escorting me. Would you care to join us?"

Aunt Margaret flushed and shook her head. "No need, dear. I have an escort."

Amy gaped at her. "You do?"

Her aunt huffed. "Well, don't look so surprised. I do have a gentleman interested in me on occasion. At least enough to tolerate me for one evening."

"I'm sorry. I didn't mean to hurt your feelings."

Aunt Margaret lifted her chin and waved her hand. "You did not hurt my feelings."

The two of them descended the stairs just as the door knocker sounded. Amy hoped it was Aunt Margaret's escort so she could see who it was before William arrived to sweep her away.

When Mr. Stevens opened the door, William and another gentleman whom Amy had never met before stood on the front steps.

William's eyes lit up, and he walked directly to her. "Good evening, Lady Amy." He took her hand and kissed it. Good heavens, he was acting like a beau. She broke into a sweat and sneaked a glance at Aunt Margaret, who seemed just as flustered as Amy, with her escort also kissing her hand.

Well, weren't they a couple of silly women!

Aunt Margaret took her escort's arm and turned him toward Amy. "My dear, may I present to you Lord Pembroke. My lord, this is Lady Amy Lovell, my niece."

He bent over Amy's hand. "It is a pleasure to meet you, Lady Amy. I see Lady Margaret is not the only woman in the family who inherited beauty."

"I agree," William quickly added.

Lord Pembroke appeared to be in his middle or late forties. He had maintained a youthful form, most likely from exercise. He had deep-blue eyes and very straight light-brown hair struck through with silver strands. But the man's most attractive feature was a bright smile that showed handsome dimples.

Aunt Margaret flushed again, and Amy almost swallowed her tongue. In all the years she'd known her aunt, she'd never seen her react to the attentions of a man. Quite interesting. She couldn't wait until they returned home later and she could pepper her with questions.

The women were assisted into their capes and they all left, Amy and William to his carriage and Aunt Margaret and Lord Pembroke to his vehicle.

"Pembroke?" William said as they rolled away from the house. "I didn't know he was even in town."

"Do you know him?"

"Yes. He's quite well known in the business circles in London. An earl, he holds a substantial portfolio and is heavy into railroad stocks. In fact, we share a membership in the same London club."

"You belong to a club in London?"

"Yes. Boodle's. I maintain a membership for the times I travel to town." He grinned. "And no, before you ask, there are no female members."

* * *

They had been at the dance for more than an hour when Aunt Margaret walked up to Amy, determination in her step. Amy and Mr. Pipers had just returned from a very lively cotillion, and he had gone to fetch her a drink.

"What is the matter, Aunt? You look angry."

Aunt Margaret took a deep breath. "Perhaps angry, but more anxious to pass along very important information to you." She drew Amy aside, away from the two women with whom Amy had been speaking.

"Excuse us," Aunt Margaret said as she took Amy's arm. "Let's stroll."

They made their way to the edge of the room where chairs lined the walls, most of them occupied by older attendees and the usual group of wallflowers. Aunt Margaret looked at the line of chairs and shook her head. "This won't work. We have to go somewhere private."

They eventually went outside the room and down the stairs to a small alcove with a cushioned window seat. Once they settled in, Aunt Margaret took Amy's hand. "I just overheard a very interesting conversation in the ladies' retiring room."

"Yes?"

"Two women were discussing Miss Hemphill. They didn't know I was in the room, so I remained quiet so they would not discover me behind the screen."

Amy's heart sped up. "What did they say?"

"Our Miss Hemphill is indeed not feeling her normal self."

She nodded. "Yes, I know that. I saw her at the sewing circle. She looks dreadful."

"What you might not know is she is apparently ill with guilt."

Amy drew back and regarded her aunt. "Indeed?"

"One of the women blurted out that Miss Hemphill had been bemoaning how her actions had ruined her life."

Amy continued to watch Aunt Margaret, her eyebrows raised.

Aunt Margaret leaned in close. "Miss Hemphill is pregnant."

CHAPTER 18

"Pregnant?"

Aunt Margaret nodded. "Yes. And feeling extremely guilty."

Amy sat and pondered that surprise. "If Miss Hemphill is pregnant, that might be why she went to London. She didn't want to see a local doctor to confirm her fears."

"My thoughts exactly."

Amy let out a deep breath. "I must tell William."

"You know I disapprove of your involvement in this matter. If you take this information to the police, it might turn them in the correct direction."

They both rose and made their way back to the ballroom. Lord Pembroke spotted Aunt Margaret the minute they entered the room and made his way to her, dodging a few men who tried to garner his attention.

That was something else Amy wanted to talk to her aunt about. Lord Pembroke seemed much too attached to Aunt Margaret for him to be someone new in her life. Was Aunt Margaret hiding secrets, too?

Amy searched the room for William, but it was so crowded she didn't see him. She made her way through the throng, excusing herself, accepting greetings from those she hadn't spoken to yet that evening, and continued to search.

The musicians began a new number—a waltz—and enough people moved to the dance floor that she was able to see more clearly.

"May I request the honor of this dance, Lady Amy?" She spun around at the sound of Mr. Harris's voice. For goodness' sake, why was the man continuing to antagonize her? She had been so focused on Miss Hemphill, she'd forgotten about the conversation she had witnessed with Mr. Harris and Mr. Miles.

A good detective followed all clues. "Yes, Mr. Harris, I accept."

His eyes lit up as he took her hand. Surely the man didn't still think he had a chance of her accepting his marriage proposal. She'd made it quite clear that she had no intention of marrying at all, and certainly not a man she'd just met who had the polish and savior faire of a turtle. Besides, when she had spotted him at the Pump Room, he hadn't exactly fallen all over himself welcoming her.

He escorted her to the dance floor and took her in his arms. Thankfully, he kept a decent amount of space between them so she wasn't forced to step on his toes to get him to release her.

"I'm sorry we did not get a chance to speak the other day at the Pump Room." He studied her, not with the polite interest his benign statement implied, but as if he was waiting for the need to defend himself. The man certainly ran hot and cold as far as his interactions with her.

Interesting.

Amy laughed, attempting to relax him so she could wangle information. Coyness in a woman never hurt. "I'm sure you saw the ruckus my dog caused." She offered him a bright smile. "I had the feeling the servers hoped I would leave of my own accord and they would not find themselves in the awkward position of having to ask a lady to leave the premises."

He laughed along with her, although the smile never reached his eyes. He still appeared guarded. They had made their way almost across the room already, Mr. Harris being quite adept at waltzing. She'd noticed more than one woman casting covert glances in his direction. If she hadn't had such a distrust and dislike of the man, she would have understood their interest.

Mr. Harris was a bit taller than medium height, but the way he carried himself spoke of command and confidence. His clothes fit his form quite well, and she doubted his tailor needed to use padding to fill out his jacket. Objectively—and a good detective must be objective—she could understand his surprise at the rejected marriage proposal.

Of course, given the two conversations they'd had, he could use some lessons in charming a young lady. But if she was going to coerce information out of him, she must be the charming one.

"And did your dog recover from its race around the room?" Mr. Harris executed a smooth turn.

"Yes, indeed. She took a lovely nap once we arrived home." She waited for a moment, then said, "I did not know that you and Mr. Miles were friends."

She knew she was not imagining things when she felt his body stiffen. "Yes. Likable chap. We enjoyed a conversation while indulging in a glass of the famous Bath water."

Well, then. It appeared he thought she was either blind or stupid—that she hadn't seen how very cozy they'd been in their conversation before Persephone charged into them. She tilted her head. "Indeed? So you had only just met?"

He shrugged. "Perhaps we had met there another time. I'm not sure."

Both remained caught up in their thoughts for a minute. "Did you know Mr. Miles is a member of a book club I belong to?"

Mr. Harris registered genuine surprise. So apparently Mr. Miles hadn't discussed his personal life with him, which led her to further believe their conversation had been related to business.

Drug business?

Deciding a switch in tactics might work, she said, "You must come one evening. We meet every Thursday at Atkinson and Tucker bookstore."

He gave a noncommittal nod.

She watched his face as she said, "We read mystery books. Murder on occasion."

"You don't say."

'Twas time to be bold. "How are you finding Mr. St. Vincent's shipping business? Will you be running it yourself now, or hire someone to do that for you?"

She attempted to put the most innocuous look on her face she could conger up. Hopefully he would think she was merely a silly, fluffy-head woman making conversation, not fishing for information.

"I will run it myself." Nothing more, just those terse words. Then, "Did my uncle discuss his business with you at all?"

Which part? The almost-bankrupt part, or the drug-dealing part?

She offered him a sweet, benign smile. "No. I know very little about shipping."

They were at a stalemate. Neither of them had gotten the information they were seeking. But the music came to an end, and Amy was once again on the search for William.

★ ★ ★

The next morning as Amy, Aunt Margaret, and William returned from church, they found the two detectives once more waiting for them in front of the house. Since she had ignored the note they'd sent for an interview, they had most likely determined the best strategy was to just show up.

"Don't you have better things to do on Sunday? Perhaps church?" She knew she probably shouldn't antagonize them, since they still held her freedom in their hands, but she was getting weary of their continued focus on her when she and William had other suspects.

There was no reaction from either of them, which frustrated her more.

They trooped up the stairs, and once inside, Aunt Margaret said, "We are headed to lunch. You are welcome to join us—"

Please, no.

"—or wait until we are through."

"We only need about five minutes of your time, Lady Amy. If you could postpone your meal that long, we would appreciate it."

Aunt Margaret glared at them. She was apparently out of patience with the men also. "Five minutes." She turned and strode down the corridor toward the kitchen, a woman on a mission.

"What is it, Detective?" Amy didn't even invite them to sit down. After all, they had said five minutes.

"What is your relationship to Mr. Francis Harris?" Carson asked.

Amy frowned. "Mr. St. Vincent's nephew?"

"The very one," Detective Marsh said.

"Whatever do you mean to infer with that question? I have no relationship with Mr. Harris."

"Yet he asked you to marry him," Carson said, as Marsh wrote in his ever-present notepad.

Had they been in the drawing room, Amy would have collapsed onto the settee. As it was, her legs were having a hard time holding her up. How the devil had they learned that bit of information? It had only been the two of them in the room when Harris made his horrible proposal, and she knew none of her staff would repeat anything they overheard. Mr. Harris must have told someone.

She stiffened and raised her chin. "I barely know the man, Detective. I met him maybe once or twice."

Detective Carson glared at her. "Did he or did he not propose to you only days after he learned the shipping business he inherited from Mr. St. Vincent was bankrupt?"

Well, then.

It appeared they were doing their work, but unfortunately, whatever they learned, they always seem to come back to her. "If you must know, Mr. Harris had the poor taste to offer marriage. I turned him down and sent him off. And, I might add, your insinuation that a man would only be interested in marrying me because he needed money is crass and unkind."

Ignoring her complaint, Carson continued. "Yet you met him in the Pump Room on Tuesday morning."

Dear God in heaven. Were they following her?

"I did not *meet* him in the Pump Room. I mean, I did meet him, but it was purely coincidental."

Detective Marsh simply raised his eyebrows. "And was the dance you had with him last night purely coincidental as well?"

Amy gasped and looked over at William, who appeared as shocked as she was. He recovered first, however. "Detectives, I demand to know why you are pursuing this line of questioning. In fact, I must ask you, on Lady Amy's behalf, to leave now. Your five minutes are up, and if you have further questions, she will answer only with her barrister present." William turned to her. "My lady, may I escort you in to lunch?"

Marsh slapped his notebook closed.

Thank heaven she had William's arm to hold on to, because Amy was having a very difficult time moving her feet forward. Her mouth was dried up like a rain-starved plot of dirt, and her heart was practically beating its way out of her body.

Once they were seated at the table, Amy calmly took her napkin, shook it out, and placed it in her lap. She took a sip of water, placed it carefully on the pristine white tablecloth, and looked across the table at Aunt Margaret. "I am going to jail."

"What?" Aunt Margaret looked from her to William. "Whatever did those awful men say?"

"Actually, they didn't say anything. They merely asked very pointed questions, all of them revolving around Mr. Harris."

Aunt Margaret picked up the platter of roast beef and added two slices to her plate. "Mr. St. Vincent's nephew?"

"Yes," William said. "They appear to be trying to link the man with Amy."

"They even knew we danced last night!" In truth, if Amy had been a weepy sort of woman, she would have excused herself from the table, hurried up the stairs, and had a good cry on her bed.

But she was not that woman. She was strong, she was determined, and if nothing else, she would solve this mystery, clear her name, and enjoy the respect on the detectives' faces when she presented them with a solved case.

Once luncheon was finished, Aunt Margaret excused herself, leaving Amy and William enjoying their tea. It was only after her aunt had departed that Amy remember she wanted to ask her about Lord Pembroke, who seemed quite taken with Aunt Margaret. This murder business was interfering with her ability to satisfy her curiosity about important things.

"I believe we should be more focused on Miss Hemphill," William said. "The fact that your aunt heard Miss Hemphill claiming remorse for something she did that ruined her life, and that she is in a family way, leads me in the direction of her being the guilty party."

Amy agreed. "Yes, I think so, too. If she did kill Mr. St. Vincent in a fit of pique because he refused to marry her, 'twas a mistake, because she has no chance now of avoiding a scandal. 'Tis quite possible she told him about her condition, and when he refused to marry her, she killed him."

William added, "Thus ruining her life, because there is no chance now of her reputation being salvaged. Had St. Vincent lived, she might have been able to convince him to do the right thing."

Amy stirred the cream and sugar in her tea. "I had wondered whether we should visit with Miss Hemphill ourselves or give the information to the detectives. But I no longer trust them with this information. They will find some way to turn this into a condemnation of me."

William offered her a sad smile. "I am afraid you are right. They are conducting this investigation with horse blinders on. They refuse to see anyone except you."

"I shall bring the note to Miss Hemphill's house and confront her with it. It sounds as though she is at a breaking point and might just confess." Amy shook her head. "I do feel sorry for the girl. She made a mistake and might have compounded her error by committing murder. I can only hope the law goes easier on women than they do on men."

"I am still curious as to how the detectives knew about Mr. Harris and his seeing you at the Pump House, proposing marriage, and dancing with you."

"I would say they are either following me or him."

"Either way, if Miss Hemphill is our guilty party, we must move quickly, or I am afraid you will receive another summons from the detectives with a directive to bring your barrister with you."

★   ★   ★

Two o'clock the following day, William arrived at Winchester House to make a visit to Miss Hemphill. It had taken Amy some time to find Miss Hemphill's direction. But apparently her driver was friends with a hackney driver who knew Miss Hemphill's flat.

"Do you have the note that was sent about St. Vincent's involvement in drugs?" William asked as the carriage rolled away from her townhouse. Unlike the previous few days, the weather was now soggy and chilly. Any hint of spring had vanished along with the sun and sweet-smelling flowers.

Amy patted her reticule. "Yes, I do." She pulled her coat close against her body and shivered. "I will be quite pleased when the warmer weather arrives and then remains. This back-and-forth with a touch of spring and then a return to colder weather is depressing."

They remained quiet for the rest of the trip, with Amy huddled in the corner watching the raindrops slide down the window. William was lost in his thoughts and studied his hands, fingers linked together, resting in his lap.

Amy turned toward William. "I do hope we are not turned away. I'm afraid I might make a ninny of myself and force my way into her house." When he did not answer, she said, "You are exceptionally quiet. Is anything wrong?"

William shook his head. "No. I just have this feeling that we are missing something. I'm running the suspects through my mind and feel as though I am looking at a puzzle with a piece missing of which I should be aware. Something that caught my eye at one point that slithered away, and now I can no longer recall."

"My, that sounds quite ominous. I, on the other hand, am hoping this visit to Miss Hemphill will clear it all up and I can go back to thinking about fictional murders, not real ones where I am the main suspect."

The neighborhood had gone from upper crust to lower middle class. The homes were smaller, one or two streetlights were broken, and in another block or two they would be in the lower end of Bath. The area where one did not travel after dark. Amy looked out the window. "I do hope we are almost there."

"Based on the neighborhood, I must admit I feel the same way."

"We should have brought a gun."

"No." The word had no sooner left William's mouth than the carriage rolled to a stop. "It appears we have arrived."

He climbed out and took the umbrella from the driver, turned, and helped Amy out of the vehicle. They made their way up the path to the front door. The steps were cracked and in need of repair, and it had clearly been some time since the wooden door was painted.

"Do you know anything about Miss Hemphill's financial state?" William asked as he dropped the knocker on the door.

Amy shook her head. "Only that she didn't have enough blunt to bail out St. Vincent's business, which is why he proposed to me, I assume. There could be no other reason, because we hardly had a fancy for each other."

Slowly the door opened, and a young girl peered out at them. She was no more than sixteen years old, with short, blonde curly hair hidden unsuccessfully under a white mobcap. "Yes, sir."

"Lord Wethington and Lady Amy Lovell calling on Miss Hemphill." He held out his card to the girl.

She stared at it for a moment as if she expected it to bite her. "Miss Hemphill rents a room here. I can take your card and knock on her door."

"That's fine." When she continued to stare at them, William said, "May we come in to wait? It is rather wet out here."

"Oh, yes, of course, my lord. Please accept my apologies." She stepped back to allow them to enter. William closed the umbrella and, not seeing an umbrella stand, leaned it against a corner wall.

"I will be just a minute."

Amy pulled the collar of her coat closer. 'Twas quite cold in the house, and that, combined with her wet clothes, brought on a chill.

They waited about five minutes before the girl returned. "I am sorry, m'lord, but Miss Hemphill is not answering her door."

"Did she go out?"

"No. I am sure she did not, because I brought her soup and bread for her lunch since she said she was feeling poorly. I would have heard her come down the stairs, since I've been working in the parlor and dining room since then."

Frustrated, Amy glanced over at William. She had no intention of leaving without speaking to the woman. "Would it be permissible for us to try to rouse her? It is quite important that we speak with her. Perhaps she is taking a nap."

The girl looked confused at their question but eventually shrugged. "Mrs. Hubbard, the landlady, isn't at home for me to ask, but I guess it would be all right."

They climbed the stairs, the worn wood creaking and groaning with their weight as they made their way up. "Which door?" William called down to the girl, who had remained at the entranceway.

"Second one on the right.'"

"Thank you." They found the correct door, and Amy knocked. "Miss Hemphill?"

No answer.

"Miss Hemphill," William said as he knocked a bit harder.

No answer.

They tried three more times until finally Amy said, "Try the door latch."

William turned the latch, and the door opened. They slowly walked into the dim room.

It was a cold, stark space. Very little in the way of personal belongings were strewn about. There was a rickety dresser, a small desk and chair, and nothing covering the bare wooden floor. Peeling wallpaper, wet from where water leaked from the window frame, gave the room a sad, neglected feeling.

No fire blazed in the fireplace, which was no surprise, since only the wealthy were able to enjoy a fire all day long.

They walked toward the bed in the center of the room. The murky afternoon sky visible from the window cast a dim light on the lump lying on top of the worn bedcover. Amy called Miss Hemphill's name and touched her on the shoulder.

The cold, stiff shoulder, belonging to a very dead Miss Hemphill.

CHAPTER 19

Amy stepped back so abruptly she trounced on William's foot. If he hadn't caught her by the arms, she would have tumbled to the floor, possibly knocking them both down. "Oh, dear." She took in a deep breath. "I believe she's dead."

William eased her aside and looked down at the woman. Her eyes were closed, her face in peaceful repose. He felt her wrist, then the side of her neck. No pulse. "Yes. I'm afraid she is dead."

Amy fought down the nausea rising up the back of her throat. To distract herself, she looked around. "We need some light."

"Wait here." William moved away.

She grabbed his arm, suddenly afraid to be alone. "Where are you going?"

"To find the maid who let us in. She will be able to supply us with a lamp, or even a candle."

Amy shook her head. "No. Not yet. Once you notify the maid, she will probably have hysterics that we will have to deal with, and then she will immediately send—or have someone send—for the police. I want to look around before the police step in."

William ran his fingers through his hair. "You're probably correct. But we still need some light."

"We'll move the drapes aside from the other two windows, and with the light from the street, maybe we can find a lamp or candle."

Their search turned up two candle stumps and one empty oil lamp. "You take one candle and I'll take the other."

They began to methodically search the room. From what they discovered, Miss Hemphill had lived right on the poverty line. There was a small amount of food—half a loaf of bread, a wrapped block of cheese, a few mint candies, and a small container of tea. Certainly not the robust diet an expectant woman needed. She had only two dresses, both of which had seen better days, but Amy did recognize one of the dresses as the one she'd worn to Lady Ambrose's sewing circle.

Amy blew out her candle stub, which had burned uncomfortably close to her fingers, and moved to the middle of the room. She placed her hands on her hips, turning in a slow circle, studying the area. "What I don't understand is why a woman with so very little would be sewing garments for the poor."

"Perhaps she wasn't always in dire straits." William rubbed a circle on the dirty window and looked outside. "You did say you were not familiar with her prior to Mr. St. Vincent's death."

"You are correct. The first time I heard her name was when someone told me she had been expecting a proposal from Mr. St. Vincent before he made his offer of marriage to me.

"If she came from a respectable family and found herself in a family way, there is a good chance they cast her out." She turned and looked again at Miss Hemphill. "Poor woman. 'Tis such a shame that society looks down on a woman for making a mistake, but the gentleman's actions are never called to account."

"Did you find Miss Hemphill?" The maid from downstairs walked into the room, took one look at the dead body on the bed, and screamed loud enough to raise Miss Hemphill from her eternal sleep. She threw her apron over her face and continued to scream. "She's dead! I saw a dead person."

Amy cast an *I told you so* glance at William. Looking very uncomfortable, he nodded toward the maid, and Amy took a deep breath and approached the girl. "Miss, you must calm yourself."

She stopped wailing long enough to peek at Amy from under her apron. "Did you kill her?"

Amy was getting mighty tired of people accusing her of murder. Did she look so very minacious, then? "No, I did not kill her. And his lordship did not kill her either. She was decidedly dead when we arrived."

The maid began to shake. "I never saw a dead person before, milady, so you must excuse me. I meant no disrespect."

Amy, on the other hand, was afraid discovering dead bodies might become a habit of hers. She patted the girl on the back. "Do you have someone you can send to the police department?"

She bobbed. "Yes, milady, I can send the man Mrs. Hubbard keeps around to do the heavy chores."

William stepped over to where they stood. "Would you please send for the police, then? And I think perhaps, given the circumstances, Mrs. Hubbard would allow you a short tea break."

The maid's eyes grew wide. "Do you think so, m'lord? She's not too fond of work breaks."

"I think so. I will speak to her when she returns—do you know when she is expected?"

She shrugged. "Not too long, I would think. She was going to walk to the shops." The girl glanced furtively at the body on the bed and shuddered.

"'Tis probably a good idea to send for the police and have your tea." Amy placed her arm around the maid's shoulders and moved her toward the door. They could hear the girl's mumbling as she headed down the stairs.

William walked to the bed and leaned over Miss Hemphill's body. He took a sniff and stepped back. Amy joined him. "What?"

"Take a whiff of her mouth and tell me if what I smell is correct."

Amy leaned over and took in a deep breath. She turned to William, and they both said, "Pennyroyal."

After scrounging around the room, they found a tattered blanket, which they used to cover the body. Then they went downstairs to await the police. As much as Amy hated to be here when the police arrived, she really had no choice. They would track her down anyway.

"With your logical, deductive mind, Amy, what do you make of the pennyroyal?" William rested his foot on his bent knee.

They sat in the drawing room right off the main entrance. The maid was nowhere in sight, so they had the room to themselves. "I'm thinking one of two things. Suicide or abortion."

"Or perhaps both." He smirked in her direction. "I don't suppose I should be surprised that you even know about abortion and that pennyroyal has a reputation for being able to rid a woman of a baby."

"Research."

He nodded. "If it was suicide, then why not drown herself? I would think it less messy and not quite as painful. Although I imagine it's not too easy to actually drown, unless you go deep and cannot swim."

"Actually, it is not very difficult to drown oneself. When the body hits cold water, you automatically gasp; it's a reflex, so when you fall in, you gasp and inhale water. The sudden coldness of the ingested water can also cause the throat to seize. Then, even if you can survive that part of it, the amount of clothing we wear would make it almost impossible to swim to the top, make it to the edge of the river or lake, and climb out onto a slippery embankment."

William just stared at her. Then he shook his head as if to clear it. "Research?"

"Just so."

A loud banging on the front door had them both jumping up from their seats. The maid was still absent, so William opened the door.

Amy groaned as Detective Marsh and Detective Carson strolled into the room. "Well, well. Why am I not surprised that Lady Amy and Lord Wethington are keeping another dead body company?" Carson grinned at her as Detective Marsh flipped open his notepad.

Botheration. Were there no other detectives in the Bath police department?

"Where is the dead body this time?" Marsh's snide remark had Amy fisting her hands, wanting to smack the smug look off his face.

"*This time*, the body is upstairs in Miss Hemphill's room." She raised her chin. "I will be happy to accompany you."

They all trooped upstairs. Amy and William stepped back and allowed the detectives to precede them. "We need more light," Detective Marsh grumbled.

"I will see if I can find the maid who let us in. We were only able to find two candle stubs."

"Not to be doing any investigation, correct?" Carson growled in her direction.

Amy sniffed. "Of course not." She glanced at William before hurrying downstairs. Just as she reached the entrance, an older woman opened the front door and stepped inside. She was plump of body and her face was flushed. She came to an abrupt halt when she saw Amy. "Who are you? Where's Sally?"

"Good afternoon, ma'am. I assume you are Mrs. Hubbard?" When the woman nodded, Amy continued, "I am Lady Amy Lovell, and is Sally the maid who answered the door?"

"Yes." Mrs. Hubbard set down the basket she carried, spilling over with goods, and began to unbutton her coat. "Now why are you in my house?"

"My friend, Lord Wethington"—it never hurt to toss out a title—"and I came to call on Miss Hemphill, who I am afraid has met with . . ." Amy struggled with how to say what they'd found. Or how to tell the woman that the police were upstairs and her maid was probably taking a much needed, but probably unauthorized, tea break.

"With what?"

She let out a deep breath. "With her end."

"End of what?"

How to get her point across without having to deal with another hysterical female? "I am sorry to say Miss Hemphill is no longer with us."

"She moved out?"

Bloody hell! Amy never cursed, but this was too much. Well, there was nothing to be done about it. "Miss Hemphill is dead, Mrs. Hubbard."

"Well, why didn't you say so, girl?" She hung her coat on a hook by the door. "Where's Sally?"

Well, then. Apparently they were not to be subjected to another overwrought outburst. Perhaps Mrs. Hubbard was not unfamiliar with tenants turning up their toes on the premises. The life of a landlady, perhaps.

"Sally was a bit emotional at the death of Miss Hemphill, and Lord Wethington suggested she take a short break from her duties to have a cup of tea."

Mrs. Hubbard raised her brows. "And will his lordship offer some blunt for the time Sally's been sitting on her arse instead of working?"

"If you require compensation for the young lady's time, I will be happy to reimburse you. She was quite distraught."

Mrs. Hubbard picked up her basket and huffed. "She is always distraught." She walked a few steps and turned. "Did you notify the police?"

"Yes, ma'am. They are upstairs right now."

The woman shook her head and continued down the corridor to what Amy assumed was the kitchen.

Remembering what she had come downstairs for, Amy followed the woman as she lumbered away. "Mrs. Hubbard?"

"Yes." She didn't stop.

"The police need more light upstairs. Do you have an oil lamp or more candles?"

The landlady placed her basket on the long wooden table and glared at the maid. "Sally, it's time to return to your work. I ain't paying you to sit around and 'recover' from the shock of a dead body."

Sally hopped up. "Yes, Mrs. Hubbard. I am well now."

"Then get that oil lamp from the drawing room and give it to her ladyship, here."

Amy followed the maid back to the drawing room, took the lamp from her hand, and returned upstairs.

"It's about time," Detective Marsh said as she joined the detectives and William in Miss Hemphill's room. She was becoming weary of everyone snapping at her as if she were a servant. She handed the lamp to Carson and backed up to stand alongside William.

"I assume you wish us to remain here to speak with you?"

Detective Marsh glanced over his shoulder. "You assume correctly. As soon as we're finished with our examination, we will have some questions for you and your cohort here." He gestured toward William. "Right now you can wait downstairs."

She would have preferred to remain while they did their examination, hopefully listening to their comments, but considering she and William were now loosely involved in another suspicious death, she didn't want to antagonize the men.

Amy and William sat in the drawing room, making mundane conversation, since there really wasn't much to say until they could speak with the detectives.

"You don't suppose they will accuse me of this death, too, do you?" Amy asked as William stood and wandered the room, touching various objects.

Detective Marsh entered the room, his partner right behind him. "Not exactly accuse you, Lady Amy, but Carson and I are very interested in knowing why you and his lordship here discovered another dead body."

William joined her again on the settee. He reached over and took her hand, which Marsh noted in his book.

Detective Carson started. "What is the chit's name, and how do you know the victim?"

"Miss Eva Hemphill and I met at a sewing circle." There was no reason to admit she barely knew the woman and hadn't been able to speak with her even once.

Marsh grinned at William. "Are you a member of this sewing circle, too?"

William drew himself up. "Detective, there should be no reason for me to remind you that a woman lies dead upstairs, and with all respect, the situation should be treated with a bit more dignity."

Amazingly enough, Marsh had the decency to look abashed and immediately cleared his throat.

"Is this the very same Miss Hemphill who had an understanding with Mr. St. Vincent before you stole him away?"

Amy flinched. "I did not steal him away. As I told you before, I had no idea she thought she had an understanding with Mr. St. Vincent."

Carson grunted. "What was the purpose of your visit today?"

"We were merely making a social call. I had heard recently that Miss Hemphill was not feeling well. We wished to check on her."

Marsh wrote furiously. He and Carson asked a few more questions back and forth, the normal ones of who had admitted them to the house, how they had determined she was dead, and so forth. Eventually, they snapped their notebooks closed. "That is all. You may leave."

Amy wasn't about to leave without some information. "Did you determine the cause of death?" She wondered if they had noticed the pennyroyal.

"That will be determined by an autopsy. The coroner will retrieve the body sometime today."

Mrs. Hubbard entered the room at that point. "Are you finished, Detectives? I need to get Miss Hemphill out of the house so I can have my maid clean the room and put a new tenant in there."

"You're the landlady?" Carson asked.

"Yes. Mrs. Hubbard."

"I have a few questions for you, too." Marsh opened his notebook again. "How long has the deceased lived here?"

"About two weeks."

Amy perked up at that answer. If Miss Hemphill had been living in such squalor for only about two weeks, there was a good chance she had been thrown from her family home quite recently.

"Did she have many visitors?"

"I don't allow men to visit, and any ladies who call must be received in the drawing room, here." Mrs. Hubbard tapped her lips with her index finger. "I don't recall anyone visiting Miss Hemphill." She gestured with her chin toward Amy and William. "Except for these two."

"Did she get a lot of mail?"

Mrs. Hubbard shook her head. "None that I'm aware of."

After a few more questions, the detectives stood. "Mrs. Hubbard, the coroner will be here today to remove the body. Please be available for more questions as the investigation into Miss Hemphill's death continues."

For the first time the landlady showed a reaction. "Do you believe she was murdered?" She immediately looked in William and Amy's direction.

The detectives headed to the door. "We won't know that until the autopsy."

Once they were outside, the detectives turned to Amy. "No leaving Bath, my lady." Carson cast his attention at William. "You either, my lord."

"Wait just a minute," William blustered. "I occasionally conduct business in London."

"Fine. No leaving Bath without first notifying us." With that they entered a carriage and slammed the door shut.

Amy took in a deep breath as the detectives' carriage rolled away. "We have to get a copy of the autopsy report. I still think Miss Hemphill had something to do with Mr. St. Vincent's death."

She was quite tired when they arrived at her house. "Would you care for a brandy before you set off for home?" Amy asked as they climbed the stairs.

"I don't mind if I do. That sounds like just the thing after discovering another dead body."

Aunt Margaret walked in the door right after them. She followed them to the drawing room, removing her gloves. "May I join you? I could use a sherry."

"Bad day?"

Her aunt smiled. "No, actually a very good day."

Amy's brows rose. "Indeed. Are you going to share it with us?"

Aunt took the glass from William. "Yes. But not today." She walked to a comfortable red-and-white-striped chair next to the fireplace and sat. "What have you two been up to?"

Amy gave her a shortened version of Miss Hemphill's demise, the odd landlady, the hysterical maid, and the same two detectives who had again invaded her life.

"The same two detectives? That is quite a coincidence."

"Coincidence or bad luck," William said. "I just hope we don't have any trouble getting a copy of the autopsy report. Given the poor state of Miss Hemphill's room and sudden demise, I think this might have a connection to Mr. St. Vincent's death."

"'Twould be quite odd if it didn't, considering she was supposed to marry him, then got tossed aside for Amy. Then we find out she was pregnant."

"And I don't believe in coincidence." William downed the last of his brandy, then stood. "I will make a visit to my club to see if I can gather more information on either Mr. Miles or Mr. Harris. They are still in my sight as suspects."

"Milady, a messenger has just delivered a letter for you." Lacey held out the envelope toward Amy.

Amy took it from her hand and looked at it, all the blood in her head racing to her feet, leaving her light-headed.

"Amy, what is it?" Aunt Margaret moved to her side. "You have gone quite pale."

Amy looked up at William and Aunt Margaret. "This letter is in the very same handwriting of the person who wrote to me about Mr. St. Vincent's drug dealing."

CHAPTER 20

Amy reread the few terse words on the letter she'd received days before.

Dear Lady Amy,

Please forgive me.

Miss Eva Hemphill

The note certainly confirmed her suspicions about the anonymous note with the information about Mr. St. Vincent's illegal and nefarious activities. Same handwriting, same author.

Aunt Margaret and William were both of the mind that the note was Miss Hemphill's confession to the murder. By killing St. Vincent, they'd argued, Miss Hemphill had removed Amy's chance of marriage.

The confirmation of the removal of Miss Hemphill from her family's home had been uncovered by Aunt Margaret, who had spoken to one of her friends who had a maid related to a servant in the Hemphill household.

In any event, the entire situation was still a mess as far as Amy was concerned. William and Aunt Margaret might be convinced of Miss Hemphill's guilt, but she was not. As far as what the police believed, Amy had no idea, since she hadn't, surprisingly enough, heard from her favorite detectives since the day Miss Hemphill had been found.

That had been almost a week ago, since it was now Saturday, and she once again awaited William's arrival so he could escort her to the Assembly Rooms. That morning he'd sent around a note saying he was going to be able to get a copy of Miss Hemphill's autopsy report and would bring it with him that night when he picked her up.

What puzzled her more than anything was the lack of visits from the two Bath police department detectives. Did they believe, as William and Aunt Margaret optimistically did, that the matter was closed, and that Miss Hemphill had murdered Mr. St. Vincent? Amy was quite certain that if that were the case, they would have told her. After all, she'd been in the spotlight of their investigation from the day she had stumbled over Mr. St. Vincent in the library.

Truth be known, the murder-mystery author in her continued to cry *no*. Why would Miss Hemphill kill the father of her child? What chance would she have of redeeming her name if he was dead? On the other hand, crimes of passion were generally not committed by those in their right mind at the time.

She sighed and folded up the well-worn note. Assuming the police would do a follow-up visit to her, since they'd been so tickled to find her at the scene of another death, she had decided to show them the note once they arrived.

They hadn't arrived.

She still had the note.

And *she* felt the murderer was still out there.

"Milady, Sir Holstein awaits your presence downstairs." Lacey tapped lightly on the bedchamber door as she voiced her message.

Sir Holstein? Of course, she'd forgotten all about the private investigator Papa had hired. Since William was expected any minute, she grabbed her reticule, gloves, and hat and left her room.

Amy held out her hand as she entered the drawing room. "Sir Holstein, how very nice to see you."

The man looked dreadful. So bad, in fact, that she wondered how his legs were holding him up. He merely nodded in her direction and took a seat.

"To what do I owe the pleasure of your visit, sir?" She was about to offer tea, but knowing how soon she would have to leave, there would not be time. With the condition he appeared to be in, she felt she should instead offer him a bed and a visit from a doctor.

"I wanted to explain why I have not reported on my progress in finding your fiancé's killer."

"Ex-fiancé."

"I have been uncommonly ill." He reached out and touched the arm of the chair, where he sat at the very edge, almost as if he wished to escape as quickly as possible.

"I am sorry to hear that, Sir Holstein. Influenza?" She really wanted to ask if he suffered from the plague, since she'd never seen anyone look so ill.

He shook his head. "No. It seems I ate a bit of bad food."

Her brows rose. "Bad food?"

He nodded and swayed slightly on the chair. "Yes. I had a terrible time of it. I won't go into details, since 'tis not proper conversation for a lady, but I have been confined to bed for a few days and am not feeling quite the thing just yet."

Quite the thing? He looked worse than poor, dead Miss Hemphill.

"Therefore, I was unable to do a proper job. I have come to tell you I can attempt to continue with the investigation or suggest another investigator with whom I am familiar to take over the matter. I will, of course, provide him with all my notes and whatever money your father paid me."

Mr. Stevens, who had already taken over night duty for the front door, entered the drawing room. "My lady, Lord Wethington has arrived."

Sir Holstein made to stand up and fell back into the chair just as William entered the room. He took one glance at the investigator and regarded Amy with raised brows.

"Sir Holstein was just leaving." She looked at the man as he struggled to rise. "Do you have a coach with you?"

"No. I will hail a hackney."

She took his arm and walked him to the door. "No, you will not. I will have my driver take you where you need to go. And please, don't concern yourself with the investigation. I will notify you if I need you to turn it over to another investigator. Right now things are going smoothly and it might all be tied up in no time."

"Is that right?"

"Yes. I will send around a note." She turned to a concerned-looking Mr. Stevens. "Please have the carriage brought forward to take Sir Holstein home."

William had walked behind them from the drawing room to the front door, and she turned to him and said, "I am ready to go."

Mr. Stevens helped her into her light coat while Sir Holstein leaned against the wall to await the carriage. With one final glance in the poor man's direction, Amy and William left the house.

"What the devil happened to Sir Holstein?" William settled into his seat and tapped on the carriage ceiling. "He looked appalling."

"Bad food." She smoothed out her skirts and settled back in the seat as the familiar clopping of horse hooves on cobblestones started up.

"Bad food? Whatever did he eat? He looks frightful."

Amy shrugged. "He never did say more than that, actually. He apparently has been laid up with this problem for some time, and from the looks of it, he is still suffering."

"Just so. Sounds as though the chap should have sent round a note rather than make the trip."

Amy grabbed the strap alongside her head as the carriage made a turn. "I imagine it was his sense of duty that made him come in person. But I agree; given the condition he was in, a note would have sufficed."

The carriage moved along nicely through the streets of Bath. William had allowed the windows to remain open, and the scent of early spring air filled the coach. 'Twould do them good to go to the Assembly Rooms for a spot of pleasure. Too much dwelling on murder and dead bodies had cast a gloom over Amy's life the past couple of weeks.

She took in a deep breath of the evening air and smiled. "The good news is now, with him out of the picture, that is one less person in the way of our investigation."

"Our investigation? I thought we had concluded that Miss Hemphill killed Mr. St. Vincent because he refused to marry her."

Amy pointed a finger at him. "No, you and Aunt Margaret concluded that. I do not agree, and I believe I said so that day. How would killing Mr. St. Vincent help the dilemma in which Miss Hemphill found herself?"

"True, but 'tis quite known that crimes of passion don't always make sense."

Amy scooted up on her seat. "On another point, were you able to obtain a copy of the autopsy report?"

William reached into his jacket pocket and withdrew papers. "Yes. I will give it to you, but basically it says she died of poisoning. Pennyroyal, as we suspected. Her pregnancy was confirmed, and the cause of death was determined to be accidental poisoning while attempting an abortion."

Amy was stunned at how sad she felt at those words. A lovely young lady who had made a mistake like many others before her, and now she and an unborn babe were dead. Amy swiped at the unexpected tears that welled in her eyes. She reached out and took the paper from William.

"Are you well, Amy?"

Unable to speak just yet, she merely nodded and tucked the papers into her reticule. Taking a deep breath, she looked out the window as they passed the various shops on their way to the Assembly Rooms.

Lord and Lady Carlisle, Mr. Miles and his mother, and several other book club members and friends from church had already gathered. Perhaps it was the temptation of full spring weather, but the atmosphere that night was lively.

Eloise nodded and patted her arm.

All the windows had been thrown open and the gas chandeliers lit. Ladies in lovely pale dresses and rich-colored gowns moved around the room on the arms of debonair gentlemen. Intricate hairdos with numerous adornments, along with the scents of perfumes and talcs, gave the attendees a festive air.

The music swept over the group, loud enough to be enjoyed by the dancers but not so loud as to hinder conversation.

Amy stood with Lady Carlisle, and Mrs. Miles, sipping on a lemonade and watching the activity in the room. "Has there been any news on Mr. St. Vincent's murder?" Lady Carlisle, who once again looked very pale and not well, placed her empty glass on a tray carried by a server.

"Nothing of which I am aware," Amy answered.

Lady Carlisle had been entertaining quite a lot on her husband's behalf. Even though she was more than twenty years younger than Lord Carlisle, the poor woman looked quite worn out. Another reason why Amy had never been enthralled with the idea of marriage. A woman must put aside all her hopes, desires, and enjoyments for the sake of her husband.

If the man wished to uproot his family and move to a foreign country, she had no choice but to go, leaving behind a lifetime of friends and family. If he decided that a much-coveted position was what he wanted, it was expected the wife would do what was necessary to make sure he attained that goal.

Lord and Lady Carlisle did not have children of their own, but his title was secured by two sons born to him and his deceased wife. At least Lady Carlisle didn't face the possibility of moving her children to a foreign land for however many years necessary.

Lady Carlisle shook her head. "One would think if you were under the suspicion of murder, the police would at least keep you informed."

How interesting. Based on Lady Carlisle's words, it appeared Amy's being the main suspect was not a secret.

"I heard that you and Lord Wethington are helping the police with their investigation." Mrs. Miles stared at Amy with an intensity that unnerved her a bit. Although the three of them enjoyed mystery books and shared an interest in the book club, Mrs. Miles had always struck her as a bit odd.

However, it was necessary to veer away from these questions. The less she said, the better. "We have offered a tip or two, but they have told us to not get in their way," Amy laughed.

"The police are very cautious about allowing interference." Mrs. Miles appeared sorry that Amy had no more information to share. Lady Carlisle seemed to have lost interest in the conversation entirely and instead studied the group of men that had congregated on the other side of the room.

William stood with Mr. Miles, Mr. Harris, Lord Carlisle, and Mr. Colbert. As she studied the men, Amy's eyes were caught by a deep-red gown flying past. She grinned at Aunt Margaret, who in turned winked at her as she floated by in Lord Pembroke's arms.

'Twas a good thing Papa wasn't present, because he had never given up on marrying off his younger sister. Had he seen Aunt Margaret with Lord Pembroke, Papa would have been hauling the poor man over to the corner to negotiate marriage contracts.

The music came to an end, and the dancers made their way to the refreshment table or over to the French doors for a bit of fresh air. Amy, Mrs. Miles, and Lady Carlisle crossed the room to join the gentlemen.

Eloise had not attended that week because she was entertaining her cousin, Mr. Burkitt. He was a charming man whom Amy had spent time with before. He joked that dances caused him to itch, so he and Eloise were off to the theater. Amy was sure he was afraid to have the marriage-minded mamas dragging their daughters to him. He was a very confirmed bachelor.

"May I request the honor of the next dance, Lady Amy?" Mr. Harris bowed in her direction.

Apparently, Mr. Harris was going to be a permanent part of their life in Bath. Although she no longer wished to physically harm the man, he was not one of her favorite people. He seemed to have formed a friendship with Mr. Miles that she found interesting. Since she now knew that Mr. Miles was involved in selling illegal opium, it was quite notable that the two men had become such fast friends.

Perhaps Mr. Harris was a new supplier for Mr. Miles, with Mr. St. Vincent dead? That led her to another line of questioning. If Mr. Miles thought what he had paid Mr. St. Vincent was too much for the drugs he in turn sold, would he have murdered Mr. St. Vincent to be able to cut a better deal with whoever inherited the shipping company?

On the other hand, perhaps the new owner would not want to take up an illegal trade at all. Unless Mr. Miles had known Mr. Harris before now.

Now *that* was an interesting idea.

The evening passed in pleasant conversation, with a few hardy dances and a light supper at the end. Feeling quite happy with herself, Amy left on William's arm and headed to his carriage. Aunt Margaret and her escort had disappeared more than an hour before, which had Amy grinning.

And speculating.

As she and William walked from the building to where the carriages were all lined up awaiting their passengers, her eye was caught by Mr. Miles and Lady Carlisle in a deep discussion that appeared not at all friendly.

Mrs. Miles stood by, looking oblivious as her son and Lady Carlisle argued. When the pair noticed several people watching them, Mr. Miles made one final comment, then turned and stormed off. After a few steps, he quickly returned for his mother and nearly dragged the poor woman to their carriage.

Lord Carlisle exited the building then, looked around the group, and joined his wife, who looked none too happy. With a brief word to her, he took her arm, and they headed toward their carriage.

"What do you suppose that was all about?" William asked as he assisted Amy into the coach. He climbed in after her and settled on the seat across.

Amy pulled her wrap closer, a sudden chill overtaking her. "I have no idea. I can't imagine what the two of them would have to disagree about so vehemently. Especially in public."

Slowly the line of vehicles rolled away from the building as she and William recounted the evening and she chastised him for not dancing with her.

"My dear Lady Amy, you were a popular partner this evening. Every time a new number started and I looked for you, you had already been taken."

Amy sniffed and raised her chin in the air, trying her best to hide her grin. "Perhaps the next time you could walk a bit faster toward me?"

He bowed. "Next time I shall race to your side."

They both laughed, just as a splintering sound echoed in the carriage. Immediately the vehicle began to sway. Amy was thrown against the wall, and as William reached out for her, he was tossed to the floor, where they both landed in a heap.

The carriage leaned to one side, and Amy reached up to catch the strap. "What was that?"

William grabbed her around the waist, hauled her back onto the seat, and held on tight. "I would guess one of the wheels snapped."

The sound of the driver's shouts to the horses surpassed the noise from the vehicle bumping along. The carriage slowed and then came to an abrupt stop. Thank goodness William still held her tightly or she would have been tossed to the floor again. Her whole body shook, and she had to force her stomach not to bring up her last meal.

She turned and looked at him, suddenly feeling light-headed. "What happened?"

Before he could answer, black dots appeared in her eyes and she slumped against his body.

CHAPTER 21

Amy attempted to swat away the annoying insect that kept tapping her cheek, but she was unable to lift her arm, which felt quite heavy.

"Amy. Talk to me, Amy. Come on, love, wake up." William's voice, raspy for some reason, filtered into her brain just as she realized she was lying on his lap. She quickly sat up and groaned, grabbing her aching head.

"Thank God." William rested his chin on her head.

"What happened?" She looked up at him and braced herself for bad news, given the serious expression on his face.

"You passed out just as the carriage came to a stop."

Then she remembered. The carriage wheel had broken, and she and William had been tossed around a bit. Her shoulder hurt, and she was certain her body would be black-and-blue in parts tomorrow.

The door to the carriage stood open, and William's driver stepped up to the opening. "It's like I thought, milord. The back wheel snapped. We're lucky it wasn't worse."

"Yes, I agree, it could have been quite serious." William moved to exit the seriously tilting vehicle. It shifted again, and Amy squealed and grasped the edges of the seat.

William sat back down. "John, reach in and take Lady Amy's hand and help her out. I'm afraid my weight might cause more damage to our situation if I climb out first."

The driver reached in and took Amy's hand. "Careful, milady. Just go slowly."

She slid gently forward on the seat and took the man's hand, then stopped and held her breath when the carriage moved again. When it settled, she took another step, and the driver mumbled an apology, grasped her around the waist, and lifted her from the carriage.

Once she was on her feet, she was able to see the damage from the broken wheel. It was a blessing they hadn't been killed. In the meantime, William had exited the vehicle and stood alongside her. "It could have been worse."

"I agree." She wrapped her arms around her middle and shivered. William took off his jacket and draped it around her shoulders. She immediately felt the warmth and inhaled the spicy scent from his soap.

"John, fetch us a hackney so I can get Lady Amy home, and then we will arrange to have the carriage brought to the mews. I'm not sure if it is salvageable, but I will have someone look at it."

He turned to Amy. "I suggest you have your cook fix you a tisane, or maybe have a bit of brandy to help you sleep. You will most likely be sore in the morning, too."

"And you as well," she added.

"Yes." He rolled his shoulders. "I already feel the effects."

"Milord, I was able to secure a hackney." William's driver walked up to them.

"Thank you so much for your driving skills," Amy said as the driver stopped in front of her. "This could have been much worse had you not taken things under control."

The man smiled, and despite the lack of light, she could have sworn he blushed.

William took her arm and walked her to the hackney, gave the driver her direction, and paid him. He helped her into the vehicle, then leaned his arm on the door. "I will call on you tomorrow afternoon to see if you are doing well."

"Thank you. Good night." The door closed, and she was on her way. As the carriage turned onto George Street, she remembered she still wore William's jacket.

★ ★ ★

Three days after the carriage accident, Amy made her way downstairs from her bedchamber to the drawing room. She was still a bit sore, but the black-and-blue marks on her body had begun to fade to an interesting yellow and green. She'd also been suffering from a headache since the accident and wondered if she had struck her head and didn't remember doing it. That could be why she had passed out.

Despite Amy's protestations, Aunt Margaret had insisted on calling a physician, who had checked her over and found her just bruised. He'd left her some laudanum to take twice a day, but Amy had decided to stop that as of today. Her body still pained her in places, especially when she walked, but there would be no more pain medication for her. Since laudanum was a form of opium, the last thing she wanted was to become addicted.

As promised, William had stopped by to ask after her health Sunday afternoon but had not requested to see her, since she was in bed at the time. He later sent a note once again asking after her health and requesting to call on her when she felt able to accept company. The visit had been set for today, and since she was weary of staying indoors, she was delighted to see the lovely spring weather. Their visit would take place in the garden.

Eloise had also visited with her Sunday, keeping her laughing with stories about the activities she and her cousin had been enjoying. She'd also told her she would be traveling to London with her cousin for a short visit. Ordinarily Amy would accompany her, as she'd done many times before, but with the murder investigation, she couldn't leave Bath and didn't want to, anyway.

She carefully eased herself into the most comfortable chair in the room and thought once more on the accident. It was quite lucky that she and William hadn't been killed.

She had barely settled into the chair when Lacey entered the room, her face registering the perpetual look of sympathy she'd adopted since Amy arrived home from the accident. "Milady, Lord Wethington has arrived."

"Thank you. Please ask Cook to prepare tea and a few sandwiches. I am hungry and slept through breakfast once again." As Lacey turned to do as she was bid, Amy added, "Oh, and please serve the tea in the garden. Lord Wethington and I will be strolling there."

"My dear Lady Amy, how are you feeling?" William limped into the room with the help of a cane, a bright smile on his somewhat battered face. He had apparently smacked his head during the accident, because she noted a bruise on his right cheekbone.

"I find each day I feel a little bit better."

'Twas so good to see William. She hadn't realized how much she'd missed him until he hobbled into the room. Maybe experiencing a life-threatening situation together had something to do with it. She now felt an attachment to him she'd hadn't before.

"What happened?" She gestured to the cane.

He smiled and waved the stick around. "Oh, this? I hadn't realized it that night, but I twisted my ankle during the accident and find it much easier to walk with the help of my friend here."

"Lacey is arranging for tea. Also some sandwiches, if you are hungry. I thought we could take a walk in the garden and have our tea out there."

"Ah, I can always use a bit of food. And a stroll in the garden sounds like a splendid idea." He withdrew a paper from inside his jacket. "Although I am glad to see you, to make sure you are still in one piece, there is a particular reason I needed to speak with you."

Amy opened her mouth to respond as Lacey returned once more to the room. "Milady, the two detectives are here and want to speak with you."

Botheration. Amy groaned. Her head immediately began to throb harder, and she wanted nothing more than to ask Lacey to refuse them entrance so she could enjoy William's visit. However, the detectives hadn't even waited for Lacey to return but trooped in right behind her.

Amy sighed. "Good afternoon, Detectives."

They came to an abrupt stop as they looked at William. "What happened to you?"

"Lady Amy and I were in a bit of an accident Saturday evening."

Detective Carson sat, with Detective Marsh taking the chair across from him. Reluctantly she took a seat on the settee, where William joined her. They formed a cozy little group, and Amy wished them to perdition.

Marsh shook his head. "An accident, eh?"

William cleared his throat to gain the detectives' attention. "Lady Amy and I were returning from the Assembly Rooms Saturday evening when my carriage wheel broke."

"No dead body this time, Lady Amy?" Carson smirked at her, which set her head to throbbing even more.

"Nasty business," Marsh said as he flipped open his ever-present notepad and pulled a pencil from his pocket. "The roads need to be dealt with. Too many ruts in the streets."

Still annoyed at their interruption, Amy said, "How can I help you, Detectives?"

"Just a few questions about some of your friends." Carson grinned. She didn't trust that man at all. She straightened in the chair as best she could and stared at him. "Indeed? Why are you concerned with my friends?"

Marsh scratched the side of his nose. "Well, we haven't uncovered any friends that St. Vincent had by talking to his employees at his shipping company, or his neighborhood. It seemed the man kept to himself. So, it appeared to us that his social life must have revolved around you and your friends, since he was your fiancé."

"Ex-fiancé."

"I have a list here of those who turned up as having an association with you, that most likely had some contact with Mr. St. Vincent."

There was no way to get out of this, since it would be impolite for her as a dignified lady to rise and march from the room, leaving William to deal with them. "Very well. Whom do you wish to know about?"

"Mr. Richard Miles."

What was it they wanted to know about him? Should she tell the detectives about Mr. Miles's drug involvement? Unless they asked specifically, she decided to remain silent about that.

"He is a member of my book club, the Mystery Book Club of Bath. We meet every Thursday evening at Atkinson and Tucker bookstore. Mr. St. Vincent attended with me a few times but was not an active member, so I don't think he and Mr. Miles were actually friends."

Carson leaned back in his chair, his eyes sharp and questioning. "Did you know Mr. Miles sells illegal drugs?"

They had done their homework. "I can't imagine how I would know that."

Unless you asked your gardener about his drug use and he then identified Mr. Miles as his drug provider.

Since they had known about her seeing Mr. Miles and Mr. Harris at the Pump Room, and that Mr. Harris had danced with her and proposed to her, who knew what these men—to whom she'd obviously not given enough credit—had also learned? Did they know she was lying?

Detective Marsh looked down at his notepad as Detective Carson said, "Lady Suzanne Carlisle."

Suzanne? Even Amy hadn't known the woman's first name. She shook her head. "Again, she is a member of my book club. All I know of her is she attends the Assembly Room dances most Saturdays, and it is said her husband is waiting for an appointment from the Queen as ambassador to France. Her contact with Mr. St. Vincent was slight. No more than conversation at the meetings he attended."

A quick flash of an agitated Lady Carlisle arguing with Mr. Miles outside the Assembly Room the Saturday before stopped her for a moment, but as odd as that seemed, that wouldn't have any connection to Mr. St. Vincent.

Marsh continued to take notes while Detective Carson shot names at her. "Mrs. Gertrude Miles."

Good heavens, were they going to go down the entire book club membership? "She is Mr. Miles's mother, and a lovely, sweet woman. She is quite fond of mystery books and enjoys our book club meetings."

"Any connection other than that to Mr. St. Vincent?"

"No."

It had just occurred to Amy that the reason for all the questions about other people, individuals whom they should have asked about long before now, was that they could not find absolute proof that Amy had killed St. Vincent and were finally considering other suspects. Surely she would have been dragged off to jail by now if they had proof.

Lacey entered the room with the tea cart. Since it appeared Amy and William would not be taking a stroll in the garden anytime soon, the maid had obviously made the correct decision and brought the tea to the drawing room.

Amy breathed a sigh of relief to have the questioning stopped for a bit. "Detectives, may I offer you tea?"

"No. But you go ahead," Marsh said as he continued to write in his pad.

Despite it being poor manners, she really needed a cup of tea and some food. She was already beginning to feel light-headed. "I believe I will indulge." She turned to William. "My lord?"

Carson snickered.

Amy regarded him with raised brows. "Is something wrong, Detective?"

"You toffs always get me. Every time we've come, the lad here is parked nice and cozy with you in this room. He stood alongside you when you found two dead bodies, and he was in the carriage with you when it went for a nasty spill. Yet you still address him as *my lord*." He chuckled, and Amy considered throwing the teapot at the man's head.

Unfortunately, the lovely pink-and-white-flowered china piece had been her mother's and was Amy's favorite, so she resisted the urge. Instead she smiled warmly. "It is called good manners, Detective. I am quite sorry you don't recognize them."

William choked on the tea he had just taken a sip of.

Some time after Amy served the tea, both detectives stood. They had also asked about Mr. Colbert, Lord Temple, and his daughter Lady Abigail. Each answer had been the same. Barely acquainted with Mr. St. Vincent.

"That is all for now. I understand the bloke your father hired to do his own investigation is under the weather."

Amy patted her lips with the napkin. "Yes, Sir Holstein apparently ingested some bad food. He is no longer working for my father."

Carson nodded. "Good." He studied her and William with a piercing stare. "We don't need anyone except the police investigating a murder."

With a nod, they left the room, and Amy let out her breath. "I really do not like those men."

William looked down at the paper he still clutched in his hand. "Now I can tell you what I tried to say before the detectives arrived."

"What is that?"

"My driver asked the coach-maker when he arrived at our mews to inspect the carriage." William opened the paper and stared down at it, then looked up at Amy.

"The spokes on the right rear wheel had been deliberately cut."

CHAPTER 22

"Deliberately cut?" Amy's jaw dropped as she stared at William and repeated his words. The wheel on the carriage they had been riding in had been damaged on purpose. In other words, someone had wanted her and William either seriously injured or dead.

Dead.

No more investigation if we are dead.

"I believe we are making the true murderer very nervous." William shifted in his seat and winced. He obviously had hidden injuries on his body similar to her black-and-blue marks.

Slowly she recovered from the shock of his words. "So am I to assume you no longer believe that Miss Hemphill killed Mr. St. Vincent?" She certainly had not been convinced, but William and Aunt Margaret had wanted to believe. Or at least had wanted *her* to believe that was the case.

William adjusted again, apparently unable to get into a comfortable position. The poor man must have been hurting. "It appears not. Unless she arranged before her death to have someone cut the wheels on my carriage. That, however, is a bit of a stretch."

Amy thought for a minute. "Do you think we should have shared that information with the police? They might stop looking so hard at me if they knew that."

"Frankly, I wanted to speak with you about it first, since we have so little faith in their investigation. I could always make a visit to the police building."

Amy took a sip of tea as she reviewed all the facts and information they had gathered thus far. "Perhaps we should hold off for a bit. They are now looking beyond me, it seems, with all the questions about Mr. St. Vincent's friends and acquaintances. It gives us a bit of an edge in finding the murderer."

"Or the murderer finding us, as it appears from the cut wheel."

"That is true." She placed her teacup in the saucer and wiped her mouth on her napkin. "However, if our serious injury or death was the plan for the cut wheel, and the police are also investigating Mr. St. Vincent's murder, is the killer going to attempt to do away with the entire police department?"

The concern in his eyes warmed her. "It appears whoever murdered Mr. St. Vincent feels we are closer to him than the police are. Since our favorite detectives had been focused on only you until now, the culprit could very well be correct in his assumption. If he noticed, as we did, that the police stubbornly continued in the same direction while we have broadened our search, then it follows that we would find Mr. St. Vincent's killer first."

Amy raised her finger. "But not if we are dead."

"Correct."

She shivered. "If the killer is right and we have a better chance of exposing him than the police, then one of the people we have been considering is our man."

William's hand stopped as it was bringing his teacup to his lips, and he regarded her over the cup. "Just so."

They finished their tea and the small sandwiches and biscuits Cook had sent in, both of them consumed with their own thoughts. Amy wiped her mouth and placed the napkin alongside her plate. "It might be a good idea to go over a few things while we are together. I find that since the accident I feel quite weary and ready for a nap after being awake for only a few hours.

"With the detectives questioning me about some of our friends, it brought to mind the argument we witnessed between Mr. Miles and Lady Carlisle last Saturday while leaving the Assembly Rooms." It had meant very little to her that night, but now, in light of the "accident" not really being an accident and the police finally spreading their net wider, as it were, perhaps it did mean something. After all, Mr. Miles was involved in nefarious behavior of which the police seemed to be aware.

William studied his shoes, his lips pursed and brows furrowed. "I can't imagine what those two would have to argue about. But then, it could have been anything at all. Perhaps they'd danced and he stepped on her toes." He smiled, and she chuckled.

"A good theory, my lord, but I've never seen Mr. Miles dance at any of those events. I'm sure he only comes to escort his mother, who seems to thoroughly enjoy the evenings out."

"Or, since he's in the illegal drug market, it is a way to innocuously maintain contact with those to whom he sells."

Amy straightened in her seat. "Do you think he is selling to people we know? Those who attend our book club meetings, sewing circles, and Assembly Room dances? I always assumed his customers were from the lower end of Bath."

William smiled at her as if she were a mere child needing a lesson on deportment. "Amy, surely you know that the use of opium is not restricted to the unfortunate members of society? It is well known to be a plague among all ranks of citizens."

"No, I did not know that. But then, I am busy killing people—in books, that is—and never reflected on the current problem with drug use. This is very interesting. Perhaps I need to add that to a plot in one of my books."

"And when you add that most likely those of our rank in society would not be visiting an illegal opium den, it becomes even more interesting. Perhaps in London that would happen and could go unnoticed to some degree with the size of the city, but in Bath"—he shook his head—"it would be much too dangerous to visit an opium den and have it not become common knowledge."

"The police said they know Mr. Miles is selling drugs, yet he remains free."

"It is my guess they are hoping to catch whoever is providing Miles with the drugs more than the local distributor."

"Mr. Harris," they both said at once.

"That would be more of a boon, to stop the flow of drugs into the country."

Amy considered what he said. "Then, if we want a connection between Mr. Miles and Mr. St. Vincent, we need to look at Mr. Miles's drug business." She stopped for a moment, starting to feel weary, something she had experienced ever since the accident.

Which, it turned out, had not been an accident at all.

"I apologize; I am getting tired. There is a connection, since Mr. Albright identified Mr. Miles as the man who sold him drugs, and we know from Miss Hemphill's note that Mr. St. Vincent was importing the drugs."

"Yes. I think we considered this before. But why kill your fiancé since he was providing the drugs?"

"Ex-fiancé."

William climbed to his feet, leaning on his cane. "I believe I will leave you now. I have an appointment with the coachmaker, and I can see you are ready for some rest."

They walked to the front door together, where William took his leave, and Amy slowly mounted the stairs to her bedchamber and climbed onto her bed, staring at the overhead canopy. The last thought she had before drifting off was to wonder why Lady Carlisle and Mr. Miles had been arguing.

★ ★ ★

The following Friday, Amy again awaited William's arrival. He'd sent a note around saying that if she was as disgruntled at being confined due to the last few days of rain as he was, they should take a ride in the park and perhaps a walk in the shops area.

Amy perked up when William's note arrived. She was truly ready to cast off the malaise that had struck her since the accident and had been compounded by the foul weather. The air had warmed, and the sky was bright blue. She was ready for some fresh air and maybe even a visit to one of the tea shops.

She washed and dressed her hair, and with her clothing covering her bruises, she looked almost normal. Persephone had been content to just lie around since the accident, keeping her mistress company while stuck indoors.

"Persephone. It's time for some fresh air." The dog looked up from where she was enjoying her nap by the fireplace in Amy's room. Lazily, she climbed to her feet and stretched.

Instead of awaiting Lacey's summons, Amy made her way downstairs and settled into a comfortable chair in the drawing room. Persephone jumped up onto the chair and collapsed onto Amy's lap. "You're getting very lazy." She glanced out the window, again grateful for the lovely, sunny weather.

The sound of carriage wheels caught her attention. She pushed the window curtain aside for a clearer view and watched as a brand-new carriage with the Wethington crest on the door rolled to a stop in front of the house.

In less than a minute, the door knocker sounded, and Lacey opened the door to William. He was no longer using his cane but did walk slowly into the room.

"Well, it appears we are looking at least good enough to face the world." William grinned as he walked forward and took Amy's extended hand. "It is a pleasure, as always, to see you, Lady Amy."

She gave him a dip and returned his smile. "And you as well, my lord."

Since they'd both missed the book club meeting the night before, they hadn't spoken since William's previous visit, when the detectives had been questioning her.

Amy retrieved Persephone's leash from Lacey, who stood at the door. William helped her down the stairs and into the carriage with all the finesse of a gentleman caller.

He cringed as Persephone jumped onto the deep-green velvet seat covering, walked in a small circle, and then plopped down, her head resting on her front paws.

"Don't be concerned. She just had a bath." Amy smoothed her hand over the fabric. "This is lovely. I can't believe you were able to secure a new carriage so quickly."

"It helps to be prompt to pay your bills. Mr. Granger, who makes such excellent coaches, had one in the making that was being held up for payment. I waved the correct amount of blunt in his face, and he quickly substituted the crest he'd already painted with mine."

Amy smoothed her skirt and looked around the carriage. "I know the upper crust are notorious for not paying invoices or paying them late. I always try to take care of my bills promptly as well. The people who do the work have families to feed. It is quite unfair to expect them to wait for their money."

William dipped his head. "Very noble of you, Lady Amy. I wish more of our ilk felt the same way." It had taken a few minutes to get them settled, and then William tapped on the ceiling and the coach was off.

"I didn't realize your carriage had been completely destroyed."

"It hadn't, but when we discussed the repairs necessary, and I took into account that it was already twelve years old, I decided to go for a new one."

"Would you think me a silly goose if I told you my heart is hammering in my chest at being in a carriage once again?" Amy attempted a smile but didn't think she'd quite made it.

William reached across the space separating them and took her hand. "Not at all. Truth be known, I am a bit uneasy myself. But for our peace of mind, I had my driver check everything about the carriage before we left.

"He was extremely upset that he did not notice the wheel had been ruined the night of the accident. I attempted to convince him 'twas not his fault, but the man still feels guilty. Especially, he said, because 'that lovely young lady' was in the carriage."

Amy grinned. "How nice of him to say that. And I agree; unless he was in the habit of always checking the wheels before taking off, there is no reason to feel guilty about not checking it that evening."

"Not at all. He'd done nothing different. After dropping off their passengers, the drivers steer the carriages over into the empty lot next to the Assembly Rooms, where they gather and have a bit of conversation and a spot or two of drink. Apparently, someone waited until all the drivers were busy before they did the damage."

William was such a nice man to not fault his driver for the mishap. So many men would have given the driver a tongue-lashing, or even sacked him. Another reason she felt William was truly an upstanding man.

It unsettled her a bit that the list of his good points was growing. And the fact that she was unsettled merely unsettled her more.

Once the carriage came to a stop at the entrance to the park, the driver quickly jumped from his perch and opened the door. He helped William down, by which his lordship seemed a bit taken aback, and then assisted Amy out of the vehicle.

"I could certainly have helped her ladyship out of the carriage," William groused at the man.

The driver merely gave William a sharp salute. "I will be waiting right here for you when you are finished with your walk, milord."

"Thank you." William took Amy's arm and moved her onto the footpath. "I hope John gets over his guilt soon. I am beginning to feel like he is my mother."

Amy laughed and looked over her shoulder at the huge man with the full mustache and beard. "He doesn't look like anyone's mother."

"Ah, but you have not met mine." His crooked smile left her wondering if he was serious or joking.

Every year Amy thought autumn was her favorite season until the following spring arrived and she changed her mind. The new light-green leaves on the trees, the sweet-scented grass, and the carefully planted and pruned flowers all raised her spirits after a long, dreary winter. She and William strolled along, not speaking of anything in particular, almost as if by mutual agreement leaving the subject of murder, killers, and annoying detectives behind for the afternoon.

Persephone was on her good behavior and walked alongside them, sniffing the ground, but otherwise not pulling and making the walk difficult. They chatted amicably, taking a complete circle around the park, stopping to speak with several others who were enjoying the lovely day.

"Would you care to ride over to Sally Lunn's and get one of her famous buns? It's been a while since I've had one," William said as they headed toward the waiting carriage.

"Yes, I believe I would. I haven't had one of Sally Lunn's buns in ages. I always think of that poem: *No more I heed the muffin's zest / The Yorkshire cake or bun, / Sweet Muse of Pastry! teach me how / To make a Sally Lunn.*"

"I thought there was a great deal more to the rhyme." William assisted her into the carriage.

Amy laughed. "There is. But I only remember the first four lines and the last four: *But heed thou well to lift thy thought / To me thy power divine; / Then to oven's glowing mouth / The wondrous work consign.*"

"Then we shall make a visit to Sally Lunn's and enjoy one of her famous buns that no one has the recipe for." He settled across from her. "One thing I want to tell you before I forget." William held on to the strap as the carriage moved forward. "It's been a pleasant day, and not one where a discussion on murder and mayhem seems appropriate."

"I agree. It was rather nice to keep all of that at bay." She studied his suddenly serious demeanor.

"I made it to my club yesterday for a short time. And I happened upon the man who told me about the argument between Mr. Harris and your fiancé."

"Ex-fiancé."

"The gentleman, Mr. Roswell, had apparently been with a friend when they witnessed the argument. His friend heard more than Roswell had and related to him recently that Mr. Harris and Mr. St. Vincent were arguing about the uncle cutting off the nephew's funds. Mr. St. Vincent was heard to say Harris would get nothing until St. Vincent died."

The carriage hit a deep rut in the road and swayed a bit, and both Amy and William grabbed on to the strap, their fearful eyes meeting. Amy held her breath and clutched Persephone, but the carriage continued on just fine.

William let out a breath and continued. "Mr. Harris then remarked something to the effect that Mr. St. Vincent's death might not be so very far off."

Amy licked her suddenly dry lips. "And Mr. St. Vincent was murdered the following week."

Chapter 23

Monday afternoon Amy climbed out of William's carriage and tugged on the hem of her jacket. "I'm not absolutely certain we can fool this man. We don't really know much about shipping products."

William took her elbow and escorted her to the front door of the RSV Worldwide Shipping Company. He studied the plaque on the door and shook his head. "Not a very innovative name."

"It's St. Vincent's initials," Amy pointed out. "Personally, I always thought shipping companies should have exotic names, like the East India Tea Company."

They had made an appointment with Mr. Harris to purportedly learn about shipping. The excuse they were using was that Amy wanted to make some investments and that William had advised her that shipping and railroads were the best investments.

Since they knew Mr. Harris had a need for cash to prop up the newly inherited business, it was assured that he would be delighted to see them.

Even though she and St. Vincent had been betrothed, she'd never been to his place of business. It was an older brick building, in somewhat good repair. The front area was dedicated to an office, with a large area in back that was most likely used to store products that arrived from his ships.

A man sitting at an older wooden desk rose as they entered the office. He was in his midtwenties, with the popular moustache and beard found on so many men. Although, with his young age and light hair color, it didn't look quite so manly.

He smiled, walked around the desk, and extended his hand to William. "Good day. I am Mr. Haverstock, Mr. Harris's clerk. I assume you are Lady Amy Lovell and Lord Wethington?"

William took the man's hand, and they shook. "Yes, we are. I believe we are expected?"

"Yes. Mr. Harris is awaiting you. If you will follow me, I will escort you to his office."

He led them down a narrow hallway, not very well lit. Amy found herself reaching for William's hand as he walked in front of her. Goodness, she had to get over this nervous reaction she had been having to things ever since the carriage accident. She had never been of a timorous nature, and it didn't sit well with her.

Mr. Harris stood as they entered the room. He smiled brightly, no doubt gleeful at the idea of getting his hands on her money after all, and without having to subject himself to marrying an unfortunate woman who had no other prospects.

His office was much more opulent than the clerk's space. But that was to be expected. No doubt St. Vincent had decorated his office with the idea of impressing potential clients with his wealth.

Which, of course, didn't exist.

"I have heard rumors that you were involved in a carriage accident on the way home from the Assembly Rooms." Mr. Harris waved them to chairs in front of his desk, then took the fine leather one behind it.

"Yes. My carriage wheel shattered, and we were sent tumbling through the vehicle. Fortunately, my driver was able to stop the carriage before there were any serious injuries."

Mr. Harris shook his head. "The city really must do something about these roads. They are not safe, and someone will be killed one day."

Amy studied him as he spoke, looking for anything in his demeanor that implied guilt at their injuries. Had he been the one to cut the wheel? Unfortunately for their investigation, he looked only curious and annoyed at the city for the poor maintenance of the roads.

They settled into their seats, and Harris rubbed his hands together. She refrained from rolling her eyes at his eagerness. Had the man no sense of refinement?

"Haverstock said you are interested in placing Lady Amy's money in shipping?" He directed his comment to William, which immediately annoyed her. It was her money they were pretending to invest, but he bypassed her as if she weren't even there.

William leaned back in his chair in a restful pose, his foot resting on his bent knee. He flipped the sides of his jacket back and stuck his thumbs into the small pockets in the font of his vest.

Harris, on the other hand, leaned forward, all excitement. *Things must really be bad in the business*, Amy thought.

"Actually, Lady Amy came to me for advice on how to invest a small portion of money she recently inherited. Since she is of age, it came directly to her and not through her father."

Harris nodded. "Yes."

Now it appeared William was purposely dragging out his comments, most likely to tantalize their target. She tried hard to hide her smile.

"I do a fairly good job of managing my own portfolio, so I took a look at what I felt was best for her ladyship, and it appeared to me that transportation is a sound venture."

"Yes, yes." More nodding. The man was practically drooling.

"I told her either railroads or shipping would be best."

For the first time Mr. Harris acknowledged her by swinging his attention in her direction. "No, my lady. If I might offer a bit of advice myself. Railroads are not going to last. Too many problems with time schedules and such. Trains breaking down, unreliable, and so forth. You want to put your money into an industry that has been around almost since the beginning of time. Shipping is the soundest way to grow your money."

Good heavens! She could almost feel the man fishing around in her pocket for the blunt to pour into his business. No one would ever accuse Mr. Harris of being circumspect.

William leaned his chair back on two legs. "Not sure I agree with you there, old boy. I have found railroad investments to be quite profitable."

Harris waved him off. "Right now, perhaps, but over the long road they will collapse. I am sure of it." He looked over at Amy again. "I can assure you any money invested in shipping—especially in this company—would give you a satisfactory return."

It was time for her to step in and have her say. "I assume you would be willing to turn over your books if I decided to invest in RSV Worldwide Shipping?"

Harris hesitated slightly. "Of course. I would just need a few days to bring everything up-to-date."

A few days to alter the books, he meant.

All this chatter was an excellent way to break the ice, as it were, but they needed to get the information necessary to decide how likely it was that the man sitting in front of them had plunged a knife into his uncle's chest.

William cleared his throat. "Mr. Harris. I must admit to some reluctance in recommending your company in particular to Lady Amy due to some rumblings I've heard in my club about your late uncle. In fact, in all honesty, if Lady Amy hadn't insisted upon it, I would not have encouraged this visit at all."

The happy, jolly, eager-to-please man disappeared in a flash, and a cautious one took his place. Mr. Harris eased back in his chair and rearranged his features into what could only be called a mask. "Indeed? Would you care to elaborate, Wethington?"

"In my financial circles there have been rumors that RSV Worldwide Shipping is a bit behind in paying bills."

Before William had finished speaking, Harris was shaking his head vehemently. "No. Not at all. If that were the case, it would only be because of my uncle's unfortunate death and the transition of the business from him to myself. It is quite possible some things had been overlooked, but I assure you, RSV Worldwide Shipping pays its bills."

They might as well get straight to the point. "Did you and your uncle get on, Mr. Harris?" Before he could answer, she added, "I only ask because he never mentioned you to me in the time we were courting."

If the man thought there was anything odd about her asking that question in the middle of a discussion on investing money, he didn't show it. He did, however, take his time in answering. "Your fiancé was my mother's brother."

"Ex-fiancé."

"My dear mother favored her brother over the others in the family. She died when I was sixteen years old and named my uncle as guardian for myself and my younger sister." He leaned back in his chair as he continued to speak. "I won't say Uncle and I were close, but we tolerated each other."

Amy flashed back to her dance with Mr. Harris, when he had thanked her for killing Mr. St. Vincent. Apparently the toleration they had for one another was stretched quite thin.

"Were you privy to his business before he died?" William said. "I just wonder how well the business will be run in the future if you only 'tolerated' each other. It would seem to me that you didn't have the information needed to run such a large company."

At least that question had something to do with the reason they were visiting. If they went too far afield, Mr. Harris might suspect something and refuse to answer any questions at all.

On the other hand, if he was in as dire straits as William's man of business reported, he would put up with quite a bit of nosiness to get his hands on her money.

"You are correct on that point, my lord. I tried several times to get my uncle to bring me into the business. Learn how to run it and all that. But perhaps he merely felt that by doing so he was contemplating his death, since I was to inherit."

Or encouraging his nephew to plan the event.

"That is true, but he did draw up a will, which is the same thing," Amy said.

William leaned forward. "There was an argument outside Mr. St. Vincent's townhouse a few weeks ago. I was surprised to hear that, since I was under the impression that you did not reside in England but had spent most of your time on the Continent. I only ask because of my concern for Lady Amy's investment, you understand."

Amy couldn't imagine how the argument between nephew and uncle would affect money she wanted to invest, but if Mr. Harris didn't question it, she had no intention of pointing that fact out to him. She had to admit, for someone who might have committed a murder, he seemed somewhat relaxed in speaking of the man.

Mr. Harris ran his fingers through his hair. "Yes. I am sorry for that, too. Especially in light of his death only a few days later. In fact, after that argument, I left for London, where I stayed with my younger sister and her husband, who had just welcomed a new child. I returned to Bath once I received the message of my uncle's demise."

William's eyebrows shot up. "You were in London when he was killed?"

"Yes. I needed time to cool off. When I say Uncle and I tolerated each other, I was being generous. He had no liking for me, nor me for him. In fact, he paid me to stay away from him." The man's shoulders slumped. "I would have liked to have had a better relationship, but he had no interest in me. He sent an allowance each month so I could live the life of a gentleman, but I would have much preferred to earn my living by working alongside him."

All the air went out of Amy's lungs. Not only had Mr. Harris not even been in Bath when St. Vincent was killed—and she was sure that if they checked that fact, it would be true—but he seemed to be almost sorry for the way he and his uncle had not gotten along.

She looked over at William, who stared back at her. They would now have to cross Mr. Harris off their list of suspects. Which, at this point, left only Mr. Miles.

It annoyed her that there was something in the back of her mind that kept nudging at her, but she could not recall it. Scattered pieces which might add up if she put them all together.

Since the reason for their visit had been settled, there was no reason to continue the conversation. She nodded at Mr. Harris. "I want to thank you for answering our questions." She looked over at William. "Did you have any more questions, my lord?"

William shook his head. "No."

Harris looked between them, obviously confused. "Would you care to have your man of business look over my books?"

There didn't seem to be any point in doing that, except to see how badly these false funds were needed. Then she remembered there was still the question of Mr. Miles and Mr. Harris continuing the drug trade that St. Vincent had. How would those transactions appear in the books? Or would they not be there at all?

With Mr. Miles being the final name on their list, seeing the business records for the last few years might give them the necessary evidence to convict Mr. Miles.

"Actually, Mr. Harris, it might be a good idea for Lord Wethington's man of business, Mr. Harding, to take a look at the records." She turned to William. "Can you arrange that, my lord?"

"Yes. Of course." William didn't seem surprised at her request, so perhaps his thoughts ran along the same line.

William stood and pulled back her chair. The two men shook hands, and they all traversed the dimly lit corridor once again to the small office at the front of the building. The clerk was busy writing but stood as they reached his desk.

He smiled and offered a slight bow. "Have a nice day, my lord, my lady."

"Thank you."

William grasped Amy's elbow, and they made their way out of the building and to the carriage.

Once they were on their way, William said, "If what Mr. Harris says is truth, and he was in London when your fiancé was killed—"

"Ex-fiancé."

"—then there is no need to pursue him."

Amy sighed. "Yes. I mentally crossed Mr. Harris off too, based on his comments. It is a simple matter to write to this sister and ascertain that he was there during the time he said. He would not lie about it, since it is too easy to disprove. That might be why the police weren't looking in his direction. They might have already questioned him and were satisfied with his answers."

William nodded. "Which could be why his name was not brought up when they questioned you. I did wonder about that at the time."

As much as she would have liked to circle back to Mr. Miles as a suspect, there didn't seem to be a strong reason for Miles to kill St. Vincent. If Mr. Miles lost his drug supplier, there would always be the chance that the new owner would not want to be involved with the drug trade. Miles would be taking a huge gamble by murdering her fiancé.

Ex-fiancé.

The situation had become frustrating. Her biggest fear was that if they could not come up with someone else, then the police would naturally turn back to her. Someone had killed Mr. St. Vincent. Someone in her garden. That was the main consideration. Had Mr. St. Vincent arrived with someone else, and had they gone to the garden together?

But she had questioned her staff, and they'd never mentioned anyone arriving with Mr. St. Vincent. Every time she answered one question, another came up. Solving a real-life murder mystery was harder than writing about one, where she could decide all the finer points to keep her readers guessing.

William sat up in his seat and peered out the window. "I say, isn't that Lady Carlisle and Mrs. Miles?" He pointed to two women, one with her arms flying about as she spoke and one patiently listening, appearing to try to soothe the other woman. They were having their discussion in front of one of the fishmonger shops.

Amy scooted to the edge of the seat and looked. "Yes. That is definitely them." She turned to William. "You must have your driver stop so we can offer our assistance."

William tapped on the ceiling of the vehicle, and the carriage came to a stop about twenty feet in front of the women.

She and William both left the carriage and hurried toward them. Lady Carlisle appeared agitated and was perspiring quite heavily. Her face was pasty white, and she kept trying to loosen the hold Mrs. Miles had on her.

The older woman looked distraught, and relief flooded her face when she spotted Amy and William approaching them. "Oh, my dears, I am so very glad to see you. It seems Lady Carlisle has taken ill."

Lady Carlisle ripped her arm away from Mrs. Miles, who was clinging to her as if she expected the woman to race down the street.

"Lady Carlisle, are you unwell?" Amy asked as she walked slowly to her. The woman did look more than a little out of sorts. Her eyes moved rapidly back and forth, almost as if she was consumed with fear and looking for a way to run.

"I am not unwell, Lady Amy. I will just continue with my walk. Thank you for your concern." She took only a few steps and then stopped and gripped her middle, letting out a slight groan.

Amy touched her on the shoulder, and she jumped. "Lady Carlisle, we have Lord Wethington's carriage with us. I think it would be best if we escorted you home."

Lady Carlisle pulled away. "No. I will walk. But thank you." She hurried away, leaving Mrs. Miles, Amy, and William staring after her.

"Should we insist?" Amy asked William.

"No. Something is troubling her, and she needs to walk it off." He turned to Mrs. Miles. "May we offer you a ride home, Mrs. Miles?"

"No. Thank you very much, but my son, Richard, is visiting with Mr. Harris and will arrive shortly. I will just spend some time in the shops." With a brief smile, she turned and headed to the millinery shop.

Amy and William looked at each other. "What the devil was that all about?" William asked.

"I assure you that I have no idea." Amy stared at Mrs. Miles's back as she disappeared into the store. After walking only a few steps, Amy gasped.

"What?"

She continued to watch where Lady Carlisle had run off to. "I knew there was something I was overlooking."

"And that is?"

"I have a strong suspicion that Lady Carlisle is not suffering from exhaustion due to too many dinner parties on behalf of her husband."

"And?" William said.

"I'm beginning to think Lady Carlisle might be addicted to opium."

CHAPTER 24

Amy growled in frustration as she attempted to adjust her dress with her bruises still not completely healed. It wasn't so much the pain of movement, since that had ceased, but she still showed some fading black-and-blue marks on her arms that the dress didn't cover. The garment was twisted about, and as much as she resisted having someone help her dress, she marched to her bedroom door, flung it open, and called for Lacey.

"What do you need, milady?" Lacey hurried into the room, took one look at the twisted mess Amy had made of her dress, and burst into laughter. "Oh, I am so sorry for laughing, but you look quite funny."

Despite her annoyance at the situation, Amy had to laugh when she turned and looked at herself in the mirror. Yes, she was a clothing disaster. "Help me straighten this out, please. Try your best to cover the fading bruises. Lord Wethington will be here shortly to escort me to the book club meeting."

"Maybe you should choose another dress, or maybe take a shawl with you."

"No. The book club room is always over-warm. Just see if you can adjust the sleeves a bit, and maybe add a lace collar to the bodice. There is one in my armoire that would go nicely with the dress."

Lacey retrieved the collar, placed it around Amy's neck, and began to move it in various ways to cover the fading mark on her upper chest. "We are seeing quite a bit of Lord Wethington lately."

"What does that mean?" Amy said as she watched Lacey in the mirror.

The maid tried very ineffectively to hide her smile. "Nothing."

Amy bent her head so she could see Lacey's face. "What you said was not nothing. Every word has a meaning, and complete sentences have an even greater meaning."

Lacey smiled. "My goodness, you are a tad touchy about his lordship."

Touchy? She was touchy? She could only be described as confused. For goodness' sake, although they'd not been much more than friendly acquaintances before the murder, she'd known the man for years. They met each week at the book club, they shared ideas, they'd danced a few times at the Assembly Rooms.

Now she was spending a great deal of time with him, and he was escorting her places where only a few weeks ago she would have gone by herself. The Assembly Rooms, the book club. For heaven's sake, last week he'd even arrived on Sunday morning to escort her to church! And joining them for lunch after church had become a weekly ritual.

Not that she was complaining. She found his company extremely enjoyable. He was always dressed as a gentleman and even smelled good. William was witty, charming, and possessed of a smile that had on occasion done strange things to her insides.

"I would not say I am touchy. I am merely attempting to keep everything in its . . . proper place." She fumbled the words, grunting as Lacey tugged on the sleeve of her dress. Even she had no idea what that ridiculous statement meant.

"There!" Lacey stood back and looked at Amy's reassembled outfit. "I think you look lovely, and his lordship will think so as well." Before Amy could retort with another unintelligible, clever sentence, Lacey raced from the room, the sound of her laughter trailing behind her.

★　★　★

When she and William arrived at the Atkinson & Tucker bookstore that night, most of the other members had already assembled. William joined a group of men and Amy headed toward Lady Carlisle, who stood with Mrs. Miles, Lady Abigail, and Mrs. Morton.

Amy noted that Lady Carlisle's appearance and demeanor were significantly better than they had been the last few times she had seen her. She appeared very relaxed, almost sleepy. "Good evening, Lady Amy; how nice to see you."

"And you as well, Lady Carlisle." Amy turned to the other ladies and nodded a good evening to them, then turned her attention back to Lady Carlisle. "You are looking so much better than the last time we met."

She waved her off. "I must apologize for that. I'm afraid I was having a bad day. You need not concern yourself."

As the group conversed, Amy studied Lady Carlisle, amazed at the difference in the woman. She was quite cheerful, smiling and nodding at the story Lady Abigail was relating. She seemed to find things funny in Lady Abigail's story that no one else thought amusing.

Lady Abigail and Mrs. Morton cast curious glances at Lady Carlisle, but Mrs. Miles seemed oblivious to the woman's behavior. Almost as if she didn't see anything odd about it, or didn't notice that Lady Carlisle's behavior that evening was in serious contrast to the way she'd behaved on the streets of Bath when she had raced away from them in an extremely agitated state.

Shortly after the last of the members arrived, Mr. Colbert called the meeting to order, and they all moved toward the chairs. William sat next to Amy, with Mrs. Miles on the sofa across from them and Lady Carlisle next to her, whispering to Mrs. Morton, giggling like a schoolgirl.

William turned to Amy with raised brows.

Amy shook her head and shrugged.

The discussion of their latest book began, but didn't hold Amy's interest. Contemplating a pretend murder was not as interesting as pondering a real one. Especially when she had no reason to believe the police had uncovered anything in their investigation that would point to someone other than her.

On another note, she was certain that once Papa discovered his man had bowed out of the investigation and Amy had not secured the services of the replacement Sir Holstein had referred to her, there would be repercussions from London. Something she was certainly not looking forward to. If Papa learned of Sir Holstein's defection, it would be much more pleasant if he sent Michael in his place to chastise her and see to hiring a replacement. She could manipulate her brother better than she could Papa.

She did feel a twinge of guilt, knowing that Papa remained in London with peace of mind because he thought Sir Holstein was on the job and therefore looking out for her. He would be livid when he learned she had placed herself in danger by ignoring the investigator's advice.

Her mind was drawn back to the discussion at hand. Lady Carlisle didn't seem interested in the book either, and it appeared most of the other members were also drifting away. Either the book they were discussing—thank goodness it wasn't one of hers—was boring, or Lady Carlisle's silliness had infiltrated the group until no one much cared what was going on.

Amy caught Mr. Colbert glowering at Lady Carlisle every once in a while. Eventually, Mr. Miles stood and took Lady Carlisle by the elbow and escorted her out of the room. By this time, no one was following the discussion, and Mr. Colbert called an end to the meeting.

"Well, that was surreal," William said as the members stood and began to avail themselves of the refreshments laid out. "Would you care for some tea or lemonade, ladies?"

Amy and Mrs. Miles both asked for lemonade, and William headed toward the table. Lady Carlisle and Mr. Miles returned. Lady Carlisle was a bit more subdued now, but still not her normal self. Mr. Miles said something to her and left to speak with the other men.

"Won't you join us, Lady Carlisle?" If something was going on with the woman, Amy wanted to know what it was. After all, she was in the middle of a murder investigation, and everything—and everyone—was under suspicion.

Lady Carlisle sat and fiddled with the beautiful gold-and-emerald necklace that seemed a bit out of place at a book club meeting. "That is a lovely necklace," Amy said.

"Fake," Mrs. Miles muttered.

Amy glanced at Mrs. Miles, not completely sure she'd heard her correctly. She didn't say anything else.

"Yes, my husband gave it to me for my birthday. Isn't it beautiful?" The woman beamed and wrapped the necklace around her finger.

"Fake."

Amy ignored Mrs. Miles. "Yes, it is beautiful. Do you know where he purchased it?"

Lady Carlisle waved her hand. "No." She giggled. "Does it matter?"

"Fake."

A bit taken aback by the three-way conversation that only she seemed to be aware of, Amy pressed her fingertips to her head, which had begun to pound. "No, I guess it does not matter. I just wondered which shop had such lovely things."

"Fake."

Dear God in heaven, if this didn't stop, she was going to explode like some sort of Chinese firecracker. Instead, she took a deep breath. "If you will excuse me, ladies, I believe I would enjoy a cup of tea."

"What's wrong?" William said as she approached him. "I apologize, I forgot your lemonade."

"That is fine. I think I prefer a cup of tea, actually."

William looked over to where Mrs. Miles and Lady Carlisle were involved in an intense conversation. Well, it appeared Mrs. Miles was intense. Lady Carlisle was still her somnolent self.

Amy leaned in closer to William. "I complimented Lady Carlisle on her necklace, and every time she mentioned it, Mrs. Miles mumbled 'Fake.'"

This time it appeared William's eyebrows would meet his hairline. "'Tis a strange relationship those two women share."

"Indeed." They both watched as Lady Carlisle gathered her belongings and, without a word to anyone, left the room.

Amy put her teacup down and nudged William. "Come. I want to hear more about this fake necklace."

William grabbed a cup of lemonade, and they strolled to where Mrs. Miles sat by herself. He held out the glass. "I apologize profusely, Mrs. Miles. I forgot all about your lemonade."

She gave William a bright smile. "That is fine, my lord." She took the glass from him and took a delicate sip.

Amy sat on one side of the woman, William on the other. "Mrs. Miles, when Lady Carlisle mentioned her lovely necklace, you mentioned it was fake."

Mrs. Miles nodded. "Fake."

"Can you tell me why you said that?"

The woman looked at her as if she were mad. "Because it's fake. All her jewelry is fake. Every last piece is fake."

William cleared his throat. "Are you insinuating that her husband gave her fake jewelry?"

Mrs. Miles straightened in her seat, indignation on her face. "Of course not. That lovely man would never do such a thing. He is a devoted husband and deserves more than *her* for a wife."

Oh, my.

Amy looked over at William, who shrugged. She turned her attention back to Mrs. Miles. "Then why do you say her necklace is fake?"

"Because she sold all the stones and replaced them with paste. Every single piece of jewelry her husband has given her. All fake. All paste." She shook her head and took another sip.

Glancing sideways at William, Amy said, "I thought you and Lady Carlisle were friends?"

"Ha!" She snorted. "'Tis hard to be friends with that one."

"Mother, I think it is time for us to leave." Mr. Miles arrived, glancing at his mother, then Amy and William. "I hope my mother has not been boring you with more of her childhood tales." His attempted smile never quite fully formed.

"No. Not at all. It's been a pleasant conversation."

Mr. Miles gripped his mother's elbow and nodded at them before walking her to the door.

William watched the couple leave the room. "If this was one of your books, now is when the reader would say, 'The plot thickens.'"

Amy continued to stare at the door where Mr. Miles and his mother had just exited. "Just so."

★　★　★

The next afternoon Amy sat at her desk, staring at a blank sheet of paper. She could think of nothing to add to the new book she had just started. She gazed out the window at the lovely spring day. Soon summer would be upon them and it would be time to think about a trip to Sussex, to one of the beaches.

A month-long vacation had been her habit for years. She and Aunt Margaret packed up and moved to a cottage they owned near the beach. There she wrote, strolled in the sand, and enjoyed food unique to that area.

Some of her best writing had been produced at her writer's retreat, which is how she'd begun to think of her time spent there. Aunt Margaret enjoyed long walks, read numerous books, and attempted to drag Amy away from her writing at least twice a day for some fun.

Her thoughts of summer, beaches, and warm weather were interrupted by the sound of carriage wheels rolling to a stop in front of the townhouse.

Within minutes Lacey was at her door. "Milady, those two detectives are back again."

Amy moaned and dropped her head into her hands. Always hopeful that their visit would be to announce the news that the murderer had been caught, she placed her pen in the ink holder and stood. "Very well. I will be down directly."

She checked her appearance in the mirror over her dressing table, adjusted her dress sleeve to cover the remaining bruise, and left the room. Just one step into the drawing room, Amy knew the detectives were not there with good news. *Scowling* would have been a kind description of their demeanor.

Both men took a seat once she sat, her heart taking funny little extra beats. Detective Carson came right to the point. "You have been interfering with our investigation."

Well, at least they hadn't come to arrest her for murder, so that was a relief. A slight relief, based on their stiff bearing.

Best to play ignorant and see what exactly they considered 'interfering.' "I'm not sure what you mean, Detectives."

"One thing we have learned throughout this investigation is that you are not a stupid woman, Lady Amy. But if you want to pretend you don't know what we're talking about, I will play your game." He pointed at her. "Did you not visit with Mr. Harris at his place of business to question him?"

She shook her head. "No. I went to his place of business because I was considering investing in his company."

"Have you other investments, Lady Amy?"

She drew herself up. "Yes. As a matter of fact, I do."

Carson leaned in, a nasty smile on his face. "How many of those investments have you personally visited?"

"Since I invest heavily in banks, and I visit my bank on a weekly basis, I would say all of them." No sooner had the words left her mouth than she realized her mistake. They were not in a jolly mood and would not appreciate her attempt at humor.

Detective Marsh glanced down at his ever-present notepad. "You said when we questioned you about Miss Eva Hemphill that you barely knew her, and had no idea she and your fiancé—"

"Ex-fiancé."

"—had been courting before he proposed to you."

"That would be correct, Detective."

Carson stood and loomed over her, forcing her to lean back. She bristled at his heavy-handedness. This was becoming too much. They were treating her like a criminal.

"Yet you and your gentleman friend were both there to discover her dead body."

Truth be known, there wasn't a great deal she could say to that. But she gave it her best attempt. "I did not know her when you questioned me before, but I met her a time or two after that at the sewing circle, and we became . . ."

Carson's brows rose. "Yes?"

Botheration. She couldn't say "friends," because who knew what they had learned about Miss Hemphill. "I became concerned about her well-being," she finished lamely.

Although she knew he did not believe that, Carson didn't question her words, since he had obviously made his point, but continued on. "You have been probing members of your book club and annoying upstanding citizens with suggestions and innuendoes."

Members of her book club? Lady Carlisle? Mrs. Miles? Had one of them complained to the police? She dismissed immediately the thought that Mr. Miles had protested about her speaking with his mother the night before, because, with his own illegal goings-on, he would be the last person to involve the law in his life to any degree.

Detective Marsh snapped his notebook closed. "And you withheld pertinent information from the police."

"What information?"

Carson sat back down and rested his spread fingers on his knees. "You learned from your gardener, Mr. Albright, that one of your book club members sold him drugs."

Drat. Somehow they'd found that out.

"Mr. Albright might have said something about that; I'm not quite sure."

Carson glared at her. "As we said, Lady Amy, you are not a stupid woman. He told you who his drug supplier was, and you would certainly remember. That was pertinent information that you neglected to report to the police."

At that point, she decided keeping quiet was her best course of action.

Detective Marsh moved to the edge of his seat as if he was preparing to stand and, hopefully, leave. "We have reason to believe your accident was no accident, Lady Amy. The spokes on Lord Wethington's wheel were deliberately cut." He glowered at her. "You and your cohort could have been killed. In fact, it is safe to say that was the intention."

She breathed a sigh of relief as both men stood. Detective Marsh then leaned down, took her by the elbow, and forced her to stand. "Lady Amy Lovell, you are under arrest for suspicion of murder and interfering in a police investigation."

Her jaw dropped as he pulled out his handcuffs, snapped them over her wrists, and moved her forward. "This is outrageous," she shouted.

When they reached the entrance hall, Lacey stood at the door, wringing her hands. "What should I do, milady?"

As they whisked her through the front door, Amy called over her shoulder, "Send a note around to Lord Wethington." They hurried her down the stairs. "Immediately!"

CHAPTER 25

"Do you know who I am?" Amy stood with her hands fisted at her hips, attempting to look intimidating but falling a bit short, with the blasted men ignoring her as they scribbled away. Her foot tapped a cadence as she stared at Detective Carson while he wrote information on the form in front of him. It appeared the man did know how to write.

He didn't bother to look up. "Yes. You are Lady Amy Lovell."

She sniffed and added, "Daughter of the Marquess of Winchester."

"I know."

"You cannot arrest a peer."

"I have already arrested you."

Amy quelled the urge to stamp her foot and instead walked around the small room that she, Detective Carson, and Detective Marsh occupied. "This is not proper. If it is discovered I have been in a room with two men with the door closed, I will be ruined."

For the first time Carson looked up. "I know nothing about your society rules, but I would say being arrested on suspicion of murder and interfering in a police investigation might be considered a bit more ruinous than being alone in a room with two men."

Amy leaned over the desk, planted her hand on the forms he was filling out, and stared him straight in the eye. "As you said, you are unfamiliar with my world. Believe me when I tell you that this is worse."

Carson held her eyes for a minute, then said, "Marsh, open the blasted door for *her ladyship*."

She straightened and smoothed nonexistent wrinkles from her skirts. "How long do you plan to keep me here?" She smirked. "Until I confess?"

"Do you have a confession to make?" the evil man smirked back.

About two hours had passed since they'd left her house and arrived at the police department. For most of that time she had been alone in the room, the two detectives only joining her for the last ten minutes. "We have sent a message to your father."

Amy closed her eyes. "Oh, no. Please, why would you do that? You know Lord Wethington will arrive as soon as he receives my message." Visions of Papa storming into the police building, waving his arms, shouting threats, then dragging her back to London filled her mind.

Carson stood and moved to the front of the desk, where he rested his hip and regarded her. "Lady Amy, you don't seem to understand how dangerous your actions are. You are not a trained investigator. You have no experience with police work. You and Lord Wethington are roaming Bath, asking questions and making someone very, very nervous."

"The true killer."

"Precisely," Marsh responded.

"Aha!" She raised her finger. "You just admitted I am not the main suspect any longer. Yet you arrested me on suspicion of murder. That is false arrest. I demand to be freed."

A knock on the partially open door drew their attention. A young man stood there in the uniform of a police officer.

"Detectives, there is a Lord Wethington here, with a Mr. Nelson-Graves, who says he is Lady Amy's barrister."

Carson returned to his chair and sat, leaning back with his fingers intertwined and his index fingers tapping his lips. "Show them in."

William entered first, his eyes flicking around the room until they landed on Amy. "Lady Amy! Are you well?" He strode in her direction but stopped right in front of her, his hands reaching out as if to embrace her. Then, thinking better of it, he dropped them to his side.

"Thank you for coming, my lord. I am well and more than ready to leave here and return to my home."

Mr. Nelson-Graves stepped up to Detective Carson and held out his hand. "I am Mr. Nelson-Graves, Lady Amy Lovell's barrister, retained by her father, the Marquess of Winchester."

Her barrister apparently felt that reminding the detectives of with whom they were dealing might give him the upper hand. In her experience, the detectives were not impressed by titles.

"Yes, I remember you from our meeting with Lady Amy, her father, and Wethington right after Mr. St. Vincent was found."

Mr. Nelson-Graves nodded. "Good. Perhaps, then, we can all sit down and discuss this?"

More chairs were brought in and they all sat, William next to her, his chair so close that the heat from his body and the familiar scent of his bath soap calmed her. She'd never been so glad to see him. She would not have thought to bring the barrister, which was why sometimes, she supposed, men did have clearer heads then women, as traitorous as that thought was.

Based on what Marsh had said, they no longer thought she had killed Mr. St. Vincent. Or at least with no positive proof, they had begun to look in other directions. That was a relief, but she had no intention of abandoning their search for the killer.

With the strange way Mrs. Miles and Lady Carlisle had been behaving of late, and with Mr. Miles being the drug dealer who might still be working with Mr. Harris, it opened up an entirely new avenue to explore.

The murder-mystery writer in her would not let go of all the hard work they'd done and the clues they'd accumulated. While the men discussed and argued about her arrest and how to settle the matter, she smiled at the words the detective had ranted about how she knew nothing of police investigations. Wouldn't he be surprised to learn she wrote books about police investigations? He would be further surprised to know she possessed an array of books on the subject.

More relaxed than she'd been for the last couple of hours, she realized her mind had drifted while the men spoke, and now there was a great deal of paper shuffling and gathering of documents by Mr. Nelson-Graves as he shoved them into his satchel.

She leaned toward William, which was no great distance. "What happened? I'm afraid I've been woolgathering."

"You are being set free. Mr. Nelson-Graves has arranged for you to be bonded out."

Amy hopped up. "Excellent."

"Wait just one minute, Lady Amy." Detective Marsh rose. "We want no more interfering in our investigation. Your barrister here has assured us you will stop following in our footsteps."

"I agree not to follow in your footsteps." An easy promise to make, since they seemed to be steps ahead of the detectives.

She looked over at Mr. Nelson-Graves, who certainly had the proper last name. His demeanor was indeed grave, and he looked now like he wanted to lock her up himself. 'Twas too bad she'd been ruminating while they spoke about how she could continue on. Although she hadn't listened to the exchange, she was sure the detectives' words about her interference had not been pleasant and had put that scowl on her barrister's face.

Surely Papa would also hear from Mr. Nelson-Graves. Her one salvation was, being under bond from the court, she would not be able to leave Bath without permission, which she hoped the detectives would not grant when Papa arrived. She did not want to be hustled off to London.

Right now all she wanted was to get William alone and discuss the latest ideas she had about Mrs. Miles and Lady Carlisle.

Good-byes were uttered, and Amy, Mr. Nelson-Graves, and William left the police department. She shuddered as they walked down the stairs to William's carriage, happy to be gone from the dark building.

"Where shall we drop you, Mr. Nelson-Graves?" William asked as they all settled in the carriage.

"My Bath office at number seventeen Stall Street, if you please."

William tapped on the ceiling and gave the driver the direction, and the carriage moved forward.

Mr. Nelson-Graves cleared his throat and looked Amy square in the eye, an act that had her squirming like a small child caught with a stolen biscuit. "Lady Amy, I feel that I must act in your father's absence. I absolutely agree with the detectives that any investigation of Mr. St. Vincent's murder must be left to the professionals."

Oh, how she ached to tell him she was a professional. A writer of murder mysteries. But as a bow of deference to her father, she remained silent on that point. "I understand." Eyes downcast, she uttered the words like a meek female, as was expected.

William choked.

She scowled sideways at him.

"I will send a report to your father immediately and advise him of this latest development. I am quite pleased with the conversation between myself and the detectives. Although they haven't said it outright, it is my opinion that the arrest on the charge of suspicion of murder was merely to get your attention and impress upon you that you are to remain out of police business."

She swallowed her retort and merely smiled and nodded her head like a good little girl.

And continued to plan their next step.

★　★　★

"Amy, I really think we need to pull back and stay out of the detectives' way." William continued his argument as they proceeded toward the business section of Bath. It was the day after her arrest. She'd spent the rest of the prior day taking a long, hot bath to erase as much as possible her memory of the police department.

After a nap and a restorative dinner, she'd spent the evening hours going over all her notes from the investigation and adding new ones they'd recently uncovered. Right now she clutched a list of jewelers in Bath she intended to visit so she could learn about replacing real stones with paste.

"Don't be a ninnyhammer, William. Yes, I know what we are doing could be dangerous, but we are merely questioning jewelers about replacing stones in my own jewelry. If my suspicions are correct and Lady Carlisle has a problem with opium, selling her jewels to pay for it makes sense. Before we can seriously add Lady Carlisle to our diminishing list of suspects, we need to learn if Mrs. Miles's accusations about Lady Carlisle's jewels being fake are true.

"Lord Carlisle is very wealthy. There could be no innocuous reason for his wife to be selling her jewels. A lady can hardly ask to have her allowance raised because her opium supplier is pressing for payment."

He shook his head. "I am not disputing doing this search but still believe my suggestion to have me do this and let you remain at home is a better idea." He raised his hand as her face grew flushed and she opened her mouth to speak. "I know what you are about to say. I know you want to do this yourself." He reached across the space and took her hand. "I couldn't stand to see you hurt again."

Oh, my.

She glanced down to where their hands joined. His so big, skin darkened from the sun, light hairs on his knuckles. Hers delicate and pale. Tiny, completely engulfed by his. She swallowed and looked up at him.

"I don't want to see you hurt," he repeated, and pulled back to lean against the soft velvet squab, leaving her hand cold.

They said nothing more as they continued their ride. Eventually they arrived at the business center where several jewelry shops conducted their trade. They stepped out of the carriage into the gloomy, cloudy day, and William gave his driver instructions on where to meet them.

Then, arm in arm, they moved away from the vehicle and headed to the jewelry store directly across the street.

A light, merry tinkle of a bell announced their arrival. The shop owner looked up from where he spoke with a gentleman. "I will be with you directly. There are seats near the window if you wish to sit, or you may look at the offerings if you so choose."

The shop was small but contained several display cases of jewels. The owner was a man of about fifty years, with a large moustache and rotund belly. It appeared he was in negotiations with his customer, who wanted to pay less for a watch.

Instead of sitting, Amy wandered the shop, looking at the various offerings. William followed behind her, commenting on sundry pieces. Within about ten minutes the gentleman left the store—without the watch—and the store owner approached them.

"Good day." He smiled at them. "I am Mr. Oglethorpe, and let me guess, you are here for an engagement ring?"

William and Amy glanced at each other, then away as quickly as possible. Her heart took to pounding, and the rise in the room's temperature made her regret not having her fan handy.

William began to clear his throat in a nervous sort of way. She decided to rescue them both. "Um, actually no. We are here about my necklace." Amy withdrew her ruby-and-diamond necklace from her reticule, annoyed to see her hand shaking as she placed it on the counter.

'Twas best not to look at William until she had calmed down. "I have heard that it is possible to replace real stones with paste so the item appears exactly the same." She looked up at the man. "Is that so?"

Apparently completely oblivious to the discord he had caused by his question, the jeweler picked up the necklace to examine it. "Yes. It is quite possible to do that. It's been known for owners to do so. Sometimes they sell the stones if they need money, and other times they keep the stones in a safe at home and wear the paste jewelry when they go about to avoid theft."

Amy nodded. "Yes. That is what I have been considering."

"Then you are wishing to replace the stones in this necklace with paste, my lady?"

She looked at the necklace as if pondering that very thing. Of course, she had no intention of doing so. Even if she needed the money—which she didn't—Papa would be livid if he knew she'd done such a thing.

Which brought her back to the reason for their visit to jewelers this afternoon. Why would someone as wealthy as Lady Carlisle sell her stones and replace them with paste? "I assume your work is brilliant, Mr. Oglethorpe, but would you have a customer that you did this for who I might speak with? As a reference?"

He appeared taken aback, her question apparently not one he'd received before. But if she were to confirm what Mrs. Miles had said, this information was vital.

"I have not done a replacement for some time, and it was in London when I had my shop there. Many of the gentlemen replaced their wives' jewels with paste with the intention of buying the gems back later."

"Did they ever?" William asked.

He shook his head. "No. I never had even one man return with the stones to have them put back into the piece. I'm afraid they found other uses for the money they received. In any case, I am afraid there is no one I can offer as a reference."

"Well, thank you, Mr. Oglethorpe. I will consider having it done, but I need more time to consider it." Amy scooped the necklace up and dumped it into her reticule. She and William left the shop.

"That was an interesting conversation." William escorted her across the street and around the corner, where another jewelry shop was located. "It is quite disheartening to know that gentlemen give their wives jewelry and then turn around and have the stones replaced."

She glanced up at him as they approached the next jewelry store. "That is not something you would do, my lord?"

He looked at her aghast. "Of course not. I think you would know that about me."

"Yes. You are right. You are much too honest and decent to do such a thing."

There was another series of throat clearing as he opened the door to the next shop and escorted her inside.

They visited six shops before they found one where the shop owner offered Lady Carlisle as a reference for switching out stones. They also confirmed it was her and not Lord Carlisle who had requested that the jewels be removed and replaced with paste. He also confirmed that she had asked about where she could sell the gems.

"Well, we have made some progress this afternoon," William said as the carriage began the journey back to Amy's house. "We now know that Mrs. Miles was correct and the jewelry Lady Carlisle wears is paste. The question that remains is, why would a woman married to a man who holds one of the oldest titles in England, and who is, by all accounts, quite wealthy, have need for money from the sale of her jewelry?"

"Based on what we've learned, most likely to buy drugs." Amy fiddled with the reticule in her lap, the sound of the necklace stones rubbing against each other oddly soothing.

They remained silent for the rest of the short ride back to her townhouse. The carriage pulled up to the front door just as another gentleman climbed the steps. He turned at the sound of carriage wheels, and Amy groaned.

"What is it?" William looked with concern at her and then at the man on the steps. The driver opened the door to the carriage, and William stepped out and reached for her.

"The man glowering at us is my brother, Michael. The Earl of Davenport."

William straightened and took her arm as they made their way up the stairs. "Should I be concerned?" he asked softly from the side of his mouth.

"No. The concern is all mine, I'm afraid." They reached her brother, who had stepped into the entrance hall. "Good afternoon, Michael."

"Do you have any idea how many other things I need to attend to in London? That the very last place I want to be right now is standing here?"

Amy removed her light jacket and handed it to Lacey. "Then why are you standing here?"

"Who is this?" Michael asked, his eyes narrowed.

William held out his hand. "William, Viscount Wethington at your service."

The two men shook, and Michael looked him in the eye, "Are you the man who has been helping my recalcitrant sister get into trouble with the police?"

"Hardly," William responded with a slight smile. "I find your sister has no problem whatsoever getting into trouble with the police all by herself."

Amy glared at William. "Traitor."

CHAPTER 26

Tuesday morning, William's foot had barely made it to the top step when Amy flung open the door, grabbed his hand, and dragged him into the entrance hall. "I remembered what had been teasing me at the back of my mind the past couple of weeks."

His brows rose, and a slight smile graced his lips. "And good day to you as well, Lady Amy."

She'd been up half the night going over her notes and moving small pieces of paper around that consisted of her suspects and the clues they'd uncovered. She'd checked her research notes and books, nodding each time as her ideas were confirmed. Once she'd put together all the parts of the puzzle, she'd sat back and stared at her results with horror.

Unbelievable.

As soon as the sun was up and the hour considered decent, she'd sent Lacey with a note to William to arrive as quickly as possible.

She grinned and pulled him into the drawing room. "Sir Holstein."

"What? The investigator? He's now on the list? I think you've gone a bit far this time."

"No. No." She began to walk in a circle, waving her arm in excitement. "The memory in the back of my mind that kept troubling me. When Sir Holstein first arrived here for his initial interview, he mentioned what a good friend he was to Lord Carlisle. My father also said so in his missive to me." She turned and looked at him.

The silence was thick as he absorbed what she had just said. William nodded. "Go on."

As she opened her mouth to speak, William sucked in a deep breath. "Are you suggesting . . . ?"

She waved him silent. "At the time we thought nothing of Sir Holstein eating bad food. It does happen. But last night when I went over all the information we've gathered the last few weeks, I had an epiphany. I checked my medical research books and looked up symptoms of arsenic poisoning."

"Poisoning!"

"Yes. And all of his symptoms when he arrived here looking so dreadful fit." She stopped pacing and looked at him. "If you remember—you were here—Sir Holstein mentioned that he'd been to their house several times for dinner."

William collapsed into the settee behind him. "You think Lady Carlisle poisoned Sir Holstein?"

Amy took in a deep breath. "Yes. In order to remove him from the investigation."

"And us? I assume you're blaming her for the carriage wheel as well? I hardly think she would take leave of the Assembly Room with saw in hand and cut the wheels."

Amy took the seat alongside him. "She would have hired someone. I doubt 'tis hard to find a man who could use the blunt to wait until the drivers were busy with their visit, cut the wheels, and move along."

William ran his fingers through his hair. "We need to stop and consider this." He stared straight ahead for a minute. "If your theory is correct, what you are saying is Lady Carlisle killed St. Vincent, then attempted to do away with Sir Holstein and us because we were investigating the murder."

"Yes."

"But what about the police? She can't do away with the entire force. They are investigating the murder, and, I might add, better than we had originally thought."

These, of course, were all issues she'd thought about the night before. 'Twas hard to think badly of someone you knew well, and who was so upstanding in the community. "Lady Carlisle is married to the man who will soon be named ambassador to France. Her husband has strong and powerful connections, right up to the Queen. I'm not saying he could pay someone to remain silent, but he could certainly put enough pressure on government higher-ups to close the case and declare it 'unsolved.'"

"And then whisk his wife off to France," William added.

Amy nodded. "Precisely. It's not as if Mr. St. Vincent's only living relative, Mr. Harris, would raise a fuss and be heartbroken if they never found the murderer. In fact, he would probably be glad he was no longer under consideration."

William shook his head. "Those are some serious accusations you are making here, Amy. Dangerous ones. If you are correct, and Lady Carlisle has been the culprit all along, we are in her sights. Lord Carlisle might be able to drag her off to France with no one the wiser, using his connections, but we have no reason to look away. She would know this."

"Hence the wagon wheel."

"But might I remind you, we are not dead."

"Yet." Amy gulped.

William rose and began to pace. The carpet would be threadbare by the time this case was solved. "All right, let's go back a bit here. My brain is still trying to take this all in and make sense of it. When you came to your conclusion, did you by any chance stumble upon a motive? We can't assume she was also in love with St. Vincent and was angry that he was marrying you, as we did with Miss Hemphill."

Amy hopped up and strode across the room and picked up a book. She flipped through the pages until she came to where she'd marked it earlier with a slip of paper. She began to read:

"*A feeling of euphoria overcomes the body after an ingestion of opium. One feels happy, relaxed, and in a state of somnolence.*" She looked up at William. "Remember seeing Lady Carlisle like that at the club meeting?"

She looked down at the page again. "*When the body is denied the drug, withdrawal is experienced. One can suffer from various discomforts, including agitation, anxiety and stomach cramping.*" Amy slammed the book shut and looked up. "Do you also remember the state Lady Carlisle was in when we met her and Mrs. Miles on the street?"

While William dwelled on that information, she continued. "Another point. If she was spending all the money her husband gives her as an allowance on opium, it follows that she would have to sell her jewelry to continue purchasing it, but without her husband aware of it."

"Yes. I concede that she is most likely addicted to opium, but we still have no motive. Why kill the man who brings the much-needed drugs into the country?"

Amy shrugged. "I'm not too clear on that point. Maybe he threatened to cut her off?"

"But if we are correct, he was not supplying drugs to individuals, but most likely to Mr. Miles, who, in turn, did the selling."

She blew out a frustrated breath. "I didn't say I had it *all* figured out."

He shook his head. "Nevertheless, we must go to the police with this information. We are in over our heads now. If what you say is correct, this is no longer a game, or a fictional murder that you write about." William stood and tugged on his jacket cuffs. "I suggest we go to the police station now and lay this all out for the detectives." He looked in her direction and then pointed toward the door.

"Um, just a minute."

He placed his hands on his hips, his frustration evident. "Amy, this is serious now. You cannot continue; it's too dangerous."

"I agree." She held up her hand when he moved toward the door. "Wait."

"What?"

His suspicious look had the words tumbling out of her. "I am waiting for one more thing."

He groaned and hung his head, covering his eyes with the palm of his hand as if not seeing her would make her disappear, like a small child would do when caught doing something wrong. "Amy," he sighed, "what now?"

"Lacey has a cousin whose dear friend's brother's wife's sister's niece, on her husband's side, that is—"

"Stop." He held up his hand. "I'm dizzy."

"—works for Lord Carlisle," she finished, lamely.

He cupped his chin and studied her for a minute. "And? What does that discombobulated string of relatives and friends have to do with this?"

"Marion—that's the woman—is checking to see if a knife is missing from the Carlisle kitchen."

When his eyes lit up, she knew he'd forgiven her the hesitation in going immediately to the police. "Yes. If we can ascertain that, there is our proof. We can dump it all in the police department and be done with it."

"I agree," Amy added.

Maybe.

★ ★ ★

Three hours later Amy still awaited word from her contact that a knife was indeed missing. She was certain the answer would be in the affirmative. With the elimination of their other suspects, this one made sense. She was still weak on a motive for the murder, but if everything else added up, the police could certainly gain a confession. If she decided to turn their evidence over to them, that is.

William had left over an hour before to an appointment he could not miss. He'd made her promise that once she had the information on Lady Carlisle, she would wait for him to return and they would go to the police together.

"I wondered if you would like a carriage ride this afternoon." Her brother, Michael entered the drawing room, pulling on his fine leather gloves. He was dressed as a gentleman should be for an afternoon out. She studied him, realizing she had never given him much thought throughout their childhood. He was seven years older than her and they were not close, since he'd been sent off to Harrow at a young age, and Amy and her mother had spent most of their time in Bath. Once Michael finished school, he had lived with their father in London, learning how to run their estates. He'd also taken up some of Papa's favorite causes in Parliament, helping with contacting other members on Papa's behalf.

She had never questioned her parents' living apart most of her life, but now that she was older, she did wonder about it. Mother had detested London and Papa loved it, so that must have had something to do with it. When they were together, they had been pleasant to each other, but almost in a formal, overly polite way. She'd never asked but had always assumed theirs had been an arranged marriage.

Since Aunt Margaret had made her home in Bath, once Mother died it had been natural for her to take over Amy's supervision, even though she was only five and twenty herself at the time.

Although Michael was a nice-looking man of thirty—and if the London newspaper society pages were correct, he enjoyed the company of many women—he had managed to avoid settling down with one woman and setting up his nursery. Amy imagined that with no mother to push him, it could very well be some time before her brother did his duty to his title.

She assumed that, with Papa a hale and hardy specimen of a man at five and fifty years, the Winchester title would not pass anytime soon to Michael, who currently held Papa's courtesy title of Earl of Davenport.

A bit taken aback by his request now, she offered him her sweetest smile. "Oh, how lovely, but I'm afraid I must pass."

He was having none of it.

"Dear sister, I heard Lord Wethington a while ago when I returned. I sincerely hope you were not conspiring with the man again. Father was most adamant that you are to stay as far away from any murder investigation as you can. I am under direct orders to escort you posthaste to London if I even suspect any such thing."

She deployed her most surprised and innocent expression. "I have not left the house all morning. Why would you think I am continuing my investigation?"

Michael crossed his arms over his chest and leaned against the wall. "Your pretend subservience does not work with me, Amy. You might fool Father, but not me. Why don't you want to go for a ride? It's a lovely day and you don't seem to be hovering over your desk, scribbling murder mysteries."

Persephone made her regal entrance, nonexistent tail in the air. Happy for the distraction, Amy scooped the dog into her arms. "I promised Persephone I would give her a bath this afternoon."

"We have servants."

"Not for Persephone's bath. She only allows me to do it."

Michael studied her a while, then pushed away from the wall. "I will return in about two hours, and I expect you to be here."

"Am I a prisoner in my own home, then?"

"Not a prisoner, but let's just say you cannot go flitting about town without me knowing where you are and with whom."

She wasn't as annoyed at his edict as she would normally have been, since she was almost certain they were about to solve the mystery of St. Vincent's murder. Once that was finished, Michael would scurry back to London and she would return to her normal, safe, and happy life.

Then Amy's brain moved from murder to romance. "Are you escorting a young lady?"

Her brother stopped and narrowed his eyes. "I might be. Why?"

She shrugged. "No reason. I didn't realize you were familiar with any of the young ladies in Bath, since you don't leave London very much."

"Miss Abernathy spends almost as much time in London as she does in Bath. As it turns out, she is currently visiting her godmother." He took his hat from Lacey and placed it on his head.

"Miss Abernathy? How very interesting."

Michael walked over to her and tapped her on the nose. "Don't get any ideas, little sister, and do not begin to plan the wedding breakfast. 'Tis only a ride." He gave her a slight bow and said, "Do try your very best to stay out of trouble." With that warning, he left the house.

Only a ride, indeed. She'd never known Michael to spend time in the company of any young lady who possessed a mother on the hunt for a husband for her daughter. But then again, as she'd noted, he was in London most of the time, and she didn't really know which respectable ladies he rode with. The society pages mentioned only his escapades.

She sat in the her favorite chair near the hearth and ran her fingers through Persephone's fur.

"My, don't we look pensive." Aunt Margaret stopped at the drawing room door, obviously—given her state of dress—also going out for the afternoon.

"Where are you off to?"

"The local chapter of the National Society for Women's Suffrage." She looked in the mirror on the wall across from the drawing room door and adjusted her hat. "We are making progress." She turned to Amy and grinned.

"I wish I could go with you, but I am awaiting an important message."

"Not the murder thing again, I hope. If you don't stop, you will find yourself permanently in London. I know my brother. He is not one to be thwarted."

Amy snorted. "You have been thwarting Papa for years."

"Yes. That is true." She smiled. "Well, good luck, then. I am off."

It grew near lunchtime, but she had no appetite. She placed Persephone carefully on a soft blanket in front of the fireplace and wandered the room. After a few minutes of the eerie silence with everyone gone, she traipsed up the stairs to her room and drew out a book to distract herself.

After reading the same paragraph three times, she wandered to the window, looking out at early summer in full bloom and admitting to herself that she really should have gone with Michael. Getting her mind off everything would have been quite pleasant, and she could have learned about the knife upon her return.

Plus, seeing her brother with Miss Abernathy would have been worth listening to the girl simper and giggle the entire time. Surely her brother was not truly interested in the girl. Amy knew Miss Abernathy from her occasional visits to London—a tittering, eyelash-batting female. She would hate to have her as a sister-in-law.

She tried again to read a few sentences but gave up. Goodness, it was quiet. The lack of sound was almost making her itch. Tired of trying to force herself to read her current novel, which held no interest, she decided to overcome her fear of the library and search for something from there to read that would take her mind off murder and mayhem.

The carpet on the stairs muffled her footsteps as she made her way downstairs. Lacey was no longer at the door, most likely busy with other tasks. Why had she never noticed how silent the house was? And furthermore, why was it troubling her so much?

Hopefully William's appointment would end soon and he could keep her company. She stood in front of the library door for a moment, then took a deep breath and turned the latch, swinging the door open.

The room looked the same, smelled the same. It appeared the servants were no longer placing fresh flowers in the room. Although Papa didn't spend much time in Bath, the room always smelled of him. Tobacco and brandy.

The first thing she noticed when she entered was the soft breeze that blew from the French doors, ruffling the curtains across the room. Someone had left the doors open, perhaps Michael. He might have used Papa's desk to do a bit of paperwork.

He'd never mentioned how long he planned on staying, but she feared he had been ordered to keep her under lock and key until the murder was solved. Well, if she received the needed proof, and she and William reported it all to the police department, Michael would most likely be on the first rail to London.

She started across the room when a slight sense of unease enveloped her. She chastised herself for being silly, assuring herself that her reaction was merely the unpleasant memory of the night she'd found St. Vincent dead on the floor.

Her heart pounding—such foolishness—she hurried to the doors and closed them. Letting out a puff of relieved air, she came to an abrupt stop, turned, then stepped back. She drew in a deep breath, and her hand covered her mouth. "What are you doing here?"

"You really should be more careful about keeping your doors locked."

CHAPTER 27

A my licked her dry lips as she stared at the very frightening gun pointing in her direction. "Perhaps that's because most visitors come to the front door and drop the knocker to be admitted to my home."

"Not me."

"So it seems." Amy ordered herself to remain calm. She'd written scenes like this in her books, but at the moment she couldn't remember one single method she'd employed to rescue her main character.

She moved a few steps from the French doors, hoping to make a run for it, or even scramble under Papa's desk for cover. "I assume you used the French doors the night you killed Mr. St. Vincent?" She might as well get that out there, since she could think of no other reason why the gun, held by a very steady hand, was pointed directly at her. She hated to admit that the detectives were right; this was a dangerous game she'd been playing.

The intruder waved the gun around, causing all of Amy's blood to race to her feet. "No, Mr. St. Vincent had opened the doors and gone out to the patio when I tapped on the glass to summon him."

Amy's eyes roamed the room, looking for anything she could use to defend herself. "He wasn't surprised to see you standing in my garden? Had you been following him?" *Think, Amy, think.* Lacey was somewhere in the house and would hopefully wander by the library, since the door to the corridor remained open.

"You might say."

She silently prayed that William's meeting was over and he was on his way here. Of course, she didn't want him to walk into a situation where he would be shot, too. If she could keep the conversation going, she might stay alive long enough to think of a way out of this mess. "Can we sit down and discuss this?"

"No reason to do that, but if you wish, we can chat for a while. I've been watching the house and I know Lord Wethington left earlier, and your brother and aunt have gone out. Allowing that most servants use this in-between time to sneak in a nap or run their own personal errands, I figure we have a few minutes." She grinned and waved her gun at the settee. "You sit there."

Amy took the seat facing the library door and tried her best to calm her pounding heart. Her guest remained standing.

"You know, we never suspected you."

"Maybe not, but you were getting too close. And the crashed carriage didn't do the job I'd planned."

Keep her talking, keep her talking. Once her panic eased and she could think clearly, she might figure a way out of this situation. "I assume you hired someone?"

She narrowed her eyes. "Do you think I brought a saw with me to the Assembly Rooms?"

Foolish question, foolish answer, her Papa always said. She didn't care how many inane questions she asked, as long as it held off the gun aimed in her direction, cocked and ready to end her life. "How do you propose to get away with this? Lord Wethington will know precisely what happened to me."

"I have plans for him, too."

Almost as if mentioning his name conjured up his presence, William appeared at the library door, took one quiet, cautious step into the room, and stopped. Thank goodness for the thick carpets that lined the corridor and muted his steps.

His eyes grew wide when he viewed the scene. Panicked that he might not realize what was going on, she quickly said, "Do be careful with that gun, Mrs. Miles."

"I have excellent aim. I've been shooting since I was a child."

Trying to give William time to assess the situation, Amy said, "How very interesting. I always wished my papa would allow me to shoot."

William motioned with his hands for her to drop to the floor. Despite the tense situation, it appeared he wanted her to pretend to faint, and his movements almost made her laugh. He held up five fingers and lowered his thumb, then the next finger. He obviously wanted her to drop when all his fingers were down.

Three. Two. One.

She swooned, and William rushed forward and wrapped his right arm around Mrs. Miles from behind. He swung his left arm downward, slamming the edge of his hand against her wrist. The gun hit the floor, landing with a thud.

Mrs. Miles screamed and attempted to wrestle herself from his grip. For an older lady, she certainly had plenty of strength. Amy grabbed the gun, and William shouted, "Bloody hell, Amy, put that down before you end up killing yourself anyway."

Holding it with her index finger and thumb, she carried it to the desk, where she gently placed it on the polished wood. She really should get her own gun and take shooting lessons. Even Mrs. Miles could shoot.

William continued to hold on to a very agitated Mrs. Miles. She cursed and stomped on his foot, but he held on, murmuring to her in an attempt to calm her. Then suddenly she stopped and collapsed in his arms. He walked her to a chair and she sat, her hands covering her face, sobbing.

Amy almost felt sorry for her.

Almost.

Amy turned her attention to William. "How did you get into the house?" Although happy and very relieved to see him, she really must do something about how freely people came and went through her doors.

"Your girl, Lacey, was racing down the stairs just as my carriage pulled up. She was frantic and said she passed the open library door and saw a woman holding a gun at you. She was off to the police department. I sent her there in my carriage."

Amy nodded as her knees turned to water now that the threat had ended. She backed up into the settee and sat. "Oh, my. I feel a bit faint."

"Put your head down between your knees. Get some blood back up to your head. You've taken a fright."

Mrs. Miles had stopped crying but was sitting quietly in the chair, looking at the floor, her hands in her lap. A pitiful sight.

William sauntered to the desk and picked up the gun, disengaged it, and placed it in the middle drawer of Papa's desk. He walked back to Mrs. Miles and stood in front of her. "Why did you kill Mr. St. Vincent?"

She remained silent and just shook her head.

Amy attempted to get her to talk. "Honestly, we thought Lady Carlisle was the culprit."

That got Mrs. Miles's attention. Her head snapped up and she glared at Amy. "That woman should have been the one with the knife in her chest."

William looked over at Amy and shrugged. "Why do you say that?" he asked.

Mrs. Miles fisted her hands in her lap and glared at Amy. "She and your fiancé—"

"Ex-fiancé."

"—were ruining my son's life. St. Vincent dragged Richard into the drug trade with promises of great wealth. That didn't happen, and my poor Richard got further and further into the nastiness while St. Vincent spent most of the money they made on Lady Carlisle."

"Lady Carlisle?" William and Amy said at the same time.

"Yes. She was his mistress, led him around by his nose. When he tired of her and put her aside, she began to demand opium from my son. By that time she had become hopelessly addicted. She sold her jewelry to pay for the drugs, and when the money ran out and she started to show signs of withdrawal, she threatened to go to the police if Richard didn't give her what she wanted."

"But why kill Mr. St. Vincent?" Amy asked.

"Because he was the leader. He started the entire mess, dragging Richard into it. If there were no more drugs for Richard to sell, our life could return to normal. It would do Lady Carlisle no good to go to the police because it would have ended with no proof that Richard had been involved."

"But what about Mr. Harris?"

Mrs. Miles shook her head. "I knew St. Vincent's shipping company was in trouble with all the money he'd spent on *that woman*. I had hoped the business would close. I never counted on Mr. Harris being stupid enough to take up the trade."

William touched her on the shoulder. "There will always be someone to deal in illegal drugs. I'm afraid the problem will never end."

Lacey raced into the room, her face flushed, her eyes wild, with Detectives Carson and Marsh right behind her. Amy had to admit it was the first time she'd been glad to see the two men who had plagued her for weeks. Lacey looked around the room and let out a huge breath. "You're safe."

"Yes. We're fine." Amy walked to Lacey and gave her a hug. "Thank you."

Detective Carson smirked at Amy and placed his hands on his hips. "More trouble, Lady Amy?"

Amy waved in Mrs. Miles's direction. "We have your murderer, Detective."

Marsh squatted in front of the woman. "I believe you are Mrs. Miles?"

She nodded.

The detectives glanced at each other. They appeared to be just as surprised to see Mrs. Miles as Amy had been. The woman had certainly fooled everyone.

"You want to tell us what happened?" Carson turned to Amy.

She took a deep breath. "Mrs. Miles arrived at my house, unannounced and uninvited, with a gun—"

"Pardon the interruption, but when someone shows up with a gun, they are generally uninvited," Marsh said.

She nodded. "Understood. Mrs. Miles said she intended to kill me because she thought I was getting too close to identifying her." She mumbled the last few words.

Detective Carson cocked his ear in her direction, a smirk on his face. "What was that last part? I'm afraid I missed it."

She straightened and looked him in the eye. "She thought I"—she waved between herself and William—"we, were getting too close."

When the detective said nothing in return, she added, "Very well, you were correct."

"Go on."

"William arrived—"

"Of course."

"—and disarmed her. She then admitted to us that she killed my fiancé—"

"Ex-fiancé," Detective Carson, Detective Marsh, William, Lacey, and Mrs. Miles all said at the same time. Stevens shouted it from the entrance hall.

She nodded. "Just so." She returned her regard to Detective Carson, waiting for the lecture she knew he was itching to deliver.

Instead he said, "Where is the gun?"

William crossed the room and withdrew it from the drawer. "I've disengaged it." He handed it to Detective Carson, who checked it and slid it into his pocket.

Detective Marsh rose and grasped Mrs. Miles's elbow to help her stand. "Put your hands behind your back, please."

Now entirely complacent, she did as the detective asked, and he fastened the handcuffs on her.

As the detectives and Mrs. Miles left the room, Detective Carson stopped and turned to Amy. "We will need you at the police station as soon as possible to give a full accounting of what went on here."

William jumped in. "Will tomorrow morning be sufficient? I believe Lady Amy could use a break from all this."

Carson snorted and followed the other two out of the room.

* * *

A couple of hours later, after a few brandies that had Amy feeling quite mellow, she and William continued to sit and discuss the events of the afternoon.

"What do you make of Sir Holstein's digestion issues?" Amy asked as she eyed the half-empty bottle of brandy, wondering if she dared take another glass. She'd never had this much hard spirits in her life.

William shrugged. "It is possible he ingested some bad food, and not necessarily at the Carlisle house. I also can't help but wonder if Lady Carlisle knew about Mrs. Miles's involvement in St. Vincent's death and wanted to spare the woman by removing Sir Holstein from the investigation. I did say theirs was a strange relationship."

Through her fuzzy brain, she agreed with William's assessment. "True. Most times they seemed like genuine friends, and other times, like when Mrs. Miles berated Lady Carlisle for selling her jewels, I felt as though she thoroughly disliked the woman."

He nodded slowly. "As I said. An unusual friendship."

"Whatever is going on in here?" Aunt Margaret smirked at Amy and William, both slouched on the sofa in the drawing room, two empty glasses and a partially filled brandy bottle on the table in front of them.

William made to stand and didn't quite make it, which made Amy even more sure she would not take any more brandy—if even William was having a problem standing. After struggling for a few minutes, William managed to remain upright. He bowed in Aunt Margaret's direction. "Good day, my lady."

Then he burped.

Amy giggled.

Aunt Margaret regarded them both with narrowed eyes. "I believe you two are . . . soused." She burst out laughing.

"I am not drunk," Amy said, although she wasn't quite sure the words that came out of her mouth actually voiced that thought.

William waved to the chair across from the sofa, barely missing Amy's head. "Won't you join us, Lady Margaret?" His legs seemed to give out, and he landed back on the sofa, a surprised expression on his face.

Her aunt placed her hands on her hips. "I think the two of you have had enough of whatever it is you have been doing and drinking."

The front door closed, and within seconds Michael entered the drawing room. "What's this I heard from Mr. Stevens that the police were here again? Are you still getting into trouble?"

Amy and William looked at each other and burst into laughter. No matter how hard she tried, Amy could not control the giggles that had overtaken her. Tears ran down her cheeks, and she swiped at them.

Aunt Margaret walked over to her and reached out her hand. "Oh, dear, I believe it's time for you to retire for the day. Whatever this is all about, you can tell us tomorrow."

"No, no. You must hear what we did." Amy hiccupped.

Michael crossed his arms over his chest. "I am very interested to hear why the police were here yet again, and why my sister is alone with a man, with no chaperone, and a near-empty bottle of brandy between them." He glared at William.

"I agree, my lord," William managed to get out without too much difficulty. She noted he didn't try to stand again. "I should not have allowed your sister to imbibe."

"Indeed."

Amy poked William in the arm. "Tell them." She was afraid to attempt to put the story into words. She was feeling more and more unlike herself.

William related the tale, beginning with Mrs. Miles's arrival and including all that followed. Amy smiled at him, grateful as always for his assistance.

After comments of surprise, and in Michael's case, even admiration, Aunt Margaret took Amy's arm. "All right, dear girl. Now it is time to sleep this off."

William managed to climb to his feet with the help of the back of the chair. "I will be off as well."

"Wait. I will walk you to the door," Amy said.

With Michael and Aunt Margaret staring after them, William and Amy made it to the front door with as much dignity as possible. Mr. Stevens tried his best to control his smile at the sight of the two of them.

As the butler opened the door, William turned to her. He took Amy's hand. "My dear Lady Amy. I will be forever grateful that you did not get shot today."

"Thank you." She swayed slightly, and William gripped her arms.

He stared into her eyes as if seeing something there he'd never seen before.

"What?"

He pulled her close and cautiously lowered his head and kissed her. A slight touching of lips. When she just stared at him wide-eyed, he kissed her again, this time with a bit more feeling.

Her insides turned to mush, and she clung to his arms to keep from sliding to the floor. William pulled back and rubbed his thumbs over her cheeks.

She viewed him through half-lidded eyes. "What was that for?"

He shrugged. "Don't know." He pulled her against him. "But let's do it again."

And so they did.

Epilogue

Six months later

Amy and William sat side by side in the back room of the Atkinson & Tucker bookstore, awaiting the arrival of the other members of the Mystery Book Club.

Since Mr. St. Vincent's murder and the work she and William had done together, they'd found themselves in a *sort of* courtship. Nothing had been formally declared, but they did spend a lot more time together than they had before the murder investigation.

And, of course, every time Papa visited from London, he made a point to invite William to dinner, and to accompany him to his club. Although William didn't seem to mind spending time with Papa, she had to admit it made her a bit nervous, always wondering when Papa would whip out the marriage contracts.

On the positive side, there had been the few kisses they'd shared since the somewhat drunken ones the day Mrs. Miles was arrested.

William flipped through the pages of *Keene's Bath Journal*, the local newspaper for Bath. Amy continued to read the latest Conan Doyle story about Sherlock Holmes. She was a bit annoyed to find that the book she was currently writing was similar. With all the mystery books being published, that situation was bound to happen, but it was always an author's concern.

"Listen to this." William turned to her and glanced back at the newspaper. "An unidentified man's body was found floating in the River Avon early yesterday morning. Attempts are being made to identify the man so his family may be notified."

Amy shuddered. "That's terrible. I wonder who the poor unfortunate man is."

The other members began to filter in, and William closed his newspaper and tucked it into his satchel. Amy closed her book and then stood to greet the others. She made her way to the small group of women who had arrived.

Lady Carlisle no longer belonged to the club, since she and her husband had moved to France after he had received the much-sought-after ambassador position. Amy hoped Lady Carlisle had received the help she needed to end her addiction.

Mr. Miles had drifted away also, which was no surprise, since his mother was currently in jail awaiting her trial for murder. As far as Amy knew, the police had shut down the drug-importing business, and RSV Shipping was currently up for sale.

"It is time to begin our meeting." Mr. Colbert stood at the front of the room. He smiled at the members; then his eyes shifted to the doorway, and he frowned. Amy turned, and an unfamiliar man stood there, looking around the room.

"May I help you, sir?" Mr. Colbert asked.

"I'm looking for a Lord Wethington."

William stood and waved the man over. The man held out a folded paper to William. "This is for you, milord."

William thanked him and returned to his seat.

"What is that?" Amy pointed at the paper.

He shrugged and opened it, his eyes scanning the missive. After a few moments, he inhaled deeply and looked over at her, his face pale. "The police have identified the man found floating in the river."

"And they notified *you*?"

"Yes. He is Mr. James Harding. My man of business."

ACKNOWLEDGMENTS

A huge thank you to Nicole Resciniti, agent extraordinaré, who encouraged me to write something different from my usual genre. You were right, I could do it.

Another thank you to my editor, Faith Black Ross, who made my book so much better.

Thank you to the tour guides and other lovely people I met in Bath, England who gave me a lot of information about the town and its history.

Thank you to my three fur babies who wait patiently in my office for me to take break and notice they are out of food.